Masque of the Gonzagas

Clare Colvin has published three novels,
The Mirror Makers, *Masque of the Gonzagas*, and
A Fatal Season. Her work has been translated in
five European languages, and her short stories
have appeared extensively in anthologies. Born in
the UK, she grew up in South Africa, the
Lebanon, and India, and now lives in London.
She writes for several national newspapers and is
opera critic for the *Sunday Express*.

Praise for *Masque of the Gonzagas*

'Gripping' – *The Times*

'I was swept up by this compelling tale of
seduction and revenge' – Robert Irwin

'A love story of suitably baroque intensity.
This is historical fiction with imaginative sweep'
– Max Davidson, *Daily Telegraph*

'The music of the story resonates in the fluency and rhythm
of the prose. A magical evocation of baroque splendour'
– Alice Thomas Ellis

'Sweeps the reader along the streets of Mantua, the valleys of
Tuscany and the canals of Venice. It pursues a fable of loss
and redemption, a carnival of miniatures and caricatures, and
a history of the conceits and deceits of the Gonzagas, as well
counterpointed and interwoven as any Monteverdi score'
– Amanda Hopkinson, *Independent*

'Marvellously baroque' – *Daily Express*

'Events glide rapidly from one meticulously imagined scene
to the next' – *Literary Review*

'A wonderful evocation of the splendours of the Italian courts
at Mantua during the Renaissance when Monteverdi's music
ruled Italy and clandestine passions were dark, and secretive
and highly dangerous' – *Birmingham Post*

'Compelling prose that flows between the actual events to
expose the dark side of the Gonzaga family and explains the
fraught relationship between duke and maestro'
– *Good Book Guide*

'Intriguing insight. Monteverdi's marvellous music runs
evasively through the narrative: you can almost hear it'
– *Classical Music*

'Clare Colvin's optically brilliant images imprint themselves
unforgettably on the mind; her words are mirrors and music
that encircle seventeenth-century Mantua like a spell,
transporting the reader to the Now of Galileo and
Monteverdi, of dukes and dwarves, warriors and poets,
courtly intrigues and passionate liaisons. This is a book to be
read more than once, with new pleasure each time'
– Russell Hoban

Masque of the
Gonzagas

Clare Colvin

ARCADIA BOOKS

Arcadia Books Ltd
15–16 Nassau Street
London W1W 7AB

www.arcadiabooks.co.uk

ISBN 1-905147-26-0

Designed and typeset in Monotype Garamond by
Discript Limited, London WC2N 4BN
Printed in Finland by WS Bookwell

Arcadia Books supports English PEN, the fellowship of writers who work together to
promote literature and its understanding. English PEN upholds writers' freedoms in
Britain and around the world, challenging political and cultural limits on free expression.
To find out more, visit www.englishpen.org, or contact
English PEN, 6–8 Amwell Street, London EC1R 1UQ.

Arcadia Books distributors are as follows:

in the UK and elsewhere in Europe:
Turnaround Publishers Services
Unit 3, Olympia Trading Estate
Coburg Road
London N22 6TZ

in the USA and Canada:
Independent Publishers Group
814 N. Franklin Street
Chicago, IL 60610

in Australia:
Tower Books
PO Box 213
Brookvale, NSW 2100

in New Zealand:
Addenda
Box 78224
Grey Lynn
Auckland

in South Africa:
Quartet Sales and Marketing
PO Box 1218
Northcliffe
Johannesburg 2115

CONTENTS

PROLOGUE
1611

Every Friday evening music is performed in the
Hall of Mirrors. Signora Adriana comes to sing in concert,
and lends the music such power and so special a grace,
bringing such delight to the senses, that the place becomes
almost like a new theatre.

Letter from Claudio Monteverdi to Cardinal
Ferdinando Gonzaga, January 1611

I watch you in the mirror. You were not quick enough to see me. You had a strange feeling for a moment that someone was there, a flicker just beyond the corner of your eye. It's gone now.

How could we live without mirrors? They are the windows through which we see ourselves. Look at you now, glancing into them as you pass by. And there is another to look at, and another. This is the Hall of Mirrors, reflecting your two images, how you are, how you would like to be. Glance at the mirror knowingly, and you see how you would like to be. Catch yourself unwittingly and there's a stranger.

Do you like our Hall of Mirrors? You're looking up at the ceiling, at the four horses and the charioteer. I watch you cross over to the other side of the room, and you see the horses galloping in the opposite direction. An optical illusion, like so many of our frescoes. We play with dimensions.

All you can see in the room is emptiness and yourself reflected in the mirrors. Can you not hear, if only faintly, music through the shroud of time? Can you not hear the people? Do you not feel the attention, the hush in the air? They are no longer glancing at the mirrors and at each other, but intent on the musicians and on the thin figure in black who directs. I have seen his back curved over his viol many times, I am more interested in watching the faces of those who watch him, so I stand at the side, my eyes on the mirror reflecting the audience.

I am watching the Duke. Have you noticed his eyes, how pale and visionary they are in the portraits? That is how they look now, absorbed in the music of our magician. I have seen his different expressions over the years,

3

the wild humour, the speaking fire as he looks at a woman, the canny glint as he juggles one debt against another, the icy hardness of a murderer. A many-faceted man, our Duke Vincenzo: mean and generous, profligate and careful, kind and cruel. And vain, gloriously vain, but why not? If you were born to that splendour, wouldn't you be?

Look at the Duchess Eleonora beside him. The serenity of her face, tempered by twenty-seven years married to the greatest libertine of our day. Not a cold man, you understand, but one so overwhelmed by the bounty of love inside him that he cannot help but bestow it on others. She is pale from a grippe. It is January in this year of 1611 and the winds blow over the Mantuan marshes even to the cloistered corners of the palace. She is in her middle years, there have been five children, and she has had year after year of this harsh climate, the burning summers, the iron winters, the marsh fevers that come with the rain. We are close to the earth here. Despite our gilding, our *trompe l'œil* and our mirrors, we are ruled by the seasons.

Eleonora is unwell. Isabella is in black. She buried Don Ferrante four years ago, but black suits her. I see her glance at the Duke, and their eyes meet for a moment, then she looks at the mirror and catches my eye, as I knew she would. There is no one as guileless and knowing as our Isabella. She wept inconsolably when Ferrante died and then was happier than she had been for years: who can blame her? Out of her isolation and back at court.

Tonight Vincenzo has only eyes and ears for the music, and for his new singer, the incomparable Adriana. She is considered the greatest, the most dramatic, the most beautiful of our day. As soon as Vincenzo heard of her, he wanted her. It was a matter of principle. Mantua must have the best art, the best music. We will show the Medici, we will show the Emperor himself. Our walls where they are not mirrored, glow with the works of Titian and Rubens. Our Director of Music is the best in Italy, the divine

Claudio. Duke Vincenzo knew as soon as he saw him over twenty years ago in Cremona, a young violist, and then again at Florence. No one can resist the Duke when he claims possession, not even Adriana, despite her protestations of honour. Have you seen her villa? Have you seen her carriages, her jewels? Are you aware of how much the court treasurer is paying her? Twenty times the salary of our Director of Music. No wonder Monteverdi looks pained. When he is not at his music, the only thought that runs through his mind is how are we going to live? He is thin because he is driven, and because there is hardly enough to eat in his house. His poor children.

But listen to Adriana, how her voice soars and laments, and we weep with her. The wonder of so much emotion engendered – the two of them, the melancholy, driven man, and the woman who lives for gifts, Adriana Cupidity Basile, look at the effect they have had on the audience, with his music and her voice. The Duke has tears in his eyes, they have become blue lakes, overbrimming onto his reddened cheeks. He has a lot to weep about, of course, and at times like this he is free to do so. At other times he keeps the demons at bay with his perpetual motion, his frantic travelling, his insatiable buying of treasures and of people. When will he ever find peace? That must be what Eleonora asks herself, though by now she doesn't expect an answer.

I know as much about the Duke as anyone. I stay in the shadows now, but he is aware of me. He may have forgotten the time, years long ago, when we talked until dawn. The philosophy of Plato, the writing of Ficino, Mirandola, Giordano Bruno, the cabbala, the alchemy of elements and much else. Keeping the spirit of enquiry alive in a world that was becoming enclosed by dogma. The Inquisitor finally arrived at Mantua – the slanderer, we called him. The books at the palace that he would have burned had he access to them.

I remember Vincenzo reading to me from Bruno: 'Unless you make yourself equal to God, you cannot understand God, for the like is not intelligible save to the like. Believe that nothing is impossible for you, think yourself immortal and capable of understanding all arts, all sciences, the nature of every living being. Mount higher than the highest height, descend lower than the lowest depth. Draw into yourself all sensations of everything created, on earth, in the sea, in the sky, in the womb, beyond death. If you embrace in your thought all things at once, times, places, substances, then you may understand God.'

Vincenzo has lived this philosophy. He has risen higher, descended lower than any of us. Yet he still does not understand God, for he has not found peace. And he is jealous of Monteverdi, he can hear through his music that Claudio is in communication with God, with the gods. As I am jealous of Vincenzo, not as he is now but as he was then: a young god of love, handsome, tall, his fair hair, as always, unruly, his eyes alight with life, a healthy mountain complexion from his Austrian mother. And I, like his father, stunted by the marshes, twisted by the wind, a thorn tree next to the ash. Everyone knows I am jealous, it is part of my nature, but no one knows Vincenzo's envy of the divine gift. Does he himself know? Look at the labyrinth ceiling for his answer, the words that are carved, twisting and turning through the maze. *Forse che si, forse che no.* Maybe yes, maybe no. What kind of a man chooses such a motto?

Step through the mirror and I will show you the pictures.

Given that his exterior features are very well known I will speak only of his interior ones, among which shines forth principally his liberality and humanity, for which he has gained both the reputation of being the most splendid duke to have been in Mantua and the universal love as much of the nobles as of the people . . .

Report on Vincenzo Gonzaga by the Venetian ambassador to Mantua, 1588

It pleases me to hope that just as the sun draws a plant's virtue from its roots into flowers, and from flowers into fruit, so Your Most Serene Highness, whom with great reason I should call my sun both for the effects which you produce in me and for the valour which shines in you, should be such that you grant me your customary kindness, for if my skill flowered for you in playing the viola, with its fruits now maturing it can more worthily and more perfectly serve you.

Dedication to Vincenzo Gonzaga in Monteverdi's *Third Book of Madrigals*, 1592

*H*ere *is a loggia* overlooking a lake, a young man sitting on the parapet, one foot resting on it, displaying what he knows is a fine calf in repose. His shirt is open at the neck, his jerkin loosely fastened. He is dressed for a morning's hunting, but he had risen late and there had been one delay after another. Secretaries flapping documents at him, messages from the Treasury. And so on, etcetera, *und so weiter*.

It is a soft spring morning, and Vincenzo is restless. There are too many people at his heels and ever more demands on his time. It is calming to look out over the waters of the lakes surrounding Mantua, their far shores fringed by willows that ripple from green to silver in the breeze. His hair is similarly ruffled by the wind, fair and resilient to the comb.

'Look at the old grandfathers along the bank, they're out in force today,' he says. 'Pike tonight for everyone.'

There, leaning against the next arch of the loggia, I can see the young man who was myself, Ottavio. He is wearing a grey cloak carefully draped at the back, obscuring his body. He is around twenty years old, his hair dark, his eyes with a darting sideways glance, as if trying to catch what is happening out of his sight. He is holding a letter in his outstretched hand, which the Duke ignores. Eventually he flicks it to attract his attention.

'She wants all her letters returned. Every one of them. She has listed the dates.'

Vincenzo sighs. 'That it comes to this. All that passion spent and now we have to make an inventory of her love letters. Why did she write so many? I don't know where they are. In this drawer or that. The hound Magnus ate one of them, I remember. I gave it to him to sniff the perfume, and he dripped saliva all over it, so I let him keep it.'

'She is very insistent, and more than a little anxious.'

Vincenzo's voice had risen a note, as it did when he felt put upon. 'What does she think I am going to do with her damned letters? Send them to her husband? Hand them out in the piazza? I've a mind to, the lack of trust she shows in me, Ottavio. No one could have been more careful with her secrets than I.'

Ottavio smiles, remembering the passages the Duke had read aloud. He says, 'Nevertheless, she is insistent. We will have to return those we can find.'

'Ottavio, will you do that for me? I can't bear the thought of looking through the letters, of people asking me what I am searching for. Do it in the afternoon when no one is in the office. You know where the keys are.'

'Tidying up after His Highness.'

'And you do it so well.' Vincenzo directs his warmest smile, his eyes shining with the love of humanity. No man or woman could resist the charm. Ottavio folds the letter and slides it into his sleeve.

Vincenzo leans over the parapet to watch the fishermen. One of them has waded into the lake and is waiting to grasp at a gliding shape. He picks up a pebble from under the lemon tree and spins it so that it lands near the man with a splash like a rising trout. The fisherman lunges at the ripples; his dog, which had seen the missile, leaps into the lake barking. The man curses the dog. The other fishermen shout at him. Vincenzo laughs.

'Such a small thing, and look at the trouble it causes.'

He glances at the entrance to the loggia, and the warmth fades from his face. A girl is standing on the topmost step, her hair loose on her shoulders, the stiff bodice of her dress giving her the appearance of a marionette; her age, around fourteen years. She is poised as though for flight, but at the same time riveted with curiosity. She stares at the Duke as if at a magnificent, mythological beast.

'Who is that?' Vincenzo's face, unusually for him, betrays anxiety.

'She is from Novellara. A second cousin, related on my mother's side. You met her mother, Donna Vittoria, yesterday. They are guests of the Duchess.'

'For a moment . . .' says Vincenzo, and paused. His unspoken thought is clear to Ottavio. For a moment he had remembered Margherita Farnese, his first wife, callously chosen in a game of politics by Vincenzo's father when she was too young, no more than a child; too frightened of love, and now condemned to a convent, the loss of her future the subject of rancour between the houses of Mantua and Parma.

The girl is looking at Vincenzo with open curiosity. He holds out a welcoming arm. '*La bella ragazza. Che bella!* Have you come to look at me, or at the view?'

Giggling bursts out from her two friends on the steps behind her. She raises a hand to her mouth, her eyes looking with adult awareness at the man before her. As he stands up, she retreats and all three girls run down the stairs in a flurry of skirts and giggles.

'Already an eye for men,' says Vincenzo. 'What is her name?'

'Isabella. From Novellara.'

'One fine day . . .' as he looks out over the water, and then, 'Now Ottavio, what are you going to do for me?'

'I am going to find all of the Signora's letters, apart from those the dog has eaten, and return them to her.'

'Tie them with a golden ribbon and pearls, so it seems we are returning something precious, rather than being thankfully rid of them.'

✳

So that is our Duke for you, Vincenzo Gonzaga, young and careless, in both senses of the word. An extraordinary vitality runs in his veins. That, more than his fine figure, more than his considerable wealth, is what attracts all to him. He seems alight with life, and those around him feel more alive. And the almost innocent joy he gets from the riches his father left him is quite touching. I can see his face now as he emerged from his first visit to the strong-rooms, and described the millions of gold scudi, the jewels, the title deeds, the files of credit notes, carefully hoarded by the miserly Duke Guglielmo. Who was no longer there to place a restraining hand on his son. Our Duke pounced on the gold like a hound among truffles.

There is, though, a sort of divine discontent in the way he uses his wealth. It is not enough to spend, he needs to create with it as well: to create beautiful things, awe-inspiring events, to create wonder. He was an adolescent when he first visited the d'Este court at Ferrara and heard the *concerte delle donne*. He breathed in the beauty of their voices and the music, and as soon as he was Duke, with access to the treasury, he set about acquiring musicians and singers from Ferrara, from Venice and from Florence, in competition with his wife's uncle, the Grand Duke Ferdinando.

Eleonora de' Medici is no fool, she knows that it is not just for art he has brought to Mantua the finest singers, and a permanent company of actors. People laugh about the Duke's musical harem, and once in a while a girl with a fine voice returns home and is never heard of again. It gives us something to gossip about.

Do you detect a note of jealousy? I have a tainted vein of the blood that runs through the family's branches, emerging now and then in twisted bodies, stunted limbs. You can hardly see, I drape my cloak so expertly it looks little more than a stoop. Unlike Vincenzo's father, who was a veritable hunchback. Duke Guglielmo il Gobbo. We are men of the marshland; our strength is in our survival, you should not expect beauty as well.

❀

Let us move to the next picture, from the profane to the sacred. You are in a cathedral, see the soaring columns, like avenues of stone trees, their branches ending in a filigree supporting the painted roof. Hear the purity of the voices praising Our Lady of the Heavens. Do you see the young man there on the left, in his musician's black robes, his face intent on the music, enraptured yet aware as he sings? Afterwards he will point out to his fellows in the choir where it was half a note too long. Not the best way to make himself loved, but even then he would sacrifice everything to the perfection of his music. Thin, with large dark eyes, a high forehead, a sensitive mouth. Claudio, son of the doctor Baldassare Monteverdi in Cremona, one book of madrigals already published in Venice, another about to come out in Milan. Just twenty-two and on a voyage of discovery. There are two qualities he has in common with the Duke: a consuming love of music and the same divine discontent. It is not enough for him to create music, he wants to claim the soul with it, his own, his listeners'. It is only a matter of time before the two will meet. The year is 1589. Grand Duke Ferdinando of Tuscany has cast off his Cardinal's robes, taken his late brother's title, and allied himself with France in his marriage to Christine of Lorraine. Neither the Habsburg Emperor nor His Most Catholic Majesty of Spain are happy to see French influence in Italy, but the Grand Duke is an astute and determined man. Claudio is aware of the politics but his interest in the wedding is to do with the musical intermedii for the comedy, *La Pellegrina*. From Cremona, he travels south with his fellow musicians to Florence. From Mantua Duke Vincenzo's 600-strong retinue sets forth for the same destination.

❋

Weddings were good for business and no city was ever more eager for business than Florence. They accepted the overcrowding, the difficulty of getting food, all supplies having been requisitioned by the Grand Duke, because in the end they would be the richer for it. No one richer than the Grand Duke whose lavish celebrations would be compensated for by the dowry of his bride. The Florentines could even tolerate the overwhelming number of Mantuans on the loose, talking in their loud, harsh dialect, walking four abreast in the street, jostling each other and anyone in their way, not out of ill will but simply because they are used to the wide open spaces around their own city and feel enclosed by hills.

The Mantuan retinue numbered 200 men at arms as well as the entire court and its attached entertainers, including a coachload of dwarfs who were getting under everyone's feet. The splendour of their trappings and costumes were a statement of vanity, designed to impress the French and the Florentines. Grand Duke Ferdinando trusted that the scale of his entertainments would redress the balance. He had borrowed Duke Vincenzo's favourite singers, the Pellizari sisters, but the composers and writers were Florentine, and the designer the great Buontalenti, the Medici architect.

Circling each other, separated by rank and society, the Duke and the musician from Cremona saw the same event from their different perspectives. Claudio, in quick glances, took in the audience of nobility, their embroidered silks, stiff ruffs and swathes of pearls. On stage, the feathered headdresses, jewels and silks of the gods and muses, and the scenery, painted with as much care as if it would be there forever. Peri, the composer, costumed as Arion the poet with papier mâché harp, sang his own composition, then escaped from forty men dressed as sailors by flinging himself into the waving ribbons of the sea, causing mirth in the orchestra at the idea of 'Lo Zazzerino' with forty sailors after him. He should be so fortunate, muttered the musicians. And so it went on, the posing on stage, the preening in the audience, over the course of seven hours.

No one had finer feathers than the Duke of Mantua, but the showiness disguised a well-informed mind. He had noticed in all the extravaganza the young Monteverdi, he had

taken soundings, he had already seen the first book of madrigals. He had an eye for promise of every sort, and knew
better than to wait until it is sought-after and therefore
more expensive. A week later a letter bearing the Gonzaga
crest arrived at Dr Baldassare's house in Cremona.

The new musician follows the others through a confusion
of corridors, up the stone staircase, through the Room of
the Zodiac, through the Room of the Falcons and the
Room of the Satyrs to the Hall of the Rivers. On its walls
are painted the six rivers that run through the Mantuan
land, on the ceiling flights of birds, at one end a stone grot-
to and above it the four black spreadeagles and cross of
the Gonzaga coat of arms. The musicians arrange their
stands and instruments before the rows of chairs and wait
for their audience. Friday night is concert night at the
palace of Mantua. Every week there are new compositions
as a diversion for the Duke.

You can trace the most influential in the court through
looking at the first two rows. Among them is always to be
found Giaches de Wert, the old Director of Music, whose
shared past with the Duke during their time in Ferrara
gives him a power beyond his position. He will talk to the
Duke during performances, pointing out particular qualities in the music. He watches the new violist, for he already
knows his compositions. He notes that the man from
Cremona is used to freer air than that of Mantua's court.
As the audience applaud at the end, the Duke, his face shining above his starched ruff with enthusiasm and the heat
of the evening, turns to de Wert.

'Mantua will be the centre of the new music. We are
leading the way, ahead of Florence. Why do you not play
nowadays, Ottavio?' the question being addressed to the
young courtier next to de Wert, Ottavio; always in the
right place.

'Because, as Your Highness has brought in so many

excellent musicians from Venice, Florence, and Ferrara, there is hardly space for a poor amateur.'

You have to use courtier's language like that when there are others present.

'What a load of balls you talk, Ottavio,' says Vincenzo. 'You play as well as anyone here,' and then to de Wert, 'Tell the new musician to compose a piece for Don Ottavio. I should like to see him play it next week.'

Monteverdi bows to the request, though his air is less of being honoured by a commission than of being doubtful about the musician. Anyone else would have accepted with a show of gratitude, and then cobbled together offcuts of other compositions to satisfy what had been a passing whim. Not Signor Claudio. He arrives at rehearsals pale from having worked through the night. We rehearse the new work for viols. And Monteverdi talks the special language of musicians when words give way to the sounds and the beat. 'Now at that point it should be ta-ta te tah, semi-quaver, allegro.' No wonder musicians stay together. No one else can understand a word that they say. Isabella arrives with her mother to watch the rehearsals for amusement, and with a little envy.

'I could sing for the Duke,' she says. 'I have a good voice. You have heard it, Ottavio.'

As I had, the summer before at Novellara. In the garden of their villa, the fields around shimmering in the golden evening light, playing the lute while Isabella sang in a high, pure voice. Like an angel, her mother had said.

Her mother says now, 'You will certainly not sing for the Duke. He might mistake you for one of the harem.'

Lucia Pellizari looks angrily at her and snaps, 'Quiet during the rehearsals.'

Isabella smiles. She is interested in everything, even a display of temper. It is a hot day. The musicians have their collars unlaced. Lucia Pellizari fans herself with a painted fan shaped like a viol. She takes the pearls from her neck and places them on the clavichord's lid. They are a present from the Duke. Sweat is trickling down Monteverdi's face as he marks time from his place at the viols. It is a sign of the marsh fever.

'From that phrase again,' he says. 'From the ta-ta te tah, and . . .'

We begin again and the music takes shape. It speaks to the heart in a way I had not heard before, like wings of angels in my chest, beating against the rib cage. I see Monteverdi's eyes watching me as an instrument of his music, and we seem to be linked as one, myself as his viol. As the movement draws to a close, I look at our audience and see Isabella, her eyes intent on me. And I realize that something still lives under the heart of ice I had assumed with my shape. 'You're like the salamander,' Vincenzo once said, 'you lack the warmth that I have.' But the music told me that somewhere within was the gift we are born with. 'Why, Ottavio,' says Isabella afterwards, touching my sleeve, 'you looked quite beautiful when you played.'

And so it was the music that first made it seem that all things were possible. That the ugly should be beautiful, the unloved should be loved. Music, the builder of hopes and dreams.

CHAPTER TWO

*I*t *is the time of Carnival*, two years later, and here is
another image in the mirror, of men in masks. Look at
that mask, gilded with curved wings, its wearer cloaked in
black, the glinting gold brocade of his doublet visible
when he turns. His companion wears silver and black. It is
the year of the gold and silver carnival.

The two men follow the Captain of the Armoury from
the painted halls to an older, darker part of the palace.
Behind them the fading sounds of revelry, ahead of them
men's footsteps, a cough from the shadows, the metallic
rattle of keys. The February air is chill and their breath is-
sues from below the masks like smoke.

'He has been talking for almost an hour,' says the
Captain. 'He has confirmed everything we suspected.'

Captain Antonio, square-jawed, light-eyed, a face weath-
ered by forty winters, a conscientious man. He knows
what the prisoner was expected to confess and he is not
going to disappoint the Duke. Footsteps echoing down
the worn stone steps, heavy metal-tipped boots followed
by the lighter tread of high-heeled court shoes. An iron
door opens into a vaulted underground room. The tapers
flicker over the scene. Three guards are standing easy near a
table at which a man is sprawled, almost falling from his
chair. His face is discoloured with bruises and blood
trickles from his matted hair. His chest shines like maho-
gany from the blood and sweat and his eyes shine too with
wild, unblinking shock.

'Here is his confession,' says Captain Antonio, holding
out a paper to the Duke, who removes his mask to read the
document.

'It's not signed.'

'He put his mark to it. Was as much as he could do.'

The Duke reads the paper and hands it on to Ottavio. He turns to the prisoner, his eyes cold in an anger-reddened face. 'So you conspired with others to fire the armoury and the theatre. On Prince Ranuccio Farnese's orders you did this. On the Farnese's orders you attempted to destroy us.'

The man stares at him as if he no longer understood words. The Captain says, 'He admits he set fire to the scenery which was stowed behind the stage, and it spread from there to the armoury. He told us that it was only the theatre he was meant to burn.'

'Only the theatre! And then the armoury. Our history destroyed in a night. The armour of Luigi, of GianFrancesco. All by this ruffian, put up to it by the Farnese. Find out the names of the others involved. Have the papers prepared for a trial.'

The Duke leaves the room without looking at the man again, one of the hired adventurers and bandits that infested the country. As they reach the end of the steps, he turns to Ottavio and says, 'If he could have the choice of anywhere in the palace he could not have chosen an area closer to my heart. The theatre and the armoury. It makes me weep to see the ruins. We shall build a great theatre in its place, and hold the most wonderful spectacles. I want the greatest architect in Italy. Who is the greatest, Ottavio?'

'Antonio Maria Viani has been working for Rome.'

'Bring Viani here. Write to him tomorrow. Tell him to come here instantly and put forward his plans.' And with that instruction, the Duke closes his mind to the scene in the prison cell.

⁂

The sounds of the Carnival grew louder as they approached the palace courtyard. Lighted windows, music, laughter. Vincenzo masked himself as they entered the great hall, to be drawn into the swirling crowd of several hundred faces glittering with gold and silver, eyes shining behind masks.

CLARE COLVIN

The air was warm and highly charged with the smoke of thousands of candles, bowls of pot-pourri, hothouse lilies and overheated bodies. The atmosphere was infectious with excitement.

'Ah, le belle donne,' said Vincenzo. He moved through the crowds, his eyes behind the mask assessing, guessing. At Carnival time, thoughts of a new adventure. The masks did little to hide the identity of those who knew each other, yet they gave the wearer an illusion of gorgeous anonymity. There was the Duchess, her fine, thin face only partially obscured by the gold-embossed mask with diamonds. And there was Agnese, unmistakable behind the feathered disguise. Agnese del Carretto, Marchesa da Grana, the dark-eyed beauty from Córdoba whose charm had caused the inconstant Duke to turn away from all other attractions. Agnese, married to a convenient courtier, and now installed at the Palazzo del Te with her own court. Eleonora, from a line of diplomatists, would not dream of showing the pain that is in her heart. She remains true to the Duke and is polite to Agnese. But she will never again see the palazzo on its watery island, not as long as Agnese is in residence. And she notices that Agnese's brocade robe is curved with something more substantial than underskirts. She is almost certainly with child.

A procession of dancers began to form, as the musicians struck up a new tune. Vincenzo bowed over the hand of Eleonora, whose fluttery gesture towards her heart indicated that she was tired, though willing to dance once more. The orchestra was playing a haunting canzonetta with an insidious, sliding beat. The procession, two by two, with a swaying motion, moved three steps forward, two steps back and hopped to one side. The first part of the procession, following Their Serene Highnesses, danced with gravity and precision. The tail end was less ordered. One gentleman, hopping at the wrong moment, trod on the train of the lady in front of him who dealt him two quick slaps with her fan, another miscounted the steps back and collided with the man behind. At the end of the procession, two dwarfs grimaced as they hopped and twirled in a parody of the lords and ladies.

Just ahead of the dwarfs, on the arm of one of the pages, was Isabella, her mask pushed back onto her hair, glowing with the excitement of the evening. Wisps of hair fell over her face, she was laughing as her eyes took in the carnival party around her with the eagerness of a child. Sixteen now, and no longer a child, but dizzily on the threshold of a new and enticing life. She stepped past the orchestra, smiling at the violist, young Claudio, looking curiously at Agnese, seated on a chair near the orchestra, attended by her complaisant husband. The head of the procession snaked round and was stepping, shuffling and hopping towards the tail so that those behind were now face to face with those they had been following. And leading the procession, the Duke with his Duchess, the heels of his shoes tapping the beat of the music against the floor, his eyes behind the mask surveying the other dancers as they passed, assessing as he went by the curve of a neck, the flash of an eye, the moment when like will meet like. Isabella is unmasked, her face open and laughing and suddenly the Duke is looking at her, and she feels his glance to the depths of her being, as she is exposed to his eyes. The curious pale light in them as they stare into hers, and then they glance to her neck and her shoulders, her breasts and her waist, encased in stiffly embroidered silk, and she knows he has seen her body under the clothes. As her hand reaches up for the mask she has need of, he smiles and she is bathed in the warmth of his charm. Unmasked, she returns his smile as he moves on. Shuffle, step, hop, turn.

'Ottavio,' she said, a long time afterwards, 'I felt naked at that moment, and then his warmth covered me, and I loved him for it.'

I would never wish to disillusion Isabella, but it is one of the tricks of the Duke. Nobody, man or woman, can resist it, but they know not to be close to the fire. One learns much through watching others. I am standing with a group of fellows who cannot or will not dance, next to me Giaches de Wert, the Director of Music. I can hear the wheeze in his breathing; old lungs suffer from the marsh fog.

'Quite a catch to that tune,' he said. 'I could almost dance to it.'

'A haunting number, Maestro. Is it one of yours?'

'No, young Messer Claudio's. A musician as devoted to music as a priest.'

'He will do well here, with a Duke as devoted.'

De Wert laughed. 'The young man is also of that opinion, he is in a hurry to impress.'

'But you yourself would surely say there is no point in hiding your talent,' drawing him out a little, to find what is in his mind.

'He has learnt much from me, but believes that all of his talent comes from himself.'

Professional jealousy then, from someone at the close of his career towards a man at the start of his. There is no point in arguing. Paid musicians are quick to feel slighted.

Isabella had masked herself again as she approached us. Her eyes shone through the blue and silver frame. 'Such a beautiful evening. Such magnificence. Do you not think so?'

'It reminds me of the balls we held at Ferrara in the eighties,' said de Wert. 'The black and white *balletto della duchessa*, the *concerto delle donne*, it started there.'

'You may have seen other such evenings. To me this is all new and exciting,' said Isabella. 'Such magnificence.' And her head was turning again, trying to see where the Duke was.

'Will you not dance with me, Ottavio?' I could see the ploy immediately. Another chance to capture the Duke's eye.

'I do not dance, Isabella.'

'You did dance with me last summer at Novellara.'

'I do not dance at Mantua.'

I had danced at Mantua, though, a few years ago, at Vincenzo's coronation. The whole city had been given free wine, there were fireworks and a banquet for a thousand. We danced, and then I saw the Duke's dwarf behind me, making a hump of his back, flailing his arms. A few drunks were laughing at his imitation of me. Why take notice of a dwarf and some drunks? But I never danced at Mantua again, despite the restlessness in my feet. Ottavio has a melancholy humour, he doesn't like dancing, said the Duke. And thus others assume characters for us, which we then adopt.

The next day was Ash Wednesday. The penitents processed to the cathedral, led again by the Duke, his forehead marked with ashes, sackcloth over his fine lawn shirt. By the evening Isabella's mother Donna Vittoria had recovered enough from the previous night's festivities to receive visitors. Isabella was at Vespers with her maid. It was a time to speak frankly to her mother.

'We are all concerned about the protection of our daughters,' she agreed, 'but Isabella is never out of the sight of either myself or her maid. What would you do? Send her to a convent?'

Donna Vittoria looked at Ottavio with blank, shortsighted eyes. 'How can I be in Novellara at this time? The Duchess needs me here, I cannot be spared. And how can Isabella be sent back alone? In this weather, through rain and floods. She cannot stay there in winter, neither can I. It is living death.'

'Then announce the betrothal to Don Ferrante. Bring forward the marriage. She cannot be both unmarried and at court.'

'It would be disastrous to hurry,' objected Donna

Vittoria. 'Negotiations are still going on over the dowry and property. Don Ferrante is hard to please. We cannot seem too eager.'

'If we leave it too long, she may not wish to marry him. I do urge you that she leaves Mantua.'

Donna Vittoria looked sympathetic. 'Of course it is difficult for you, Ottavio. I am sorry if you are caused pain by her presence.'

A reminder of last summer when Ottavio's approach to Donna Vittoria for Isabella's hand had been rebuffed. She had tried to be tactful. It was a case of the best match, and it was necessary for Isabella to marry into a different branch of the family, otherwise, who knows? Her eyes had been drawn momentarily to Ottavio's draped cloak. He had left Novellara shortly afterwards and returned to Mantua.

'It's not for any reason of mine,' said Ottavio, 'but because of the Duke. He has noticed her.'

'Nonsense, Ottavio, he's not interested in young girls, only in married women and his actresses. I should know, I'm close to Eleonora. Besides, he is devoted to Agnese. She is having his child, as you must know. There is even a note in the *avvisi*.'

Lying on the table next to Donna Vittoria were two recent news pamphlets, from Venice and from Rome, which she had read avidly for their gossip. She picked up one of the papers. 'Where has it got to? No, this one has the scandalous lies about His Holiness. I don't believe a word of it. Who tells them all these things? Paid informers, I suppose. The menanti have their spies everywhere.'

'And occasionally pay something other than money for their information.' Only a year ago one of the correspondents, accused of slander, had been arrested and brought to Rome where his right hand had been cut off, then his tongue, before he was hanged.

'In any case,' said Donna Vittoria, 'we can neither leave Mantua until spring, nor speed up the negotiations with

Don Ferrante. So that is where it rests. You will have to trust me as a mother who knows her child.'

An unsatisfactory response, but there could be no further argument. Ottavio bowed over Donna Vittoria's hand, and left her apartment. He felt urgently in need of getting away from the palace and all it contained. He collected his overcoat and hat, and called for a torchbearer at the gates. In the piazza of the cathedral, a band of hooded monks processed, bearing a shrine lit by oil lamps and chanting a *misera culpa*. A few penitents in sackcloth were following them, but most had done enough for the day. A dank mist caught at the throat, the light of the torches in the square illuminating its eddying swirls. Ottavio walked through the archway that linked the piazza of the cathedral with the Piazza dell'Erbe, under the shadow of the Tower of the Cage, where Vincenzo's father, Duke Guglielmo, had had an outdoor cage suspended for prisoners. Away from the gilded palace and the lights of the piazza, the city's darkness gathered him to it. Narrow, high-walled streets, shuttered windows, and the sound of boots echoing on paving stones. Now the sound was coming nearer, and he could hear the heavy tread of men and the iron-rimmed wheels of a cart. He waited in the shadows, his hand on the hilt of his sword while his torchbearer held the flame high to illuminate the faces of the men. As they drew near, he recognized two of the Duke's guards. On the cart, drawn by a hooded porter, was something shaped like a body wrapped in canvas. Several steps behind the cart, with a torchbearer, walked Captain Antonio. He hailed Ottavio.

'I was searching for you earlier. To report on the prisoner.'

'What has happened?' An unnecessary question, looking at the cart.

'He died. Last night, not long after you left. I'm sorry about it. I shall put in a full report.'

Ottavio crossed himself in the presence of death. 'His

Highness will be unhappy. There goes his evidence against the Farnese.'

'Who was to know this bravo had so weak a heart? We thought he was stronger. His brother is outside the gates waiting for him. Even ruffians have families.'

The soldiers moved on, the torchlight and the sound of the cart receding down the street. Ottavio shivered in the night air. He remembered the man's eyes looking at him, the expression of shock in them, one might even say, of outraged innocence. Who would ever know the truth of the matter? Nowhere was healthy in the city, neither the palace nor the streets outside. The torchbearer asked, 'Where to, signor?'

'To the cathedral.' He felt the need for a blessing against the night, for the security of sanctified walls. As he entered the cathedral the choir were singing the last psalm of vespers. Dark smoke rose into the air from the torches and candles, pale scented smoke drifted from the incense burners. The cathedral musicians and choir were a separate establishment from the ducal palace but he saw two of the Duke's musicians among the congregation nearby, one of them being Messer Claudio, intent on the music. Ottavio waited until the Bishop gave the final blessing, and as the Sanctus sounded he crossed himself for the second time that evening and felt the darkness leave him.

Now the congregation was moving towards the door of the cathedral, Isabella with her maid among them. He stepped forward and offered to escort them back, and the three of them crossed the square in the light of the torchbearer. As they approached the open gates a horseman rode out, muffled from the cold, but unmistakable by his bearing. The Duke, as always careless of a guard when in his own city, confident of the people's goodwill. With a single torchbearer against the dark, the horseman rode towards the narrow street along which the deadcart had rolled earlier. Isabella watched until he was lost to view.

'You see,' said Ottavio, with a note of satisfaction, 'even on a night like this, even on Ash Wednesday, he cannot stay away from his lady on the island del Te.'

Isabella turned to him, her face calm. 'It must be wonderful to be loved like that,' she said.

CHAPTER THREE

The musicians' rehearsal room is in uproar. Rumour has followed rumour over the future of the pastoral comedy, *Il Pastor Fido*. The latest commotion involves the actors of the intermedia on the harmony of the elements, who have gone on strike. Lucia Pellizari declares she is in favour of their action. It was bad enough for the actresses to be obliged to drape themselves in flimsy gauze as nymphs but at least they had the figures for it. But when you demanded of distinguished old actors that they wear only a few leaves to cover their private parts, of course there was going to be trouble. Who wants to see naked old men anyway?

A voice from the cornetti spoke up in favour of naked men, of whatever age. Why should it be only women who disrobed? The intermedia were recreating the legends on the walls of the Palazzo del Te, on which there were naked people of all sexes, including old men.

But fortunately no old women, said the basso, which started another argument as to what point in your life you were regarded as unworthy to take off your clothes.

Gianbattista Guarini is in despair at the actors, said the viola bastarda. He now believes his poetry is unstageable, that the Duke should withdraw the whole event and produce it as a concert only.

Words, music, actors, singers, dancers, scenery, machinery, it's all too much for one play, said the trombone. His Highness wishes to outdo the Grand Duke's *Pellegrina*, but the Medici has Buontalenti.

Listen, I will tell you exactly why Guarini is going back on the idea of staging his work, cried Lucia Pellizari, pitching her voice higher to be heard above the rest of the orchestra. He is embarrassed to be caught in the contest

28

between two women. Agnese, Marchesa da Grana, tenant of the Palazzo del Te, wants to stage the work there for her greater glory, to show that the centre of culture is at her own court. Our Duchess feels she has exceeded her station. That's the crux of it, and Guarini is unhappy at being caught up in their power struggle.

And of course the Duke's mother is on the Duchess's side, added Lucia's sister, Isabetta Pellizari.

Ah! La madre! cried several voices in unison, and the basso's rumbling voice, The Habsburg mother will win.

After which the gossip diminished to the tuning of instruments as the rehearsal, speculation satisfied, begins.

※

In another part of the palace – the Duke's apartments – other voices were raised. Vincenzo walked fast through a succession of rooms, each double door being opened by a footman at his approach. He was followed by his secretary, to whom he had been dictating a letter when interrupted by his mother.

Like a brocade-clad battering ram, Duchess-Mother Leonora advanced on the retreating Duke, anxious to drive home her argument. To his protests that all had been arranged, that the actors and musicians were in full rehearsal, the date set for the night of the full moon in May, she replied that it was yet a month away and there was time to cancel.

'The poem must not be staged,' she said. 'It is immoral and pagan, and is not approved by the Church. It's disgraceful that you should have such a work performed in public.'

'The public will not see it, only those at court of sufficient artistic sensibility,' said Vincenzo, adding under his breath but not low enough, 'which may not include you.'

Incensed, she redoubled her moral assault, all the energy of her ample, under-exercised body ringing in her voice until, at the moment she judged his anger close to the point where he became irrational, she wheeled and retreated, presenting an unassailable back, off which further comment glanced harmlessly like toy arrows. Vincenzo walked through the remaining set of double doors to his study, the desire to slam them thwarted by the footmen.

'Madre del Dio, quale madre!' and he slumped into a chair. The secretary and Ottavio exchanged glances, and both assumed a sympathetic air.

'Ottavio,' he said, 'is it wrong to have a dream?'

Shaking of the head from Ottavio, together with soothing words of agreement.

'In these times of repression, of attacks on our very thoughts, is it wrong to try to create a better world, to create an Arcadia? A place of wonder, and music, and spectacle.'

'It is highly commendable, Your Highness, and everyday I hear people praising you for it.'

The Duke glanced at Ottavio's composed face. 'You will have to be my Ambassador to Rome,' he said.

From the other side of the door came the sound of more voices, and the footman entered to say that one of the musicians had arrived to deliver a new composition. In the usual course of events it would have been delivered to the Duke's secretary, but there was a mood of anarchy, as happens when too many wills are fighting for supremacy. Then whoever comes knocking at the door is given entrance, if only to divert the gathering storm of his rage.

'Yes, let the man in,' said the Duke impatiently. 'Let me see his work, he may present it to me.'

So there in the ducal presence was the young musician in black, holding in his hand the score of the poem by Tasso which the Duke has commanded to be set for soprano and alto. The eyes of the latest diversion met those of the Duke. He bowed as he delivered the score and waited as the Duke glanced at it.

'We will hear this at the concert in the Hall of the Rivers tonight,' said the Duke.

The composer's face lost its deferential air and he said abruptly, 'The musicians won't be able to rehearse it to my satisfaction. They are entirely taken up with *Il Pastor Fido*.'

There was a silence so dense that it seemed to fill the room with a tangible fog. The secretary looked down at his desk, disassociating himself from the scene.

'Oh,' said the Duke, 'Your satisfaction? What about *my* satisfaction? I should like to hear it now.'

Signor Claudio bowed, regaining his deference, and said, 'Your satisfaction will only be met when the piece is well rehearsed, Your Highness. It is difficult for a singer to perform a part he has not mastered, and it would damage the composition. It will be ready for next Friday's concert, when it will better suit your taste.'

'Then I await next Friday with anticipation,' said the Duke. 'I shan't be disappointed, shall I?' Instead of anger, the other ducal weapon of charm immersed the young man in its irresistible strength. Claudio returned the smile, and his eyes shone with the reflected warmth. So the two men stood for a moment, the young musician of single purpose, not yet twenty-five but with the awareness of his gift, and Duke Vincenzo, in his thirtieth year, rich, feared, beloved, and at the mercy of the labyrinth of his mind. Which way to turn? What path to choose? Ruler, politician, soldier, scholar, lover, father, all contained in one man. And already within him the awareness of passing time.

❈

It is the night of the full moon in May and the courtyard of the Palazzo del Te is alive with conversation as the guests of the Marchesa da Grana take their seats. Chairs have been set out, interspersed with the statues and wrought iron pergolas. The torches set in brackets on the surrounding arches add a yellow warmth to the light of the moon. There is the sound of many voices chattering, the rustle of acres of material in motion, silks, velvets and brocade containing energetic bodies attempting to compose themselves to two hours of sitting still. Some will continue walking around the edge of the courtyard between compositions. The court of the Marchesa is young, and not inclined to be still, even to hear the music they love.

So the Marchesa has won, then? Not at all, for this is only a concert. Guarini has withdrawn *Il Pastor Fido*. Some say it is because of the intransigence of the actors, others that the two Eleonoras have prevailed. Agnese refuses to be downcast. She will have a concert, and she is aware that the strength of her position rests in the Duchess's acceptance of her. For a while, when the arguments had been raging, she had felt vulnerable. But now, seated next to the Duke, she feels restored to her position as favourite.

Look at his attentiveness. The gentle swell of her robes demands his concern. He is holding a private conversation with her while around them the audience gossips and preens. She laughs, her head inclines to his. And then the chattering dies down as the musicians take their places, and the singers arrive – the Pellizari sisters, one in pink and silver silk, the other embroidered in flowers, followed by the tenor and the bass. The other singers are ladies of the court who pride themselves on their voices. Agnese would have sung, for she is a member of the Accademia degli Invaghiti, musical gentlemen and ladies of Mantua, but the tension of the preceding weeks together with her condition had led her to decline to take part.

Music, singing, laughter, mingled in the evening air, warmed by the flames, the many people and the remains of the day. The human warmth of the court, pleasant enough for those present, was even more enticing to the inhabitants of the marshes. At eight in the evening the air was filled with agitated clouds of mosquitoes, their high-pitched whine audible during any pause in the music. Audible, too, was the clapping of hands against exposed flesh, muttered curses that rose into a crescendo of complaints. The incense burners had proved ineffective against the mosquitoes' frenzied attack. The Pellizaris slapped at their exposed shoulders as they sang, the musicians scratched their heads furiously between phrases, bows in hand. Then as suddenly as they had arrived, the mosquitoes departed, so weighed down with blood that many landing on the water fell through the surface and drowned.

The Duke, who had been gallantly shielding the Marchesa's bosom with his hand, called for more incense in case of a second attack. The night air began to smell like the inside of San Pietro, the smoke wafting opaque in the moonlight. A few muttered that they might as well have held the pastoral concert behind closed doors in the first place and been spared the torture.

The Duke signalled to Ottavio to call for Monteverdi.

'Your Highness.' The musician's face was covered with swellings that itched from the insects' poison. It was always those from outside Mantua who suffered the most, as if the mosquitoes found a particular sweetness in them.

'I should like to hear your composition again, the Tasso, I have a special affection for it.'

'I am honoured,' and while the audience talked among themselves the musicians conferred quickly as to which among them knew the work best. Lucia Pellizari, her Venetian skin punctured with the Mantuan pests, said, 'Your pupil knows it as well as any of us. I cannot concentrate on a new song. I feel as if I have a hundred hot needles in my face.'

And that is how Isabella sang for the Duke on the night of the full moon in May, in company with the *concerte delle donne*. She was wearing blue and silver, as on the night of the Carnival, and her hair glinted pale in the moonlight. And I, Ottavio, stood at one side of the courtyard where I could watch both the audience and the musicians. Her voice was high and clear, above the florid notes of the other singers as she sung of the harmony of love. Her face, unmarked by the marsh pests, was shining with the joy of the music, and the emotion its composer had brought to the words. She glanced at the Duke with eyes of innocent seduction. He smiled, whispered something to Agnese, and they both looked well pleased. The song ended, the singers bowed to the applause, and for most of the audience that was where it ended. A delightful new composition, delightfully sung.

But I had seen as Agnese moved from the Duke's side to talk to her guests, Vincenzo's eyes turn back to Isabella. She was alone for a moment as she crossed the courtyard from musicians to the audience. I had seen the expression before, the sharpened gaze, the head held as if scenting the air. Isabella may have confused it with admiration, even, in her youthful egotism, with love. But it was simply the hunting instinct of the Gonzaga, who has caught sight of the prey.

CHAPTER FOUR

I *sabella looks at herself* in the mirror. She is pleased with what she sees. She had spread her hair out in the sun to dry after rinsing it in lemon juice and the maid is right, it is lighter. She stares into her eyes, admiring their clearness, turns her head sideways as she tries to see the profile which always eludes her. The Duke had said it was like the portrait of Simonetta Vespucci by Piero di Cosimo. She raises her hair in both hands to see how it would look arranged so. She decides it resembles a mass of silken gold.

She reflects upon life at court. It is all so exciting. She would hate to be anywhere else. Two years ago when she first arrived, she felt constrained by the formality, by the need to walk sedately with that curious gliding motion the court ladies adopted, to know whom to greet and how. She would long for the summers in the country, but now it is the opposite. She has no wish to return to Novellara and miss the great game at court.

It is a game, really, she thinks. Everyone is plotting to better themselves, to move ahead on the chequer board. And if they land on the wrong square, they lose several lives. At the very least, they are not seen in court again. Cousin Ottavio is skilled at the game; he has been playing it for years. A pawn to the Duke, moved here and there to block a knight or a bishop. Their branch of the Gonzaga has had its disagreements in the past with Mantua, yet here they are, received very happily by the Duke and the Duchess, because of Ottavio.

She wonders how the negotiations are going with Don Ferrante. She had met him last summer, and he had pleased her even though he was older than she would have liked. He had a good figure and an attentive manner, but how slow he had become during all the talk about estates and dowries. She is no longer pleased with him. It is neither chivalrous nor courteous to spend so long quibbling over an odd nought. She remembers tales that her grandmother told her of the court during the days of her namesake, Isabella d'Este; the gallantry, the high romance. Who then would have talked about money and whether this estate was of a higher yield than that? Unless Don Ferrante comes to protest his love, she tells her reflection, I'll call the whole thing off.

This unheard-of proposal gives her a sensation of illusory power, and she imagines herself, unbeholden to Don Ferrante, as one of the ladies at court, the names that they used to have – Tortorina, Chiarina, Diana piu calde del sole – somehow they had more style then, so her grandmother said. The air was freer. But the gentlemen at court are all on their mettle, knowing that otherwise they will seem pale beside the Duke. She thinks of the musicians: such a different life they lead in their sober costumes, looking on as the instruments they play enable the jewelled courtiers to make their moves across the board. Claudio, so serious, such a perfectionist, with a biting edge if he feels someone is not giving of his best. He was quite wounding when she was inattentive during her lesson, a few days after she had sung at the concert. A man both sensitive and proud, being talented and poor. And Ottavio was sensitive too, with the touchiness of one filled with self-dislike. When she was a child and he not much older, she had tried to climb on his back and he had thrown her off with such violence that she had cried for an hour. Now he always dressed in subdued colours, grey or black, with a cloak. But on horseback, he took on a new form, like a centaur, and she had seen the way he could move with it as it leapt.

She sees him now in the mirror, the dark form watching her. He has come in silently and caught her unawares.

'You have a letter there,' he says.

'Yes, I have.' It is still in her hand. She would have hidden it if there were time.

'Who is it from?'

'A friend. It's private.'

'May I see?'

'Certainly not. You have no right.'

'I saw the Duke's dwarf as I was approaching. Was it he who brought you the letter?'

'Not at all,' lies Isabella. 'The dwarf is everywhere, all over the place, up and down the corridors. Like too many other people, I may say.'

She can see he is not satisfied. When he leaves, she waits for a few minutes in case he has an afterthought and returns, then she unfolds the letter again. It is a poem, from the Duke. Not his own, but it doesn't matter. A few lines from *Il Pastor Fido*, with the hope that she will sing the words one day.

> Quanto il mondo ha di vago e di gentile,
> opra e d'Amore.
> Amante e il cielo, amante
> la terra, amante il mare . . .

All that is fair or good in the world is the work of love . . . She smiles as she re-reads the letter.

※

In another part of the palace, Vincenzo listened to Ottavio as the barber massaged his scalp. The essence of rosemary scented the room. The barber listened too, his face impassive, the dark eyes glistening as if oiled.

'The negotiations with Don Ferrante have reached a delicate final stage,' said Ottavio. 'We are in the process of drawing up the contracts, and then the marriage will be able to take place.'

'So Ferrante is still arguing over money, is he? He owes me 10,000 scudi, and I know he falsifies the monies from his estates to give the impression he is less rich. But the family will go ahead with the marriage?'

Ottavio hesitated for a moment, then in a quiet voice, 'It is a good marriage, one that we would not like to see jeopardized.'

The barber's hands paused in their massage as the Duke turned his head towards Ottavio. 'I am not sure I believe what I hear,' said the Duke. 'In what way may the marriage be jeopardized?'

The barber waited motionless, eyes lowered. Ottavio raised his hands in a gesture of conciliation before the cold fire of the Duke.

'Only that Your Highness's court is so supremely civilized she may become reluctant to leave it for the sober responsibility of marriage. We should like to leave shortly for Novellara, with your permission.'

'If you feel it is necessary, then of course I shall not prevent it. I would not keep anyone here against their will. But before you depart, I wish to give a present to Isabella. Because she sang so well at the concert, and to remind her that we should like her to sing at Mantua again.'

Donna Vittoria raised her eyes from the latest *avviso* from Venice to greet Ottavio.

'What did the Duke say?'

'He will be happy to allow us to leave court, but first he wants to give Isabella a present.'

'What sort of a present?' asked Donna Vittoria. 'Did he say?'

'I could hardly ask, particularly with his barber who, as you know, is also his procurer, listening in to every word.'

'Shame on you for listening to gossip, Ottavio, and double shame for repeating it.'

'I think we should leave very soon, Madama. I know she has already received a letter from the Duke.'

'Dio, the thoughtless girl! She is compromised if anyone

hears of it. I shall have a talk to her, and we will arrange our departure at once. What a pity. It's difficult to see how our Duchess can spare me.'

Donna Vittoria sighed and folded the paper.

'What news from Venice?' asked Ottavio.

'Little of note. They have arrested the so-called philosopher Giordano Bruno, and he is awaiting trial.'

'On what grounds?'

'For speaking wickedly against the Church. On Italian soil, as well. It must have given joy to the Protestants. It says here that when the informant first told him he would be delivered to the Inquisition, Messer Bruno said that if he would let him go, he would teach him everything he knew. It sounds like the Devil speaking.'

'It sounds like a frightened and desperate man,' said Ottavio. 'So nowhere is safe, not even Venice.'

※

Vincenzo has had enough of the pressures at court. There have been too many disputes to deal with, too many people asking favours. He needs a few days away to relax among those who don't tax his brain. His chief huntsman, Ippolito, has arranged some sport for him and he has decamped to his villa near Marmirolo, close enough to return within a couple of hours, yet blessedly free of the court. The Duke's entourage clatters out of Mantua and on to the open road. Back in court, several people also breathe more freely.

Now was the time, Ottavio suggested to Donna Vittoria, for Isabella discreetly to be sent away. He distrusts the Duke's talk of a gift. But Donna Vittoria says it is difficult to leave suddenly. Eleonora is unwell, and needs her company. And besides, you cannot just creep away without formally being granted permission. But Her Highness will do this instead, said Ottavio. Tell her that Isabella is suffering from the Mantuan air, and she will have every sympathy, knowing how bad it has been for her own health.

Donna Vittoria then said that Isabella could not make the long journey back to Novellara on her own. In the end, they reached a compromise solution. Isabella would stay with her aunt at her convent on the road to Brescia, having taken leave of the Duchess, and Donna Vittoria would join her the following week. Like all compromises it wasn't satisfactory to anyone, least of all to Isabella.

CHAPTER FIVE

The waters of the River Mincio widen into lakes that surround the city like a vast moat. The banks are dense with silver willow, and yellow mustard flowers grow among the rushes on the small islands. Water lilies raise their golden cups above the green plates of their leaves. On the surface of the lake drifts what seems like white scum, the fluff of poplar seeds, borne here and there in the wind. Where it has accumulated in corners of the city it is as if someone has shaken out an eiderdown of goose feathers. It lies on the island of Te like a first fall of snow.

Isabella's coach rolled over the long bridge and she looked out at the water on each side. From the open window, she smelt the stagnant odour on the warm air. Seated beside her was Emilia, her maid, dressed in sprigged cotton. Opposite, in figured velvet and starched ruff, the Duke's dwarf.

There are times when you would give a few years of your life just to turn the clock back to undo what was done, to unsay what was said. Isabella was in such a frame of mind. She felt the blood rise to her face as she thought back to the previous evening. It was all to do with the Duke's dwarf, Archimedeo, who had suggested himself as company for the journey. During the last few days he had been entertaining her with stories and jokes. Many of them had to do with the Duke, and she had a hunger to hear his name, a hunger that those around her seemed perversely to deny.

'I am coming with you on the journey. There is no need for the dwarf, he will simply make trouble,' Ottavio had said.

She had said, her blood warm from the wine and her mood frivolous, that she would have both of them to accompany her. It would be a departure like that of a princess in a fairy tale, accompanied by her hunchback and her dwarf.

Or words to that effect; not perhaps put quite as curtly, she hoped to God, as she tried to recall the exact sequence in which they fell out of her mouth. But as soon as they had reached the air, she knew she would have given anything for them not to have been said. She tried to talk of something else to distract his attention, but she could feel the wave of silent anger, she saw his face darken, and then he had turned on his heel and left.

The next day Ottavio had called to take her to the carriage, his face impassive, his eyes cold. As he handed her in through the door, she waited for him to follow, but he said, 'I shall be riding ahead with the guards,' and closed the door in her face.

'Someone's in a bad mood today,' chuckled the dwarf. 'Never mind, I'm feeling cheerful,' and he began to sing.

So they rolled on through the countryside, with Archimedeo cracking jokes, Isabella politely laughing when necessary, and ahead of them Ottavio on his steel grey horse riding with the guards. After a while the dwarf said, 'Here's another Carissima Isabella for you. I'm sorry for the late delivery, I have been carrying it around for a day.'

Isabella unfolded the letter, a poem in the Duke's hand, though not by him. She smiled as she read it, but frowned as she reached the postscript.

'He says to wait for his return, he has a present for me. And now I'm leaving.'

'Oh Zeus,' said Archimedeo. 'I knew I should have got it to you sooner. I'm going to be in trouble again.'

Ahead of them rode Ottavio, feeling the air on his face. The plains of Mantua shimmered in the early summer heat, stretching towards the distant hills of Brescia. There was harmony in the sound of the breeze murmuring through the trees and grass, the birdsong, the creak of the saddlery, the clop of horses' hoofs. Harmony everywhere except in himself. Like a black note of discord in the peaceful landscape, he rode on, half listening to the guards, half immersed in his own bitterness. The sooner Isabella was married, the sooner he would be rid of what was a tie of emotion that had rubbed raw. The sores could only be cured with ice in the heart. To have allowed other sensations when she saw him in such a light was to have made a fool of himself.

The guards talked of this and that, the sun shone warm on his face, the horses snorted. Their ears pricked forward and they made little whinnying noises as they saw other horsemen riding over the marshes a mile or so ahead. The guards watched the figures warily. The road to Brescia was safer than the road to Venice, but their job was to anticipate trouble. Huntsmen, said one of the guards, and their tension eased. They had come to a stretch of forest land that edged the left-hand side of the road. A boy was driving a herd of goats along the grass on the right, as if in a pastoral scene. The horsemen could now be seen more clearly as they approached. Two of them had their gloved hands extended, on each of which was perched a falcon. The nearest to the road hailed the guards, and rode towards them. His teeth smiled white from his sun-scorched face, and Ottavio recognized the Duke's huntsman, Ippolito. Among the others he saw a young cousin of Vincenzo, known for his prowess at sport rather than at court, beaming with the virtue of those who can drink deep all night and gallop over the countryside all day.

'Don Ottavio,' called Ippolito. 'Come and join us for some sport.'

Ottavio saw the falcon perched on his wrist, its sleek body, the feathered ruffs ending in claws that gripped the glove tightly, the chain that bound the bird to the handler. The falcon was unhooded, its curved beak in profile. One round, bright eye watched him.

'I am accompanying milady Isabella on her way to her aunt,' said Ottavio.

'You can spare a while, and they are travelling slowly,' said Ippolito, and indeed the coach had come to a complete halt as the goats spilled across the road. Ippolito held his gloved hand towards Ottavio.

'Come try the Duke's falcon,' he said.

'Where is the Duke?' asked Ottavio, with sudden unease.

'He has one of his headaches, a martyr to excess, the poor man. We won't be seeing him today.'

Ottavio rode out onto the open lands away from the road, through the tussocks of reeds and long grass. After they had ridden some way Ippolito loosed the chain on the bird and shook the glove, so that the falcon was dislodged from his perch, and rose into the air with a slow spread of his wings.

'He will come back when I call,' said Ippolito. 'Here, take the glove.'

Ottavio pulled on the heavy leather gauntlet, its surface scuffed with claw marks, and watched the falcon as it flew upwards to the sky. Its wings moved with majesty, like the wings of angels, and he felt his spirit soar with it as it circled ever higher. Free as a bird, they said, and so it was. Unbeholden to any elements, unheeding of earth, of weight, of anything but its wild need to rise upwards to infinity.

'When I whistle, raise your right arm and he will come to you,' said Ippolito. 'Watch the way he comes down.'

He placed a small piece of raw meat on the glove, and looked up at the bird, giving a long, melodious whistle. From the sky, the circling falcon spiralled down and then swooped like a stone dropping to the glove. Its talons hit the leather and gripped tightly. Ottavio's hand shook under the weight and velocity. It tore at the piece of meat and then raised its head to look at its new handler. Golden, round and bright, its eyelid so fast it appeared unblinking, the eye watched him with a more than human intelligence.

'He is the sweetest bird we have,' said Ippolito. 'Come a little further into the marshland, and we will find him some prey.'

Ottavio followed him, bearing the falcon, which Ippolito had hooded, on his wrist. As the horse stumbled, the falcon swayed and gripped the glove more tightly with its talons. Ottavio sensed the trust that the bird must have towards its unseen handler, clinging on in its darkness, a trust that bound the two of them together as one.

❈

The dwarf, stepping on to the seat of the coach, leant out of the window and called out to the goatherd, 'If you can't control your goats you should keep away from the road. You're holding up the traffic.'

The boy looked up at the dwarf with smiling incomprehension. Apart from the coach, the only other vehicle on the road was a donkey cart plodding slowly in their wake. But people from the town were irascible and had to be humoured. He waved a leafy twig at the goats and called to them. Some listened and came towards him, others went in the opposite direction. A river of white and black fur, curved horns and bulging wall eyes weaved in front of the coach.

'We could be here till nightfall,' said Archimedeo, and then, clapping his hand to his head, 'I have just had a brilliant idea. I'm amazed that I have only just thought of it.'

He turned to Isabella, his face alight with the brilliance of the idea. 'We are only a mile from the villa by Marmirolo. Why do we not take a small deviation and then you can say goodbye formally to the Duke and he can give you his present?'

Isabella's face reflected the light that was in his, but she said, 'No, we cannot possibly. It is not the same as at court, and in any case Ottavio would not hear of it.'

Depression settled on the features of the dwarf, and he said, 'I knew I should have delivered the letter sooner. I shall be in such trouble now.'

He stared gloomily out of the window, and then, 'Look at Don Ottavio, he is just a speck on the horizon. He will be away for hours yet, and we shall be sitting here in the road. Why don't we leave the guards here with a message for him? We shall probably be back before he has missed us.'

Isabella glanced at her maid for her reaction. Emilia had been in a state of some agony for the last hour, from the effects of drinking too much tisane at breakfast and the uneven road. She was on the point of asking to retreat into the trees. The idea of getting away from the road to seclusion found favour with her.

Archimedeo brightened again, and he climbed down from the coach to hail the guards who had ridden some way ahead. He returned, hauled himself back in and said, 'There, that's done. You will be able to say goodbye to the Duke, and I shall save myself from a boot up the backside.'

The coach moved on, scattering the remaining goats, and shortly after turned to the left onto a track that ran through the trees. Branches brushed against the sides of the coach, for no one had visited the villa since last autumn. A stone wall surrounded the villa's grounds, running beside the track for a quarter mile until they reached a tall iron gate, with pillars each side surmounted by the stone eagles of the Gonzaga. Three guards were sitting at a table to one side, rolling dice. The dwarf leaned out of the window and called, 'Guests for His Serene Highness.'

One of the guards lazily rose to his feet and pushed the gates further open to accommodate the width of the coach. They were now driving along an avenue of poplars. A heady sweet scent drifted through the windows. On one side of the avenue was a long channel of water. From its dark mirror water lilies thrust the golden globes of their flowers towards the light. A chorus of frogs croaked vociferously. The sun filtered green through the leaves.

Some two hundred paces on, the avenue opened out into a park, in the centre of which was the villa, a classical building in the style of the Palazzo del Te, though smaller. The coach came to a halt in front of the flight of steps that led to the main door, and the dwarf bounded out of the coach and, bowing low, extended his hand to help Isabella.

Inside, the villa was cool and shaded, the walls painted with frescoes by the master, Giulio Romano, each room having a different theme. In the room where Isabella and Emilia thankfully retired, there were pictures of nymphs pouring water from jugs on to their naked bodies. The main hall was frescoed with the chase – mettlesome stallions and mastiffs in full cry after a stag. Archimedeo said regretfully, when they rejoined him, 'We may have to wait a little while. The Duke is having a late morning.'

Isabella no longer minded, for there was so much to see in the frescoes. After she had looked at the hunt she moved on to the salon where a mural feast was in progress. Satyrs poured wine down the throats of nymphs. Two putti were cramming grapes into the mouth of a girl wreathed in flowers. A cherub was kneeling under a nanny goat, milking it with his mouth. On the ceiling above was a horse and charioteer, the perspective taken from below, exposing their rears. Isabella was intrigued.

She was on her own, the dwarf having taken Emilia for a tour of the grounds, when she heard footsteps approaching. The doors at the far end of the salon opened, and there was Vincenzo. He exclaimed, 'Carissima Isabella,' and ran his hand through his hair as if to tame its unruliness before polite company, then clasped her hands in both of his and kissed her on the cheeks. She smelt a fresh scent of acqua di limone on his newly shaved skin.

'Forgive me for being forward,' said the Duke, 'but you cannot know what joy it gives me to see you here.

How unhappy I would have been if I had returned to Mantua and found you had left without a word.'

Isabella smiled. 'I would have been unhappy, too.'

He was looking at her like a young boy eager for approval. 'Carissima Isabella, not looking a day older than when I left,' and as she laughed, he said, his tone changing, 'I have thought of you day and night.'

'You have done nothing of the sort,' said Isabella, with a hint of alarm. As if he sensed her about to take flight, he said, 'Come, you must have something to eat after your long journey.'

'It wasn't very long, hardly two hours, and then we have two hours more before we reach the convent.'

He had clapped his hands for a servant and gave an order, then turned to Isabella again. 'A convent, did I hear?'

'My aunt and some of her worthy friends undertake work for the poor. It's not a closed order.'

'My little songbird in a convent? How could they do this to you?'

'It's only until I am married,' said Isabella. The manservant placed on the table two Venetian glass goblets, a jug of white wine, a plate of almond cakes and a bowl of peaches. Then, his eyes discreetly lowered, he left the room. Isabella sat opposite the Duke. He poured wine into their glasses and, examining the peaches, picked the ripest and gave it to her, then sat back in his chair and watched her.

'You must have something as well,' said Isabella. 'Otherwise I shall feel self-conscious.'

'You look so beautiful when you eat,' said the Duke, 'I can hardly take my eyes off you. Do you remember at the Palazzo del Te, after the concert? You were near a plate of figs. You took one and split it open, then sucked the flesh from the skin.'

'What appalling manners,' said Isabella. 'I am ashamed

of myself.' But secretly she was flattered at the thought of the Duke retaining in his mind this insignificant act. She reached for a knife to cut the peach.

'Bite into it whole,' commanded the Duke. So she did, and the juice ran down her chin and on to her hands. He reached forward, and wiped away the juice with his handkerchief. His hand touched hers.

'I had such a bad headache this morning, and since seeing you it's gone,' and he lifted her hand to his forehead.

'A headache? Poor Vincenzo.' It was the first time she had spoken his name to him and she was not sure if she should have, but he simply smiled, with that curious light in his eyes.

'So you are marrying Don Ferrante? When will this happen?'

'Quite soon. Before the end of next month.'

'And do you wish to marry him?' He was staring at her as if to read the thoughts behind her words.

'He pleased me well enough, until . . .'

'Until . . . ?' he encouraged.

Isabella looked down at the half-eaten peach.

'My mother says that you always love your husband once you are married.'

'Your mother is very wise, but you haven't answered my question.'

'That,' said Isabella, 'is the only answer you will get,' and tears started in her eyes.

'Oh come now, Carissima Isabella,' as the handkerchief was used again, and then Vincenzo, getting to his feet, said, 'I have a present for you. Because you sang so well, and to remind you not to forget me when you are married.'

Isabella smiled again. 'A present?' and she followed him through the double doors into the next room.

They were in another frescoed salon, this one smaller, with a canopied couch, shaped like a boat and gilded. The walls were thronged with field birds, painted with meticulous accuracy, and dimpled putti holding garlands of flowers.

'Each room is prettier than the last,' said Isabella. The Duke closed the doors behind them and opened the lid of a small lacquered chest on a table. It seemed to Isabella now as the door shut that they had entered an enclosed and heightened atmosphere. She could hear no sounds from outside, and the windows on to the gardens were shaded from the light.

※

The Duke turns and there is something glittering in his hand.

'May I?' he says, standing in front of Isabella. He leans forward, his arms encircling her as he fastens the clasp of the jewels behind her neck. His chest is touching the bodice of her dress, his breath warm on her neck. He stands back and looks at the necklace with a critical eye, then says, 'It suits you well, come and see,' and leads her to a mirror on the wall.

She looks at herself in the glass, her neck now adorned with sapphires and pearls. The Duke's image, reflected behind her, watches her mirrored eyes.

'I couldn't have chosen better,' he says. 'You see how close the sapphire is to the blue of your eyes, the pearls to the smoothness of your skin.'

And he turns her to face him. 'Carissima Isabella,' he whispers, 'does it please you?'

'Oh yes, it does,' she says, her hand touching the necklace, and her heart is suddenly painfully thumping in her chest, as she realizes she has stepped into unknown country. A voice in her head says clearly, 'Go now and no harm will be done.' She gathers herself to speak, but doesn't know what words will now extricate her with grace. How can she say, 'Thank you very much for your jewels', and then disappear out of the door? It seems ungracious when he has been so kind, and so concerned about her. She hesitates a moment too long as he looks at her expectantly. And his eyes are so full of love, and there is an air of vulnerability in his face. He leans forward and kisses her on the mouth. Isabella feels the softness of his lips, the caress of his moustache. He raises his head and looks into her face.

'Is that your first kiss?' he asks.

'Yes,' she says. It is not. She has already practised with the page.

'Maybe yes, maybe no,' he murmurs, and bends his head towards her again. She sees the two eyes merge into one as they reach her and closes her own eyes as his mouth touches hers and she feels his tongue darting over her lips. This was something she had most decidedly stopped the page from doing. But with Vincenzo it is different, it is not an intrusion but an intimacy of his love. Her lips part to the pressure of his tongue. It feels right, and her mouth opens wider. His hands behind her back clasp her more tightly and she can now feel his heartbeat through his light jerkin. He groans, 'Ah, how beautiful!' and his breath sounds loud and harsh. She draws back in sudden apprehension. But he hushes her gently, and whispers, 'Dolce,' as if soothing a nervous mare. Then one hand is at her breast, and now, she knows not how he got there, it is inside the dress, inside the chemise, and against her bare skin. She feels the heat of desire through her body, and wants to love him more than anything.

He is murmuring, 'Carissima Isabella, mia fanciulla,' and other endearments, and he has edged her towards the couch onto which, her knees having turned to water, she sinks. He is kneeling over her, his hands are pushing aside the material of her skirts, and exposing her legs, and now his hands are where none but a husband's should be, and she cries out in alarm. Or rather, her mind is crying in alarm, her body is saying something quite else. His mouth is kissing her breasts, now naked to the air, and she smells the scent of rosemary in his hair. And then he raises his head, and looking at her with eyes that have become quite dark, whispers again, 'May I?' And she says, 'Yes,' because that is what she wants, and also because it would be useless to say 'No.'

His body is over hers, her legs are being pushed wide apart, and suddenly there is tremendous pain. A battering ram of flesh is pounding at her, and her mind is filled with terrible images: bodies impaled on stakes, torn apart between two horses, Vlad the Impaler, the nightmare of her childhood. And now the battering ram is inside her, she is impaled on his flesh. As it thrusts ever deeper, Isabella screams.

CHAPTER SIX

*H*igh *overhead the falcon glided*, circling as it waited for a creature to betray itself by a movement. The riders looked upwards, their lips drawn back from their teeth, their eyes half closed against the light.

'I think you have already killed every bird in the land, Ippolito,' said the Duke's cousin.

'No, there are always more,' said Ippolito. 'And there are rabbits and mice. He won't lack for food. Look, he can see my handkerchief if I raise it. His eyes miss nothing.'

From the grass a lark flew upwards, its throat bursting with song. It spiralled ever higher, carelessly throwing out the notes of joy in life, in the sun. As it diminished to a speck against the blue, its voice filled the air to the horizon. The falcon hovered, its wings trembling, and then dived. The song ended in mid-note.

'I wish that he had let it live,' said Ottavio. 'There is one less song in the world.'

The Duke's cousin laughed. 'I believe the salamander has a soft heart after all. It's only a field bird.'

Ottavio looked at him and his two friends, and as they laughed their teeth seemed to him like the teeth of wolves. Ippolito shrugged as Ottavio gave him back the glove. 'What can you do? It strayed within his sights.'

Ottavio looked towards the road. 'I must return to the coach,' he said, and then stared in both directions at the empty road.

'The coach has travelled further than you thought,' said Ippolito. The falcon landed heavily on his glove and he took the lark from it and dropped it into the bag by his side.

'Yet the guards are still there,' said Ottavio, seeing at the roadside two horses, and in the shade of the trees two recumbent figures. He glanced at the Duke's cousin and saw that his face was set in the broadest grin. Ottavio had the sensation of a man waking to find a thief has been in the night.

'Fine guards they are,' he said. 'I must leave you.'

As he turned back for the road, he heard the laughter of men enjoying their sport.

The guards, hearing the approaching horse, stumbled to their feet, and had resumed a semblance of alertness by the time he arrived.

'Where is the coach?' demanded Ottavio. 'Why are you not with it?'

One of the guards, brushing dried grass from his tunic, said, 'We were waiting for you with a message. The dwarf told us to say they had gone to visit the Duke.'

'You idiots!' shouted Ottavio, and as they querulously asked why, he said, 'You should have come to tell me directly. We have lost too much time. Where did they go?'

'Why, to the Duke's villa,' said the guard, pointing to the track through the trees.

Ottavio left them to their complaints about his bad humour and galloped along the track by the wall, brushing past branches, until he reached the iron gate. It was closed. He called through the bars, 'Let me through, I must see the Duke.'

The gatekeeper looked up from the game of dice. 'The Lord Duke is not receiving visitors,' he said. But as Ottavio refused to be turned away, he shrugged, 'I shall ask him, if you insist,' and he walked slowly up the long avenue, leaving Ottavio staring after him, willing him to walk faster. Half an hour later he returned.

'They are on their way,' he said, and opened the gates as the coach rolled towards them. The coachman drew up beside Ottavio, who dismounted, flung the horse's reins at the coachman's boy, and opened the door of the coach. He heard the sound of sobbing as he got in. The maid was crying into her handkerchief, now and then murmuring,

'Madre del Dio'. The dwarf was examining his fingernails with some attention. And Isabella was staring in front of her with expressionless eyes.

Ottavio cried out, 'Isabella!' but she seemed not to hear. The maid re-doubled her sobs.

'Be quiet!' snapped Ottavio, and then to the dwarf, 'What has happened to Isabella?'

'You will have to ask her,' said the dwarf. 'I wasn't present.'

'You toad, you pander!' and he pulled the dwarf from his seat and thrust him out of the coach. 'You can walk from here.'

'I cannot,' protested Archimedeo, and Ottavio heaved him onto his horse, at which he protested again. 'I hate horses, I shall fall.'

'Hang on to the saddle, you piece of ordure,' and Ottavio, ordering the coachman to drive on, got back into the coach, slammed the door, and drew up the windows for privacy against the listeners outside.

'Isabella,' he called, shaking her gently by the shoulder, but her eyes mirrored no sign of recognition. He turned to the maid, who was rocking to and fro as she sobbed. Then Emilia found her voice, and cried out, 'She is dishonoured . . .' before a fresh storm of weeping overtook her.

Ottavio gripped Emilia's shoulder and shook her more firmly. Emilia protested in the midst of her tears and, taking a breath, said, 'He has violated her. He has despoiled her. She is ruined.'

Isabella's face remained unchanged by the maid's outburst, as if she had not heard. She gave no sign of recognition as Ottavio, leaning close to her ear, asked very quietly, 'Is this true?'

'Madre del Dio, it is true! He took her by force,' cried the maid. At Isabella's neck, the blue fire of sapphires sparkled in clusters of pearls.

'Where did this necklace come from?' And as Ottavio

understood, he tore it from her neck. Pearls and sapphires scattered over the floor of the coach. As the maid's sobs increased to a crescendo, Ottavio began hitting the backrest to either side of Isabella, pounding it with his fists inches from her face, and shouted, 'I shall kill him! I shall kill him!'

Emilia wailed and cried out in fear, for Ottavio had taken his dagger from his belt and was stabbing at the upholstery. He drew the dagger down and horsehair burst from the gashes in the leather as if the carriage was being disembowelled. His violence had broken through Isabella's trance and she cried out, 'No, Ottavio!' and burst into tears. 'He didn't force me. I loved him. Don't harm him. I loved him, Ottavio.'

And deep within him, a huge wave of anger overwhelmed him, bursting out in a sound like a bull in its fury. Isabella and the maid were transfixed with alarm. The dagger clattered to the floor and Ottavio subsided on to the seat beside Isabella, his head in his hands while deep, heaving sobs shook his body. The women's alarm turned to dismay, to hear a man, against the natural order of things, in tears. Isabella drew him to her, trying to comfort him, and for the first time her arms encircled his back, as his head lay against her breast. She rocked him to her, murmuring, 'There, dolce, Ottavio,' as earlier the Duke had soothed her. Ottavio's breathing became quieter, and the maid watched in amazement, her own sobs stilled. So the three of them were borne along in the closed coach, which grew ever hotter from the lack of air. Isabella fanned Ottavio's forehead, the maid dabbed at her face with a handkerchief. And then Isabella said in a quiet voice, urgently, 'Emilia, I think I'm bleeding.'

Ottavio retreated to the corner of the carriage, and sat with his head in his hands, hearing the rustling of skirts, Emilia's soft cries of concern, and then the sound of material being torn into bandages. The women's voices were so subdued that he didn't catch what they were saying, but eventually Isabella said in clearer tones, 'We have done now, Ottavio.' For the rest of the journey she sat pale-faced, looking straight ahead of her, with the air of one willing it to be over.

The coach drew up in front of the villa, and Emilia who had been retrieving sapphires and pearls from the floor, helped her mistress to her feet. Isabella helped Ottavio to his. As they descended from the coach, Signora Caterina Maria, waiting there to greet them with the other ladies of the convent, was unsure who was supporting whom. She kissed Isabella, and said, 'My child, you all look so exhausted.'

Isabella smiled, tears in her eyes. 'We are tired. It was such a long journey.'

❄

The marriage to Don Ferrante took place within a fortnight. Isabella took the sacrament with modest grace, some said an air of resignation. The bridal party left after two days of celebrations, and Don Ferrante made no attempt to detain them. Ottavio stayed away from court, at the villa of his elder brother half a day's ride from Novellara. A fortnight had passed when a messenger arrived with a letter from Donna Vittoria summoning him to attend her. He found her sitting in a shaded room in a state of agitation. A letter lay on the table beside her.

'I can't bear the thought of travelling in this hot weather, but what can I do? There is a crisis in their marriage.'

She gave Ottavio the letter from Don Ferrante which revealed at some length the cause of her agitation, in that Isabella was shunning her marital duty; that when Ferrante got into bed, she would get out, that she spent nights curled up in a corner of the room weeping, refusing all comfort. Don Ferrante could not bear the shame of a bride who rejected him, and if she could not be made to see reason, he would have to send her away.

'Well,' said Donna Vittoria. 'This is a pretty fine mess. Whatever has got into Isabella? I brought her up to be modest, but this sort of hysteria is against all reason. Ottavio, what do you know of her mind?'

'Not much more than you, Madama,' said Ottavio. 'If you cannot persuade her to accept Ferrante, how can I?'

'It is all very odd,' said Donna Vittoria. 'The marriage is brought forward because my sister writes to tell me Isabella is pining for Don Ferrante, then once she is married she spurns him. She has refused to go to confession. I think you know something more about this than me. Look at this, Ottavio.'

She handed to him another letter, a bill from the palace's treasury with a claim for damages from the Master of Horses.

'Upholstery ripped to shreds. What possessed you, Ottavio, to behave like a vandal?'

'There were only a couple of tears. They've exaggerated the damage in order to claim more. But don't worry, Madama, I'll pay whatever they ask.'

'I wish I had not left court. The answer lies there somewhere,' said Donna Vittoria.

Ottavio recognized the danger they were in. If Donna Vittoria found out the truth, she would go to the Duchess with her complaint. The Duchess would confront the Duke, and the repercussions would be immeasurable. Isabella's reputation and marriage ruined, the entire family out of favour and subject to the derisory gossip of the court.

'Perhaps I do know something of Isabella's mind,' said Ottavio. 'I am returning to Mantua, and on the way I could see her and talk to Don Ferrante. If I can reconcile them, it will save you the journey.'

In the shade of Don Ferrante's orchard, Isabella talked to Ottavio. She was in love with Vincenzo, she said, she had tried to forget him but she could not.

'After the way he behaved towards you?' Ottavio asked

incredulously. 'He fooled you, he seduced you and, if I may say so as a witness to the result, he did not even do it very skilfully.'

Isabella blushed. 'Nevertheless I love him, and I am waiting for him. I shall wait for him for ever.'

'And if he tells you not to wait, to accept your marriage?'

'That would be a different matter,' said Isabella. 'But he will not. We are linked in our souls, I know it.'

Ottavio raised his eyes to the heavens in despair, and went to Ferrante to tell him he would seek advice from doctors in Mantua.

'Do you think that will help?' asked Ferrante. His face was shadowed with anxiety and he seemed, in a short space of time, to have aged.

'Before I help you, tell me one thing. Do you love Isabella?'

Ferrante looked at him, pain and anger in his eyes. 'I could not love any woman more. I feel ill at her distress, and even more so if I have caused it.'

Ottavio embraced him, with words of reassurance, and departed for Mantua on the same day.

※

The palace was in chaos, caused by the imminent annual exodus to the Gonzaga summer villa on Lake Garda. Maids hurried along the corridors carrying clothes and linen, porters were heaving trunks downstairs. There was a buzz of excitement at the thought of the journey from those who were going on it and at the expectation of less work from those staying behind in Mantua.

Ottavio announced his presence to the guards before the main doors to the Duke's apartment, and waited. Eventually the doors were opened to admit him, and the Duke's secretary showed him into the library. He waited again, and then the doors opened for Vincenzo. Before Ottavio could speak, Vincenzo had embraced him, saying,

'Welcome back, my friend. You have been missed.'

Ottavio disengaged himself from the embrace. 'As you know, there has been a reason for my absence, and now there is a reason for me to be here.'

The Duke drew back and returning to formal speech, said, 'I trust the wedding celebrations went well.'

Ottavio glanced round the room. The secretary had withdrawn, but now a clerk had come in to look through the shelves for a book. There were voices outside which presaged another invasion.

'Is there somewhere more private we can talk?' asked Ottavio. 'I don't want what I am going to say to be overheard.'

'There is not an inch of privacy in the whole palace, as you well know,' said the Duke. 'Come, let's go up to the loggia and get away from these people.'

So there they were at their old meeting place on the loggia, Vincenzo sitting on the balustrade overlooking the lake, Ottavio standing nearby, talking in a low voice for fear that even here they might be interrupted.

'Isabella is in danger because of you,' he said. 'She agreed to marry Don Ferrante, but now she has rejected him. Because of you.'

Vincenzo, for the first time, looked shamefaced. 'I am sorry for what happened. I should not have been so impulsive.'

'I would not have thought impulsive was the word to describe a campaign of seduction, conducted with the help of your familiar, the dwarf, and aided by your cousin.'

'Oh come now, Ottavio, you have always thought too much of conspiracies. This was accidental. In different circumstances it might never have happened.'

'But it did, and now a girl's life is ruined, because of you. She will not allow him in the same bed.'

'She kicks him out of bed? Poor Ferrante,' and Vincenzo laughed. 'How humiliating for him.'

'She doesn't kick him out. She gets out herself and sleeps on the floor.'

'No wonder he is unsuccessful. To let your bride sleep on the floor. What an idiot he is.'

'But she doesn't sleep, Your Highness. For most of the time she lies there weeping. Because of you.'

Vincenzo ceased laughing. 'I would not have hurt her for the world.'

'But you have, and now she is ruined. Ferrante is losing patience. If he sends her away, there is nothing left for her except a convent. A young woman at the beginning of her life condemned to the veil. But you know about that already. That was the fate of your first wife. You remember Margherita?'

'Don't talk about her,' said Vincenzo. 'I cannot bear the thought.'

'And this will be the same, with Isabella.'

'What can I do?' Vincenzo looked at Ottavio, with an air of helplessness.

'Tell her to love her husband as she loved you. Write to her as persuasively as you know how.'

'You cannot dictate to the heart.'

'On the contrary, the heart can dictate to the heart, and you must do so, to save Isabella. You know how to use your powers of persuasion.'

Vincenzo looked out over the land as he considered. Ottavio waited silently. Then Vincenzo said, 'I shall write. Come with me, Ottavio and keep everyone at bay.'

So while Ottavio stood near the Duke's desk in the library, and a footman outside repelled invaders, the Duke wrote his letter. It took around half an hour, and finally he settled back in his chair and read it through, and, with an air of approval, said, 'Ottavio, I think this is well argued. Would you like to cast an eye over it?'

'No, it is between you and Isabella.'

The Duke folded the letter and sealed it before giving it

to Ottavio. 'I think that will settle matters,' he said. 'Now you can take it to her.'

Ottavio took the letter from him and slipped it into his sleeve.

'Tidying up after His Highness,' he said, and bowed.

The Duke looked away. There was, after all, nothing that could be said. Ottavio left his presence, left the palace, and set off in the afternoon heat and dust to reach Isabella before nightfall.

※

Don Ferrante's villa lay in the western reaches of the state of Mantua, a three-storeyed building in classical style set in grounds shaded by poplars and limes. Inside, the light was dim from the shutters still closed against the heat of the day. Isabella was unwell, said Don Ferrante. She had retired to her bedroom and he had not seen her for two days. Their only method of communication was through her maid who was now sleeping in the same room like a watch-dog, though God knew he had no intention of setting foot there again unless invited.

The two men dined in a room that was silent but for the ticking of the clock and the footsteps of servants bring-ing in food. Eventually Ferrante began to talk of general matters: of the chaos in France, of the war against the Protestants, and the possibility of it spreading to Italy. Ottavio observed him, assessing his character. His head, round, the hair short and the colour of iron, a muscular neck and shoulders, dark eyes, a choleric face, the temper tightly controlled. A vein twitched in Ferrante's temple and tension, like a wire, coiled through his body. A danger-ous man if crossed, thought Ottavio. The letter in the leather wallet of his belt was a weapon that could be turned against both its carrier and the recipient.

'I must talk to Isabella tomorrow,' said Ottavio. 'I have messages from her confessor in Mantua and from the doctor.'

'If she is well enough, you may do so,' said Ferrante. 'She is seeing no one tonight. She is always more nervous in the evenings.'

Isabella, that it has come to this. The evenings when she used to enchant us with her voice, now a time of shadows and fear. Ferrante rose from the table and bade Ottavio good-night. His heavy footsteps sounded on the tiles of the hall, while Ottavio sat alone with a flask of wine and the ticking of the clock for company.

In Don Ferrante's orchard there was a stone seat at the end of an avenue of pleached limes. Isabella chose it as the site to read the letter. She was leaning on the arm of her maid, weakened as she was from sleepless nights and days without eating.

'Did he write willingly?' she asked Ottavio, holding the unopened letter in her hand.

'He wrote with great concern for you,' said Ottavio.

'How did he look? Did he talk about me?'

'He looked harassed from the preparations for the journey to Lake Garda. He complained of a headache.'

'How like him,' she smiled. 'His head always suffers. Did he talk about me?'

'Read the letter, Isabella.'

She sighed, broke the seal and unfolded the letter. She looked at the writing for a moment as if recalling other letters in that hand, and then began to read. Her face became pale. She turned the page, and finally looked up with eyes that were empty of any remaining dream.

'So that's how it is,' she said, 'and very prettily expressed. But why should I have expected anything else?'

'He wishes you well, Isabella. He said he would not have you hurt for anything.'

'Of course not, he has a loving heart, even if a selfish and greedy one. Even if capricious, unthinking, uncaring . . .' and she began to cry. After a while she looked up with tear-clouded eyes and said to Ottavio, 'So I am to love my husband as once I loved *him*. Do you think that is good advice?'

'It is the best in the circumstances,' said Ottavio.

'Well,' she said, folding the paper, 'that is how it is. Ottavio, what am I to do with this letter? I do not want to destroy it, but I cannot keep it here. If Don Ferrante finds it he will kill me.'

'Do you have no secure place for it?'

'There is nowhere that would be safe. Ottavio, I shall have to entrust it to you. Keep it for me. One day when I am old, I shall want to re-read it, and see how it seems in the light of the years. I might even laugh, who knows?'

'I shall keep it for you until you ask for its return,' said Ottavio.

She held out the letter. 'There you are. See how I trust you, Ottavio. My life in your hands. Does it give you a feeling of power?'

'Of responsibility, only. And the wish that you will forget and begin living again.'

She turned a full smile on him, of gleaming white bone. She said quietly, 'May the House of Gonzaga go to perdition, and may I help it to its end. A plague on all of you.'

'Time will heal your wounds, Isabella.'

'And time will undo. Take the letter, Ottavio. I have done with it. Come, Emilia.'

Isabella rose from her seat and walked back to the house, followed at a distance by her maid. Ottavio put the letter back into his wallet, unread.

※

Years later, on an evening in Venice when the light from the water washed the city in a lambent haze, I told the story to Claudio, for by then the name of Gonzaga had fallen into such disrepute, the scandals seized on by the *avvisi* so many and various, and Isabella's name dragged through the mire with the rest, that it no longer seemed a secret which needed to be kept.

Claudio laughed in the short, bitter way he had when the Gonzaga were mentioned, and said, 'How many lives they have ruined. The power they have to despoil.'

'And the power to build,' I said.

He nodded, his mind seemingly absorbed in other thoughts. He was growing old, and his concentration would wander. After a while he said, 'The subject for an opera.'

'Isabella, the Duke, myself?'

'Under classical names,' said Monteverdi. 'Vincenzo as Apollo, or Jupiter.'

'Or Caligula?' I suggested. 'The tyrant of pleasure?'

Monteverdi smiled, and the habitual melancholy of his face was lightened by the spirit that still lay within.

'Maybe. Maybe not. We shall have to wait and see. There must be a death.'

And of course there was, but so many that our minds could not have encompassed the thought on that evening. It is as well not to know the future, or else how could we live?

PART TWO
1594–1605

In his pavilions, which were many and beautiful, the lord Duke stayed and was served in the grand manner, for as well as the usual guard of arquebusiers, he also had with him a most numerous and complete household, wherefore he continually and to his great splendour maintained a most abundant table.

Report by the official chronicler of the Mantuan crusade to Hungary, 1595

This humble petition comes to you with no other aim but to beg Your Highness to kindly direct that I receive wages amounting to a total of five months, in which situation my wife Claudia and my father-in-law also find themselves, and this sum grows even larger since we do not see any hope of being able to get hold of future payments save by the express command of Your Highness, without which support all that I have been building up will be ruined and undone . . .

Letter from Monteverdi to Duke Vincenzo, 1604

CHAPTER SEVEN

There is a portrait of Vincenzo at the time when he had, if he would only have realized it, achieved his dream of Arcadia in the palace on the island. For, after all, this was a man who claimed that love was everything, and there was a perfect, unquestioning love in Agnese, who never knew about Isabella, though she came to know of others. Yet in this portrait painted during the fullness of those years of beauty, love and music, there is in his eyes a blankness, as if he is looking at a vacuum.

That expression was rarely seen in real life, for he moved in an element of diversions. A flow of demands from the ducal office vitalized the entire palace. We must send two of his best horses to his cousin the Archduke, and last Friday's composition, together with two of his singers, must be despatched to Ferrara for the Duchess Margherita, his sister. And there was a carved gold bowl and spoon in the studiolo that must be sent for Agnese's beautiful baby, my son. And the Pope had written from Rome. It would be only courteous to call upon His Holiness, so why don't we write back and announce our visit? Myself and three hundred of my company.

While people scurried to put His Serene Highness's wishes into action, he would move on to another diversion, so that the paths of his friends, followers and servants crossed as they traversed the acres of the palace to arrange the transport of the Duke's gifts with the Master of the Horses, of singers with the Director of Music, of precious antiques with the keeper of the studiolo. His mind unoccupied for a moment, he would take books from the library shelves, reading them not with a contemplative mind but with voraciousness as if somewhere in their pages was the answer to his quest.

There he is in his library, books open on the desk in front of him, staring at the gilded leather on the walls as at a chasm. In this contemplation Ottavio found him, and saw the reflection in his eyes of the confusion within. For only a moment, as Vincenzo's face was at once animated by the news Ottavio had brought of the impending visit to Rome.

Their relationship had gone through changes since the fall of Isabella. The useful confidant became the accuser and absented himself from court. But no one escapes the Duke unless the Duke so wishes. It took a few months, but at a nicely judged moment arrived the message from Mantua. A sizable portion of land in the west of the state with the title of Count attached. Ottavio returned, for you do not reject the Duke's gift. The court took note. The man from a lesser branch of the house of Gonzaga, who compensated for his physical imperfection with a sharp tongue, had grown in stature by the strength of the title. In due course, on the birth of Isabella's first child, ducal gifts arrived at the house of Ferrante. A carved silver bowl and spoon for her son, a velvet cloak embroidered with pearls for the mother. These gifts, too, were accepted with a brief letter of thanks.

A year or so passed in which the Duke indulged in a frenzy of travelling and entertainment: to Rome, to the sea air at Genoa, to his Habsburg relations in Innsbruck and Vienna, to his uncle the Grand Duke in Florence, to the pleasures of Venice. In Mantua, the Duke's players performed their *commedia dell'arte*; the Duke's musicians and singers gave their concerts; the Duke's armoury manufactured fireworks whenever there was cause for a celebration, such as the birth of the youngest prince, brother to Francesco and Ferdinando. The Duke's heart warmed to Eleonora and the tiny child wrapped in its woollen shawl. A soft down on its head, the pale blue eyes with milky gaze taking in the new world, the mouth always mobile and searching for the breast. They called the boy Vincenzo after his father. It was only appropriate, said Eleonora, for of their sons, he was the one at birth who most resembled him.

It was during this celebration that two letters arrived from Rome. The Mantuan ambassador wrote in his ornately curved script of the scene at mass. In front of the assembly of ambassadors and cardinals the Pope had broken down and cried into his handkerchief. The Holy Father's voice had quivered with emotion as he told the assembly of the Turkish invasion of Christendom. Five handkerchiefs, the ambassador had counted them, had been soaked with his tears. The second letter was from Pope Clement VIII himself calling upon the Duke of Mantua, as a Christian prince, to join with the Imperial forces in ridding Hungary of the infidels, who were advancing on Buda and Pest.

Vincenzo's face was animated by a new sense of purpose. All the travel and entertainments were as games compared with this great adventure of life and death. This was the call he had been waiting for, he declared. The Holy Father would not lack help as long as the Gonzaga ruled Mantua. And besides, his dear, pious mother, God rest her soul, may she be in glory, would have wished it. He took down from the library shelves Tasso's *La Gerusalemme Liberata*, his mind dazzled by its images of clashing steel, of blood on the sand. He had found in its pages his role, that of crusader for the faith.

On a fine morning in June, the piazza of San Pietro was congested with horses and soldiers, coaches and wagons. Porters and pages dodged through the crowds with luggage and messages. Whinnying and snorts from the horses, shouts from the men, cheers from the onlookers, tears from the ladies. The army had emptied the Mantuan court of its men. The sun glanced off the polished breastplates as the company set off across the bridge for the road north. There they go, wave upon wave of them – seven marquises, an array of barons and courtiers, dozens of pages, and companies of fighting men. And there, rolling along

CLARE COLVIN

behind them, the carriages and men with the necessities of
the Duke's daily life: his valet, his barber, a team of cooks
and carvers, several doctors, an alchemist and five singer-
musicians with their orchestral instruments. It is a full complement for a concert – a castrato, two tenors and two bass
singers, plus a musical director appointed for the crusade.
The Duke's eye has lit on Claudio Monteverdi for the post.
Young, in reasonable health, able to turn his hand to any
form of music, and with a new composition which the
Duke intends to be heard by a wider audience. Vincenzo
rides on, high with the sense of adventure, while at the rear
of the procession roll the reminders of his purpose, a
dozen cannons on iron-rimmed wheels.

Ottavio was riding a magnificent black horse, a gift
from the Duke. In his ears sounded the music of an army
on the move – horses' hoofs on the sun-hardened ground,
the clank of steel, the creak of leather. The cavalcade rode
by the ripening cornfields, the heat of the day glistening on
their faces. He drew level with one of the household carriages. Archimedeo, standing on the seat, leaned out of the
window and called, 'That's a fine beast you're riding, O
Ennobled One.'

'Go bury yourself, rat's droppings,' said Ottavio.

So the travelling court transported all its rivalries and
quarrels, which would multiply when they joined the other
battalions of the Holy Crusade – the Medici mercenaries,
the Papal Auxiliaries, and the Imperial Forces. That day was
delayed for the Duke. He sent the main army with his
Captain, Count Rossi, on towards the Hungarian battlefield
and diverted with his court towards Innsbruck. 'After all,'
he said, 'we are so nearby, and my sister the Archduchess
would never forgive me if we didn't visit her.' From there,
it was a short step to the Danube and a boat ride to Vienna,
to be entertained by the Habsburg Archdukes. The crusade
was on hold, for the Duke at any rate, while he was distracted by the Viennese season of parties and tournaments.

'Why are we here?' the Duke suddenly asked, around the middle of September. 'I nearly got killed in the last tournament. Better to die in glory on the battlefield, and besides, I am the supreme commander of the Mantuan Army. I should be with them.'

Thus echoing what Ottavio had heard others muttering for the past couple of weeks, the Duke set off with his entourage along the Danube. Late in the evening, they set up camp beside one of the riverside villages. The villagers built a bonfire in their honour and a band of Magyars arrived to play for the gathering. Through the night air, the plaintive notes of the gypsy fiddles caught at the senses, now rapid, now slow, soaring upwards then dying away to a tremolo. The Duke's restlessness was stilled, as he listened to the new and unusual sound. Nearby, his musical director watched the chief fiddler in rapt attention, his eyes taking in the way the bow moved, the way the hand touched the strings. The Duke and his musician caught each other's eyes in the firelight, as they shared the same thought: here was a sound that expressed the emotions so persuasively they must acquire the knowledge for themselves.

When the gypsies paused in their playing, Claudio and the bass singer, Gian Battista, examined the instruments, and soon they were talking in the musician's universal language of sounds and practical demonstration. The head of the Magyars, a small man with face lined by age and weather, offered Claudio his bow and fiddle, nodding with approval as Claudio practised a few phrases. The notes became a tune, an old Lombard folk song. As they recognized it, the company began to sing the words – *Forse che sì, Forse che non*. In the night air, a harmonious blend of tenor, baritone and bass joined in the chorus to the final nostalgic lines,

> Maybe no, maybe yes,
> The world won't always be like this.

Comrades gathered around the fire, their voices celebrating a simple joy in living, in a communion that can only come about in the open air of another land, away from custom and etiquette. Vincenzo rose to his feet, his eyes filled with tears, and embraced his musical director. Turning to the assembled company, he declared, 'We have Orpheus in our midst. This man can charm the stones to sing. No musician comes close to him. He is touched by the gods.'

Claudio's face in the firelight reflected the warmth of the Duke's, and there were tears in his eyes as well. Suffused by love and approval, he glowed. 'The Duke's love,' said Ottavio, watching the scene, 'is more dangerous than his hatred, for it makes a prisoner of you.'

The evening was the last harmonious one, as the next day they reached the battlefield camp. After two months of use, the camp was as dismal as a shanty slum. The ground had been churned by horses, their hoofs trampling the grass into mud. From the communal latrines, when the wind was in the wrong direction, came an overpowering stench. Around the kitchens were strewn bones of animals that had been spit-roasted. The Duke's cooks came back from their inspection indignant at being expected to work in such conditions, and declared that the sour cabbage rotting in barrels the Germans had brought smelt worst of all.

The commanders were, after their enforced time together and their lack of success against the Turks, in a quarrelsome mood. Aldobrandini, commanding the Papal Auxiliaries, questioned the judgement of Archduke Matthias of the Imperial Forces. The Archduke was suffering from dysentery, and frequently retired from meetings. The Grand Duke of Tuscany had sent the rougher elements of the Medici in the persons of Dons Giovanni, Antonio and Virginio, who, like their men, were more interested in the spoils of war than in its purpose.

In the Duke's tent, Carlo Rossi listed the Mantuans already killed or wounded. The wounded included the faithful Captain Antonio of the Duke's armoury who had lost his scalp to a Turkish scimitar. It had been a frustrating and painful siege, but now the Duke had arrived, they felt a new impetus for a final assault on the fortress of Plintenburg that dominated the bend of the Danube. Whoever held the fortress would control the area for miles around. Drive the Turks from Plintenburg, and they would be able to reclaim the lands of the Danube.

Vincenzo gave orders for his cooks to prepare an eve of battle dinner for the commanders. From the musicians' tent came the sounds of instruments being tuned, of voices being exercised as they prepared for the evening. And thus it was that we first heard the vespers which Monteverdi had written, played on the organ which had been transported from Mantua, and sung by the quintet. From the moment that the first chords sounded, and the bass voice of Gian Battista rang out over the camp, men paused and listened.

Through the fields and swelling into the night air the music rose towards the heavens, and towards the Turks watching from the towers of Plintenburg. And when the final chords died away, there was silence. Even Don Giovanni de' Medici was lost for words, until from the Mantuan ranks a voice called, 'Bravo, Mantua!' At which, the commanders all offered their congratulations to Vincenzo for this reminder of the high purpose of the Holy War and the auspicious sign through the music that God was on their side.

CHAPTER EIGHT

*N*o one *pays much attention* to the viewpoint of a dwarf. When you are trying to address a man with your head thrown back in order to catch a view of the face rather than of the breeches you can understand the difficulty. It diminishes everything you say.

At court Archimedeo would approach people when they were sitting down, therefore closer at hand and more receptive. Here on the battlefield, the constant movement of men and horses made him feel as if he were in a living forest of leather-booted, armour-clad, mud-spattered legs, and that was only the men. With the horses it was worse. He would look up to see iron-rimmed hoofs, huge bellies with foam-flecked hide, and hear the grinding sound of stomach and intestines lurching to the animal's pace. Sometimes their tails would proudly rise, which was a signal to move away fast, as steaming manure erupted from their bowels.

A huge black beast stood near him and discharged an acrid stream of urine which hit the ground and splashed his feet.

'Mind me!' shouted Archimedeo. Ottavio, standing in the stirrups while his horse relieved itself, looked down and said, 'What, Archimedeo? Still alive?'

'Despite your efforts to drown me in horse piss,' said Archimedeo. He saw the malicious light in Ottavio's eyes.

'I am so sorry, Signor Archimedeo,' he said with exaggerated courtesy. 'I didn't see you down there.'

'May you fall from your horse onto your ugly back,' cried Archimedeo, but Ottavio had ridden on, and the words were no more discernible to him than the buzzing of a gnat.

The dwarf's-eye view of the battle, in contrast with the

tangled proximity of the camp, was of a distant panorama. At dawn the army moved on Plintenburg. Archimedeo watched from one of the wagons on the edge of the camp as they rode out. The Duke wore his chased silver and steel armour, the white crescent of Mantua on his arm. His knights rode either side of him, a company of steel and horseflesh. The musketeers marched ahead in solid formation, their faces set in the implacable expression of those who are to kill or be killed. A second company of Mantuan cavaliers rode out from another section of the camp, with Rossi at their head, followed by Aldobrandini and the papal auxiliaries. Archimedeo, wrapped in a cast-off cloak of the Duke's that enveloped him from head to foot, watched the fighting men as they advanced towards the citadel to the sound of marching feet, drums beating, and the thunderclap of cannons that signalled the start of the day's offensive.

'This is a good vantage point, Master Archimedeo,' as two of the musicians, the Signors Claudio and Gian Battista, climbed on to the wagon.

'Any nearer and we would be too near,' said Archimedeo. 'The Turks have a long range.'

A trumpet sounded. A horse screamed. The shouts of men rang out in the air. The smell of gunpowder reached them on the wind. They could see a mêlée of horses and men near the main gates of the citadel where the cannon bombardment had been strongest. The enemy were too close for gunfire and there was a confusion of hand-to-hand fighting. There would for an instant be a gap in the field, a vacuum which horses and men would charge to fill, the clash of metal, shouts and screams and rallying trumpet calls increasing to a crescendo, and then momentarily diminishing as soldiers on both sides retired for breathing space.

'If one side was composed of men who never tired, the battle would be over quickly,' said Archimedeo.

'All men work to the same rhythm. They eat at the same time, they rest at the same time, whether infidel or Christian,' said Claudio.

'Thank God we're not the trumpeters,' said Gian Battista, as the trumpet broke off in mid-note.

The day advanced, men and horses returning to camp and reinforcements going out. The blood wagon went by, bearing the badly wounded and dying. They saw the Duke's cousin carried by on a pallet, his arm half severed at the elbow, his face waxen with pain and loss of blood, yet still insisting he was needed on the field.

'He won't go hunting again for many a day,' said Archimedeo. 'Let's see how Don Ottavio fares, whether his proud horse, which is a present from the Duke, bears him back as arrogant as when he left.'

'It's like a game of Calcio,' said Claudio. 'Look at the way they group and re-form as a team. But the stakes are higher – life and death. Listen to the tumult.'

He watched the battle, his eyes shining, his lips drawn back in a smile, recording in his mind the sights and sounds. Gian Battista said uneasily, 'If they were to lose, we would all be massacred.'

'Archimedeo would be spared,' said Claudio. 'He would be dressed in a turban and put in charge of the harem.'

'After the appropriate operation,' said Gian Battista. Archimedeo shrieked and the musicians laughed.

'Of course the ladies at court would breathe more easily then,' added Gian Battista, his laughter edged with the day's tension.

'They say the Turks inhale a grass which makes them battle-mad,' said Claudio. 'Their cruelty knows no bounds. Here come another band of exhausted soldiers, and there go the Medici, stirring themselves into battle.'

Filing past were a company of the knights who had ridden out at the beginning of the day, their faces grimed with dirt, blood and sweat.

'Good day, Don Ottavio, back already?' called Archimedeo. But Ottavio appeared not to hear him, his ears resounding with the clamour of fighting, his eyes still seeing the eyes of the enemy, reddened like his from rage and fatigue.

'Let him go. He has fought bravely,' said Claudio. 'He has helped save you from the Turk.'

As dusk fell, the Duke's company returned, but the siege of the citadel continued in relays throughout the night. The next day the Duke went forth again and fought through the entire day, his bravery conspicuous to all. Two evenings later, a message came from the Turkish defenders agreeing to surrender, on condition that it was to the Pasha of Mantua.

The Duke was in his tent, his battle-weary muscles being massaged with aromatic oils when the Turkish envoys arrived. He received them, wearing his dressing-robe, while they made their obeisances, and his esteem was massaged by their syrup of flattery.

Only to you, the most chivalrous of enemies, would we surrender Plintenburg, said the younger envoy, his eyes filled with melting admiration.

Were there not among the Christians a prince of such magnificence and valour, we would have fought to the end, said the elder, assuming a similar expression.

The Duke called for them to have food brought to them, and left them while he consulted with the other commanders. Don Giovanni looked at him suspiciously. Only to you? he asked. What ransom will you take? The expense of taking this accursed fort must be paid for.

But, touched by the appeal to his chivalry, Vincenzo said the objective had been to defend the Holy Empire and to drive back the Turks, not to fill the Medici coffers with gold. The Medici scowled in the background as he promised safe passage to the Turks when they left Plintenburg. No one but Vincenzo was surprised when news came back to camp later that the Turks had been robbed on the road of their jewellery and plate by a band of Medici mercenaries, led by Don Giovanni. The poetic saga playing in his head was suddenly ousted by cynical reality.

The Turkish army was still in the area, and now the Imperial forces took up a defensive position at Plintenburg, unable to withdraw for fear of it being re-taken. But there was no enemy to come to grips with. The Turks launched raids on villages, disappearing long before any defence forces arrived. After the taking of the citadel, the uncertainties soured the victory as the commanders disputed the best way to proceed.

In the evenings the disputes waxed and waned, according to the mood brought on by the wine. In a succession of parties, each commander entertained the others. Vincenzo's tent, it was generally agreed, served the best dinner, his cooks having set up their own field kitchen. A week after the victory, now a diminishing glow on the horizon, the commanders were only eating together because they knew that whoever was absent was likely to be slandered by the others.

This is harder work than fighting, said Vincenzo, as he heard the raised voices of the Medici through the darkness outside. It was early October, and the weather, after a succession of warm days and clear nights, had broken. The Medici entered, shaking the rain from their cloaks and thrusting out their mud-bespattered boots to be removed by the page, before setting foot on the carpets laid over the tarpaulin floor.

Others arrived and the boots ranged up: the black leather of Aldobrandini, the Spanish kid of Archduke Matthias, the canvas and tan of Carlo Rossi. The page poured wine for the assembled men, and they raised their glasses toasting each other, the Duke, the Emperor and the Pope. There was in the air the sense of abandon, a need to forget the curious and unsatisfactory position of work half completed, and the winter on its way.

The Duke's cooks had provided a dinner of artichokes cooked in oil, a risotto and spit-roasted lamb. There was an abundance of wine. The commanders complimented him on his table and Archduke Matthias gave a toast to the Duke's musicians, who had reminded them on the eve of battle of the purpose of the crusade. At which the Duke said, 'Why are they not here tonight? Ottavio, fetch Claudio and his band to entertain us.'

Through the rain to the musicians' tent went Ottavio, to find the sort of reception he expected: distinct lack of enthusiasm from the musicians, half-way through their evening meal, and objections on their behalf from their director. Two of the musicians were ill, the others tired, the instruments and voices alike untuned. They had nothing planned. The Duke's pages were perfectly able to sing and play the lute, which at that time of the evening was all that would be required.

'We both know that, Signor Claudio,' said Ottavio, 'but His Highness has asked for you, and the commanders of all the forces are there. You cannot refuse him.'

That much was evident, agreed Claudio, but you will have to excuse those who are ill. The small troupe tramped along the rain-sodden track to the Duke's tent, where they found the commanders full of wine and in expansive mood. Before long the concert had become a succession of roundelays with parts divided amongst the gathering, each competing with the strength of his voice.

'Play us one of the Magyar tunes,' called the Duke. 'That catch they were singing on the banks of the Danube.'

So Claudio played on his viola the uneven beat of the gypsy music. The Dons Giovanni and Virginio linked arms and danced, scattering all before them. Archimedeo clambered for a place out of range on the table.

'Play something faster, Claudio!' shouted the Duke, 'make them dance till they drop.'

'The fastest music is a Gallic jig, thus,' and Claudio, and the Duke, his face flushed with wine and exuberance, called out, 'The dance with swords! Lay swords on the table for Giovanni.'

Don Giovanni leapt on to the table, said Archimedeo clambered off to find a safer place. The crossed swords glinted in the light of the tapers. The tent had become smoky from the flames, and the iron brazier of hot coals. The air was as warm and dense as that of a stable. Don Giovanni began to dance among the swords, his bare feet avoiding the steel edges.

'Play faster, Claudio,' called the Duke. Giovanni's feet danced nearer the steel, as he matched the tempo. The Duke glanced at his face which was streaming with sweat, at the shirt clinging damply to his arms, and then at the feet, close to the swords. Vincenzo's eyes glinted like the steel in the firelight, his face reddened from the heat.

'Faster, Claudio,' from the Duke, and then, 'A hit! A hit!'

Giovanni's right foot had touched a blade, and blood spurted from a cut in his instep. He swore and looked down as he continued to dance. His foot touched the swords again.

'Enough, the swords have won,' called out Aldobrandini.

'The fiddler has won. He plays like the devil,' said Giovanni. 'But what would you expect from Mantua?' He hopped to a chair, and held his foot out for the page to bathe in a bowl of water.

'Of course His Serene Highness knows all about sword dances,' continued Don Giovanni. 'Bind the foot tighter, boy. Of course, there was the Scot, Il Critonio, do you remember? Duke Guglielmo's favourite who danced to a blade one night in a back street. At least I have survived my sword dance.'

There was a silence. The triumphant humour drained from Vincenzo's face and he looked furious. One of the

Medici laughed. The Archduke rose to his feet and said, 'Well, well, the night draws on. I must return to my tent.'

'But the fun has only just begun,' protested Don Giovanni. 'I can no longer dance, but others will. It is time for the dwarf to entertain us, what is he doing here else?'

And indeed, the same thought had occurred to Archimedeo who, aware that he must provide a diversion, had clambered on to the table among the swords, and bowing to the company, said, 'I shall teach the Medici how to dance.'

'Take the pace slowly, Claudio,' said the Duke. 'I don't want my little man sliced to pieces.'

Archimedeo, tossing his head imperiously in imitation of Don Giovanni, placed his hands on his hips, and jumped among the swords. His bow legs, supporting the chunky body, moved with a lack of co-ordination that spoke of more drink consumed than was good for him.

'The dwarf is drunk,' called out Don Virginio de Medici.

'I am not,' said Archimedeo, stopping his dance. 'I can drink any man here under the table.'

'Is that so?' said Don Virginio. 'Try this flagon, then.' He held out a pewter stein filled to the brim with red wine.

'What's this, a thimble?' asked Archimedeo, holding it up. 'Watch me down this in one!' And he held the stein to his lips, tilting his head back. Red wine dribbled from his mouth on to his waistcoat.

'The dwarf is cheating,' cried Don Giovanni, his bandaged foot resting on the shoulder of the page sitting in front of him. 'His waistcoat is consuming most of the wine.'

'Enough,' said the Duke, taking the stein from the dwarf. 'We want him ready to fight in the morning.'

Archimedeo half fell from the table, and said in a slurred voice, 'I can take on any one of you here.'

'Another challenge from the dwarf,' said Don Giovanni, but now that Archimedeo was obviously incapable of further amusement, they lost interest in him and began to gossip about the Emperor Rudolf, whose lands they were defending at great cost to their men and themselves. The Medici maintained that the Emperor, who consulted astrologers and alchemists every hour of the day, was weak in the head, and, moreover, suspiciously reluctant to marry. The Emperor's cousin, the Archduke, and Vincenzo, who had a weakness himself for astrologers, and who had been given a coach and four by the Emperor during his stay in Vienna, accused the Medici of slander. From his resting place on the floor Archimedeo groaned.

'Ottavio, get him out of here before he pukes on my carpet,' the Duke called sharply.

Ottavio picked up the fallen dwarf by his collar and the seat of his breeches and carried him out of the overheated tent into the night air. Archimedeo groaned and retched.

'Not over me, you won't,' said Ottavio and dropped him face down on to the ground. There was a splat from the mud in which the dwarf landed. Ottavio returned to the tent from where the Archduke, pale in the face from an attack of stomach cramps, was emerging. Don Giovanni, wearing only one boot and using the page as a crutch, was stumbling back with his brothers towards his tent. Aldobrandini, wrapped in his cloak against the cold night air, thanked the Duke with elaborate courtesy for his hospitality, and followed the others, his path veering in a gentle curve.

Inside the tent, a servant was fanning the dying coals of the brazier, while the Duke gazed reflectively at his glass of wine, listening to the music Claudio was playing on the page's lute. The other musicians had long since returned to their tent.

'Ottavio, where has everybody gone?' he said.

'It's late, it is nearly morning.'

'At least we still have music. Claudio is turning Marco's lute into a divine instrument.'

Claudio smiled, his eyes shadowed with weariness.

'I must get to bed,' said the Duke. 'Where is young Marco?'

'He took the wounded Don Giovanni back to his tent.'

'The poor lad. We won't be seeing him again tonight. Is Archimedeo recovered?'

'He's probably asleep by now,' said Ottavio.

'I am getting a headache. It's the suspense of waiting and doing nothing . . . It drives me mad.'

Ottavio pressed his hands into the Duke's shoulders, easing the tension of the muscles. 'Claudio is falling asleep,' he said.

'What is he doing here? He should be in bed. Claudio, son of Apollo. One day you'll write music about our victories, but for now, farewell, go to bed.'

'This is what war is about,' said Ottavio, as Claudio left the tent. 'Waiting, discomfort. There's very little glory.'

'Tomorrow I shall find the Turk. There was glory when we took Plintenburg. There will be glory again.' And the Duke allowed himself to be led to his bed where he immediately fell unconscious.

The rain fell steadily the following day, and the camp was a quagmire of churned mud. Then the weather lifted, and the Duke set out with a force to search for Turkish marauders, who mysteriously failed to appear. It was his last expedition, for he fell ill with fever and inflammation of the skin. St Anthony's Fire, said his doctor. Bed rest and bleeding is the only cure.

Confined to his tent, Vincenzo became despondent. There was illness all round him. The men were wasting with dysentery, which had even felled Aldobrandini, who was a pale and sweating shadow of himself. In the adjoining tent to the Duke, Archimedeo lay in a fever.

'Ottavio, how could you leave him lying in the rain?'

said the Duke. 'You are a man without any heart. You will buy him a new suit of clothes at the least.'

As he recovered from his illness, the Duke's enthusiasm for the expedition turned to detestation. On a Sunday, he decided to take mass at the cathedral at Gran, which the crusaders had relieved in the month before they reclaimed Plintenburg. It was a clear day in late October, and the spires of the cathedral were sharp spikes against the sky. As they rode into the cathedral square they could see the damage that the building had suffered. The faces of the stone statues on the portico had been axed into blankness. Inside the cathedral the painted eyes of the wooden images had been gouged out. The faces of saints on the frescoes were scratched with knives.

'See the work of the infidel,' exclaimed Vincenzo. The Prior, who had met the crusaders at the door, looked at him with sadness.

'The damage is terrible but it was not the Turks who did this,' he said. 'They respected our cathedral. This part of the town was relieved by a band of German Lutherans from the Imperial forces. They called our cathedral a temple of idolatry. They were battle-mad, the heretics. We could not stop the destruction.'

'We fought for this?' said Vincenzo. 'What was the purpose?'

A few days later, he gave orders to strike camp, and without consulting either the Emperor or his fellow commanders, the Mantuans set off back to Italy, leaving behind them the graves of their dead.

CHAPTER NINE

H *ere* *is* *another* *mirror*, with edges of carved ivory.
Isabella watches herself as she combs her hair. She
looks into her eyes, reading her thoughts. She sees the eyes
of a woman who has no illusions, and yet they are not the
eyes of the disillusioned. Rather of a woman who is calmly
waiting for whatever life will bring. What it brings at present is children. She is pregnant with her third child. She
faces up to nature's game with the knowledge of an experi-
enced player. Her breasts already feel heavy and she leaves
her gowns unlaced to accommodate the expanding curve
of her stomach. She knows that there will be discomfort
and then terrible pain, but after that another soul to love, a
small being to tug at her heart. She has love to spare.

She thinks of the Duke's last message to her. Love your
husband as once you loved me, he had said, and although
she had never felt that same elation in her heart when she
looked at Ferrante, after three years and two children he
was woven into her life, his shadow blocking the memory
of the life before. Reminders arrived occasionally in the
shape of letters from her mother, who though now infre-
quently at court knew the latest gossip from Mantua. And
then there was the time when, a month or so after the
birth of the first-born, presents had arrived from the palace.
She had been sitting at the same ivory mirror in her bedroom a few nights after that when she had seen Ferrante's
image in the glass behind her. His hands had rested on her
shoulders, the thumbs pressing into the first vertebrae.

'The Duke sends gifts for you and the baby. Why is
that?' he had asked.

'The Duke is a generous man. We should be glad to be
favoured,' she had said, looking back steadily at his face in
the glass as his hands had momentarily tightened on her

neck. Since then the pearl-embroidered cloak had lain un-worn in her chest for fear that the sight of it would revive his suspicions.

Now his voice interrupted her contemplation of the glass. She could see him behind her, wearing a dressing-robe over his long shirt as he sat on the edge of the bed waiting for her to come to him. He was holding a letter from Ottavio addressed to her. It had been sent from the fields of Hungary in the last few days of the campaign as the costs to Mantua in men and money and the rain-soaked October skies had cast a pall over the camp.

'The glory of war, like love, exists only in songs? What does he mean?' asked Ferrante. He read all her letters.

'Ottavio is a melancholy soul who believes that because he hasn't found love, it doesn't exist. But we know better.'

'I know better, certainly,' said Ferrante. He rose from the bed as she got up from her seat at the mirror. His hands encircled her waist and rested on her stomach, claiming possession of her and the child.

※

As her mind cast a cloud over the time before her marriage, a similar cloud descended on the Duke's memory of the Hungarian expedition. By the time Carnival arrived, the battle where so much was lost for so little gain was trans-formed into a shimmering epic of gallantry. A tournament in the piazza enacted the defeat of the Turkish janizaries by the brave Mantuans. The Duke's players celebrated the de-feat of the Turk in *commedia dell'arte* with the villains dressed in turbans and curved slippers. The Duke's young sons, Francesco and Ferdinando, took part in a pastoral of nymphs and shepherds. A concert was held in the Room of the Rivers for the new madrigals based on the heroic stan-zas of Tasso in *Gerusalemme Liberate*. Who would have thought from the celebrations that the expedition had cost Mantua 100,000 crowns? Money continued to be paid out to the families of the dead and wounded, for the Duke did not want anything to tarnish his popularity as a war hero. What would his ancestors have thought, those *condottieri* like GianFrancesco who fought only for money, and then only for the highest bidder? Those who held this opinion were careful not to say so. Ottavio, as he sat next to the Duke during the concert, had listened to the compliments with a smile that masked a heaviness within. Vincenzo, addicted to love for so many years, had now found a new addiction in war.

The singers turned from the metallic glitter of Tasso to the *madrigali amorosi* with which no concert would be complete. *Questi vaghi concenti* . . .

> These charming songs that the birds
> are singing as day breaks,
> are, so I believe, about the pains
> and torments of love . . .

Vincenzo looks at Ottavio and raises one eyebrow then looks back at the singers. Ottavio follows his glance. Among the sopranos, a girl with a fresh, clear face, and a high, pure voice, sings with an air of devotion as if the madrigal was Holy Writ. Her large, dark eyes are watching a point at the back of the room, for she is concentrating entirely on the notes and the music, rather than on their effect on the audience.

'I don't remember this new singer,' said Vincenzo. 'Where does she come from? Who hired her?'

'She is from Mantua, daughter of the violist, Cattaneo. She has only newly joined the choir. She is very young.'

'What a beautiful voice. How young is she?'

'Too young, Your Highness. Far too young.'

The Duke stared at the girl, his face framed by his high-standing lace and pearl collar, like the fanned tail of a white peacock, his eyes as hard and bright as sapphires. She appeared oblivious of the ducal attention, her face concentrated only on the sound.

'Too young? That's only because you're growing old, Ottavio. But in any case, I am a patient man.'

The Duchess Eleonora, seated at the right hand of the Duke, glanced at her husband with a half smile of understanding, and a sadness in her eyes.

> If she whom I desire to please
> found pleasure in my anguish,
> then, for her sake, would I wish
> my tears to be eternal . . .

The audience applauded, and the singers bowed. The girl now took in the faces in front of her, saw the array of stiff court dresses, the pomaded hair, the jewels on throats and hands. She bowed again, but her eyes turned towards the musicians, towards Monteverdi, as if seeking his approval. Only when his expression had reassured her, did she make a final bow to the audience. Her eyes, still reflecting the joy of the music, met those of the Duke.

❄

A mirror image of an earlier meeting of eyes? No, each one is different. The little Cattaneo was born under a different star. Isabella had a mercurial curiosity and a boundless belief that the world was a great game, with the dice in her favour. Moving to the whirling eddies of her imagination, she lost sight of reality. Cattaneo has an anchor in the music, and in the enclosed world of the musicians. That is not to say that she is undisturbed at the Duke's evident interest, but once away from the range of his eyes she sends the memory of them to the back of her mind. She is well aware of the Duke's reputation, and the transitory nature of his affections.

It is different for the Duke as well. Love has become for him a competition, not with any other man, for he knows there is no one at court who would dare to compete with him, but with his younger self. He lives in the shadow of past loves. Sometimes they surface in his mind, and he will smile with remembered affection or derision. 'That terrible writer of letters, do you remember Ottavio, how she pursued me? And then demanded the return of all her letters? What a pest.' Or 'There is no lovelier woman than the Marchesa da Grana, and isn't the boy Silvio the sweetest tempered, liveliest child?' But he never mentions Isabella, except just once, soon after the concert. His voice was casual. He was looking at some papers at the time as he said over his shoulder to Ottavio, 'Is Isabella well? Have you seen her?'

'She is well, and with child again.'

'Ferrante is making sure she will never come to court. Is this the fourth?'

'The third. She has two sons already.'

He put the papers down on his desk and looked directly at Ottavio. 'Are they dark like Ferrante?'

'The second is dark, the eldest is fair.'

'He is . . .' and now he hesitated in a moment of unusual shyness 'He is . . . Ferrante's child?'

'Of course. Isabella, as you may recall, is fair. The child resembles her.'

'Ah, of course . . . the fair Isabella. Remember me to her.'

※

In the early summer's evening at Don Ferrante's villa, the assembled company are sitting on the terrace in the dusk. Ferrante's two nieces are singing the songs that Ottavio has brought from the court. He accompanies them on the lute. Several of Ferrante's cousins, his nephews and his brother have arrived for the evening's entertainment. On the lawn are people who work on the estate and leaning out of windows various servants of the house.

Isabella winces from back pain and Emilia rearranges the cushions behind her. The birth is expected during the following month, and she is moving around with the ungainliness now familiar to her. Her legs are extended on a footstool. Beside her on another footstool sits Scipione, her eldest boy, fair and with the wide eyes of the curious. They are directed towards the shape of Ottavio's cloak with an appraising stare.

In the air above them swallows wheel in their evening flight, their restless cries presaging the dark. There is the whine of a mosquito and the slap of a hand against a face. Above them the stars are beginning to show as specks of white in the fading sky. The nieces end their song and bow to the scattered applause. Ottavio tunes the lute, and says to Isabella, 'Come, sing for us as well, so that we don't forget your beautiful voice.'

'In a few months, perhaps. At the moment I am too tired and heavy.'

'In a few months it will be the same excuse,' said Ottavio, and noticed Ferrante's glance of anger.

'What a pity you will not sing,' he added. 'Signor Claudio said he was thinking of you when he set this poem.'

'What is it called? Does Claudio remember me?' Isabella's face showed new interest.

'"O come sei gentile", by Guarini. We will sing it for you, listen now.'

The strings of the lute combined with the voices of the two girls, and the echoing tones of the lower register from Ottavio. The listeners from the terrace, from the lawn, and from the windows, were silent, enchanted by the nostalgic sweetness of the tune.

> O, how charming you are, dear little bird!
> And how much my amorous state resembles yours!
> You a prisoner, I a prisoner;
> you sing, I sing . . .

The nieces began the next verse, and Isabella's eyes filled with tears. They streamed down her face unheeded, unseen by the nieces who were absorbed in the pleasure of singing. Ottavio felt the strings of the lute pluck at her heart.

Ferrante, suddenly alert to her distress, leaned towards her and asked, 'Are you unwell?'

Isabella began to sob openly. The girls faltered in mid-song. A disconcerted murmur was heard from those watching. Ottavio rested his hand on the lute strings as Emilia moved to Isabella's side in concern. A whispered conversation and then Emilia said to the company at large, 'Madonna is unwell. It is close to her time.'

There were expressions of sympathy as Isabella left the terrace, supported by Emilia. Gradually everyone, after talking among themselves for a short while, bade good-night to Don Ferrante and dispersed. Ottavio stayed until the last had gone.

'I must go to Isabella,' said Ferrante. 'It should not have been yet – it is over a month before her time.'

From the shadows, where he had remained unnoticed in the general exodus, came the voice of Isabella's son.

'It was the music that made her unwell.'

Ferrante glanced at Ottavio. His eyes darkened as if the boy had expressed his own suspicions, and he left the terrace. Ottavio said, half to himself, 'When we grow older, young man, we learn that some things are better left unsaid.'

CHAPTER TEN

It's a stab in the back, a cut to the heart, and any other simile that denotes wounded pride. Benedetto Pallavicino is to be Director of Music at court, now that Giaches de Wert has finally died. Something has gone wrong in the arena of natural justice. After following His Serene Highness through the mud of Hungary, after the compositions, the published works, now to hear that the post is not to be his is hardly bearable.

'But, Claudio, why should you have expected to be appointed over Pallavicino?' asked Ottavio. 'He has been here longer, since the days of the Duke's father. He is senior in years to you. He is a composer too.'

'An indifferent composer,' said Claudio. The voice of an affronted artist is similar to a child which doesn't get its way. His eyes glowed large and dark; his face seemed thinner; there was about him the air of an exotic animal that has been consigned to the common herd.

'A *respected* composer,' corrected Ottavio, 'even if he lacks brilliance. But this is the way life goes at the court – and Pallavicino would have had de Wert's support. The Duke always listened to de Wert's advice. He and Giaches de Wert went back a long way.'

Common sense does not come into it. Claudio remembers the Duke's arm round his shoulders, he hears his voice – an Orpheus among us were the words. He sees in the firelight beside the Danube the Duke's face, luminous in its warmth. And now to hear he is not to be Director – it's like a slap in the face with a wet fish. Ottavio sees the intensity of the hurt in his eyes, and says, 'You *will* become Director. You must be patient. It would be a mistake to show them you care and, after all, Pallavicino is not young.'

'So I am to wait for the man to die,' Claudio's voice had a waspish note.

'Or until he retires, and in the mean time you have more time to compose. The post brings with it more duties than you would expect.'

'And a larger salary,' said Claudio.

Then there's more to it than hurt pride, thought Ottavio. The young man wants to set up a household. He needs a larger salary because he is thinking of taking a wife.

'Who is it, then?' Ottavio laughed, and then added, 'May I give you a piece of advice? Never wait for the money or the right moment – you will find it has passed you by.'

'What do you mean?' The question hung in the air as the door to the music room opened, and the little Cattaneo stood on the threshold. She paused uncertainly and said, 'I'm sorry to disturb you, Signor Claudio – I'm early for the lesson.'

Ottavio laughed again as he caught Claudio's eye and saw a discernible heightening of colour in his face. The composer distractedly began sorting the scores, saying to the girl brusquely, 'I will be ready in a few minutes.' Ottavio was still smiling to himself as he arrived at the Duke's apartment, but it was one piece of gossip that he did not intend to pass on, for fear of renewing Vincenzo's interest in the girl.

❈

The word is going round the court. *Il Pastor Fido* is on again. Guarini has dined with the Duke and Duchess. There is, as always, an excuse, a visit by the Princess Margherita of Austria, on her way to strengthen the Habsburg dynasty with her marriage to Spain. Something truly special must be planned. The new form of *drama per musica* in Florence by the composer Peri and the poet Rinuccini at the Carnival had set the pace. Grand Duke

Ferdinando's face had been suffused with undisguised pride as the audience applauded the final scene of *Dafne*. Was this not, he asked, giving Vincenzo one of his uncomfortably sharp glances, the advance they had all been seeking? Of course, Vincenzo said later to Eleonora, in the privacy of their bedchamber after seven hours of music and a banquet, it would have been a greater advance had the music composed by the Grand Duke's precious Peri actually been dramatic. In any event, Mantua had to reply, and *Il Pastor Fido* would allow the full range of their theatrical and musical skills now that they could draw on the talents of the new theatrical designer.

There was at this time a reconciliation between Duke and Duchess and the pastoral would be a celebration of their love. Eleonora smiled at the momentary triumph of hope over experience. She was wearing the loose robes of approaching motherhood. Her uncle the Grand Duke had sent one of his physicians to attend her, despite the several already established at Mantua. Vincenzo decided it was an excuse to spy on their marriage and sent him back.

Summertime brought the annual exodus to Lake Garda. Eleonora remained in the healthy air of the country villa. Vincenzo, stricken by restlessness, returned early to Mantua via Venice. News of his impending arrival galvanized the designer into producing plans for costumes and stage sets, with intricate instructions. He consulted with the Director of Music over casting and with the Quartermaster over the necessary carpenters, painters and scene shifters to be organized. The ducal barge arrived earlier than expected at the palace quayside after a night journey from Venice, missing by half an hour the departure of three boatloads of court musicians and singers who had gone for a day's picnic to the upper reaches of the lake.

※

It's a late summer day, and there is a haze over the city. The smell of stagnant water which, despite the work of the city's night-soil and garbage collectors, is contaminated with effluent, assails the nostrils of those entering or leaving port. The musicians row as swiftly as the morning's early heat allows from the city's detritus to the clean dark mirror of the upper lake. The Duke, standing on his gilded barge, stares at the water in the port with distaste and tells Ottavio to remind him to devise a sufficiently punitive law against depositers of ordure.

Meanwhile, the musicians, safely out of range of polluted waters and ducal whims, rest on their oars, looking back towards the city. The towers of the Castello San Giorgio and the ducal palace dominate the skyline; square, uncompromising, the fortress of the *condottieri*. To the left is the graceful cupola of Sta Barbara, Duke Guglielmo's offering to the glory of God and of Mantua. The haze in the air gives the city the quality of a mirage; its mirror image reflected in the water seems more substantial.

The musicians row to the point where the river runs into the lake, where there is a clearing of grass among the willow trees and a pebbled shore. They draw up two of the boats and fasten them to the willow trees. The third boat remains out on the water, with the serious fishers among them casting their lines. The Pellizari sisters and Cattaneo's daughter spread cloths and cushions out on the grass and Gian Battista opens a flagon of wine. From the boat comes a triumphant cry as the fishers haul in a thrashing pike.

The young Claudia Cattaneo has never felt happier. She sits on the rug in the dappled shade of the willow, watching the Pellizari sisters' two small children splashing in the water, smelling the burning wood from the fire that Claudio and her father are building, listening to Gian Battista tell a joke in a sonorous voice. She is wearing a garland of marguerites and roses because it is her birthday, and that is what girls wear on their birthdays, Lucia Pellizari had said, weaving the flowers together. Isabetta Pellizari is carving a large melon and handing slices to all within range. From the fire wafts the smell of freshly caught fish being cooked. Lucia's small son falls flat into the water and runs to his mother. She distracts him by weaving a garland of daisies and willow twigs. He laughs with pleasure and struts around, showing off his new crown.

'Like a little prince,' says Claudia, and realizes in the sudden quality of the silence that something has gone wrong, like a cloud across the sun. Then Gian Battista calls out, 'When will the fish be ready? We are all hungry here.'

'Have some bread to fill your face,' says Isabetta, thrusting a loaf at him. Claudia drinks more wine from an earthenware goblet and looks up at the branches of the willow. The leaves hang heavy from the twigs in the exhaustion of late summer. The young tenor who has joined the court recently has brought a lute with him and he begins to play it idly, picking out a few bars of a song. Father Cattaneo is arguing with his wife about how long the fish should be grilled.

Claudio steps away from the fire to avoid being involved in their dispute. He walks over to the shade of the tree and sits down in front of Claudia. They say nothing, their eyes sending silent messages. Claudio takes Claudia's hand and she smiles as he smiles, she is filled with joy. They are oblivious to all around them. The tenor smiles and begins singing, *Amor, se giusto sei* . . . Love, if you are fair . . .

'Claudia and Claudio,' says Lucia. 'The names are made for each other.'

<hr/>

The Duke had spent the morning listening to reports from his secretary, and now, towards mid-day, he has had enough. Thoughts of water play in his mind. He has half a mind to ride over to the Palazzo del Te and the coolness of its pools and grottoes, but it means going through the heat of the city. He looks at some of the drawings for the pastoral, but they are incomplete without the designer there to discuss them, and the man is not to be found. He shouts for Ottavio, who seems to have skulked off as well, and by the time he finally appears, the Duke is becoming impatient. But Ottavio has news to alleviate the ducal ennui. Dr Donati has arrived from the University of Padua with news of scientific significance. Anything that will add to the Duke's knowledge of the spheres is seized on, and Vincenzo immediately asks for Dr Donati to attend him. Send him up to the loggia, he says over his shoulder, his thoughts still on pools of cool water.

※

The musicians have had their fill of fish and fruit, bread and wine, and are reclining on the grass. Old Cattaneo has retreated into the trees for a sleep. The Pellizaris are amusing their children by clapping hands and singing rhymes. In the pauses between their talk and laughter, there is an early afternoon stillness, an exhausted silence among the birds. Gian Battista lazily gets to his feet. He has taken off his stockings and walks into the lake. His feet stir up a cloud of mud. The others look on, feeling in their minds the coolness of the water against skin.

Gian Battista calls to Claudio, the new tenor Francesco, and the Pellizari brother. The men are going to swim. They leave the picnic with the women grouped around it and move away to the next inlet in the lake, which is hidden from view. Not long after there is a sound of splashing, of bodies displacing water, and shouts of enjoyment. Lucia wanders over in the direction of the noise and comes back smiling.

'They have all folded up their clothes neatly on the bank and are splashing around without a stitch on,' she says.

'If we were to steal their clothes, they would not be able to come out of the water,' said Isabetta. But no one is unkind enough, or bold enough, to do that. On the other hand, they are inclined to try the water themselves. 'They will be gone some time,' says Lucia and unlaces her overdress. She steps out of it and walks into the lake, raising her lawn chemise to her knees. 'Mud is good for the ankles,' she says. Claudia, in her chemise and still wearing the garland on her head, walks into the water. She feels the water edging up to her knees, and lifts the chemise out of the way. She wades further in, and the water is up to her thighs. Glancing around to make sure she is not seen by any of the men, she lifts the chemise over her head and throws it to Lucia.

'Claudia!' calls her mother sharply, but too late. Claudia raises her hands to her head to adjust the garland which has nearly fallen off, and walks on till the water is up to her waist. The lower half of her body is cool, the upper half warm in the sun, the heat of the rays like a benediction on her head. She crouches down to immerse herself in the water, and as she stands up it runs down her shoulders in sparkling drops. She looks towards the city a long way off, its towers rising above the lake and feels a sense of freedom at being so far from its influence. As she glances towards the palace, she sees a glint, as of a mirror in the sun. She looks towards it. The light wavers and flashes, and then seems to be glinting directly towards her. She wonders if someone is signalling with a mirror. In the heat of the sun, she feels a shiver run through her body.

❈

Dr Donati's face was like that of a bird: a thin beaky nose, very bright, small, dark eyes alive with intelligence, and a lined skin the colour of yellowing parchment. Despite the heat, he was wearing his scholar's black gown, the plain white collar of his shirt emerging above his doublet. In his presence, Vincenzo became like a respectful and eager student. He showed him to a cushioned seat on the loggia, called for wine and fruit to be brought to the table, and waited for him to tell the news from Padua.

Archimedeo, whose presence was not required, but whose curiosity compelled him to be there, climbed on to the balustrade, to see and hear better what was going on. Ottavio sat the other side of the table, and poured wine into silver goblets. He compared them in his mind to an aviary. Dr Donati's darting eyes, and black robes, like a bright little blackbird; Archimedeo in his red and green jerkin perched on the balustrade like a parakeet; the Duke's high stiff collar, his hair carelessly on end, his slashed doublet with the undershirt showing through like pale slanted eyes, a peacock; and himself, bent towards the table, in his dark clothes, a crow.

Dr Donati gathered them to him with his bright-eyed glance, and talked about the work at Padua. Dr Galileo Galilei has been working on an instrument, which originally came to him, in an imperfect form, from the Netherlands. This instrument would make it possible to observe the planets with the eye, rather than through geometry. They believed it would open new worlds to them, and that they would discover the true movements of the heavens. They would be able to ascertain, through practical observation, whether the earth did indeed move round the sun.

There was a moment's silence at the stating of this possibility, as the men contemplated a world overturned. The earth round the sun, not the sun round the earth. The theory was already current, but as a matter of argument not of certainty. To know for sure ... The Duke's face was alive with anticipation. And now Dr Donati mentioned, almost casually, their disappointment at the lack of interest by the Grand Duke Ferdinando of Tuscany in the development of their work. In the days when his brother ruled, there had been a greater interest in questions of the universe. The Grand Duke was a cautious man in his munificence. His interests lay in the world immediately around him.

Vincenzo's interest was heightened by the reluctance of his uncle-in-law to subscribe to the search for knowledge. Dr Donati signalled to his assistant who stepped forward with a case. It is a lesser instrument than the one Dr Galilei is working on at present, but it would show them its optical qualities.

The assistant laid the case on the table and Dr Donati lifted from it a thick wooden stick. At either end, he showed them, was a curved optical glass. And now to demonstrate its power – and this one did not have the range of the newest instrument – he suggested His Serene Highness surveyed his lands.

His Serene Highness lifted the stick to his eye and said, after a moment, 'I can see nothing but a blur.'

'It is pointing at the wall at present,' explained Dr Donati. 'May I guide you to a better view.'

He moved the instrument, squinting along its line.

'Ah,' said the Duke, 'I see green,' and then, 'Why it is as close as if only an arm's length from me. I see leaves as if they are growing here on the loggia. I see the bark on the tree trunk. Why, this is amazing.'

He stared through the lens, silent for a moment in awe. And then, 'I can see the pebbles on the shore, and a bird. Ottavio, this is extraordinary. See for yourself.'

Ottavio looked through the lens and it was as the Duke said, those distant points suddenly within reach, as if they themselves were standing on the far shore. He moved the instrument to the right, following the shore line, and now he saw a human form, a woman standing in the water, in a white chemise.

'Dio, Lucia Pellizari in her chemise!' he exclaimed.

'What!' cried the Duke.

Ottavio murmured, 'She's becoming fat,' and then, unsteady in his hand, the telescope moved further to the right and he saw a girl standing in the water up to her thighs, and as he trained the instrument in her direction, she lifted her chemise above her head.

'Ah! The little Cattaneo is naked.'

'What!' shouted the Duke and snatched the instrument

from his grasp. 'Where? I can see only water.' And then, 'There she is. How pretty. She is looking at me, and she is naked.'

'You can see her. She cannot see you.'

'No, she is looking at me. She is not too young, Ottavio, that much I can see from her shameless display. What a lovely pair she's got, and pointing straight at me.'

'She thinks she cannot be seen. If she knew you were watching she would die of shame.'

'Nonsense,' said the Duke, 'she would be like the others. La cattiva Cattaneo. This is a wonderful instrument, Dr Donati. Never mind the heavens, what it sees on earth is enough. I shall pay you handsomely for it.'

'Regretfully, I cannot part with it, for we need it for our research,' said Donati.

'I shall pay well for your research,' said the Duke, still looking through the lens. 'Ottavio, I think I'm falling in love.'

'Surely not.'

'Go and see Benintendi in the Treasury. We must arrange for Dr Donati to be rewarded for his trouble.'

The Duke turned back to the lake, and the scene through the telescope. 'It's as if they're already playing the nymphs in *Il Pastor Fido*, oh, and now she's fleeing. What a delicious arse she has. And now I have seen all of her.'

※

'Claudia!' called her mother urgently. 'Come in at once, the men are returning.'

Claudia ran through the water towards her mother who was holding out her clothes, flapping them at her to emphasize the need for haste. She scolded as she thrust the clothes at her. 'Into the bushes with you and make yourself decent. And you, too, Lucia and Isabetta, wandering around in your underclothes. It's always the same, a few glasses of wine in the sun and everyone forgets themselves.'

The women retreated out of sight behind the willows

and the men arrived, cheerfully dishevelled with wet hair and bare feet. It was lucky, Signora Cattaneo said, that no one from court could see them now.

'And what if they could?' asked Gian Battista, enveloping her in a hug. Signora Cattaneo scolded and then laughed. The men began to load the plates and cloths on to the boat. Cattaneo stamped on the embers of the fire.

'Where is Claudio?' asked Signora Cattaneo, and Gian Battista waved a hand in the direction of the willows. Signora Cattaneo raised her eyes to the sky in despair. 'Let's hope the ladies are dressed.' She called, 'Claudia!' as a reminder to her daughter that she is close at hand.

✷

Claudia has her arms over her head as she struggles to put her dress on over the chemise which clings to her damp skin. Her head emerges from the material and she finds she is looking straight at Claudio. His eyes are very dark and brilliant, the air is still, there is a profound silence. She can only continue looking at him, an immense warmth in her heart spreading through her limbs, through the air, towards him. She smiles and at the same time feels tears in her eyes, as he moves closer. Neither says anything, and then there is no need as he bends his head towards her.

She hears her mother call, and from the trees nearby, Lucia's voice, indulgent. 'Claudio and Claudia.' She moves back from his embrace but her hand remains in his.

'Whenever I see you I am happy,' he says.

She knows the truth now, she understands why she feels so joyful and so close to tears. She knows she should not tell him, but she cannot be quiet, she is overwhelmed by her knowledge. 'I love you, Claudio,' she says.

His face is so full of light it is wonderful to look at. She has never seen him so happy. And now the tears in her eyes overflow.

'I'm going back to the boat,' calls Lucia, from the trees. 'Come, Isabetta, the lovebirds will follow.'

Standing under the willow trees, Claudia feels an immense relief that all will be well. She loves him, he loves her, they are destined for each other. The heat of the day has diffused into a late afternoon warmth. Around them the birds have begun to sing again, and there is a murmurous hum of insects.

'We must go,' she says, as she hears her mother call again. She is aware of a noise close to her ear, the whining note of a mosquito, and then there is a sharp stinging sensation. She cries out, and slaps at her neck. On her hand is a mess of black insect and her own blood.

'They're vicious,' she says, and walks faster through the trees, as she hears the sound of mosquitoes newly awake in their search for flesh. The relentless whine of the one she killed remains in her mind as the boat slides back towards Mantua and the swollen bite on her neck throbs insistently.

A few days later, she has a fever, and lies on her bed soaked with sweat and on fire with heat. It is the low fever of the marshland, from the Mantuan air, says the doctor. It will pass. And so it does, but a shadow remains.

CHAPTER ELEVEN

*M**arket day*, and the city is crowded with farmers from the region. They began arriving at dawn with their produce, stalls piled with vegetables and fruit, sheep and poultry ready for slaughter. They call out their wares and shout greetings at faces they recognize. They have broad open faces, weather-darkened skin, eyes that are used to long distances and wide skies. From isolated homesteads they arrive at their meeting place on the Piazza dell'Erbe. Those not in charge of the stalls gather in groups to trade news and livestock, their voices raised in the distinctive dialect, like donkeys braying, observes Ottavio. He listens to snatches of conversation as he moves through the crowd. He can efface his presence so that he's unnoticed – it's a skill he has learnt.

The townspeople meet and gossip in their own groups. Here are several weavers, the fine material of their clothes at odds with the worried expression in their eyes. Mantua's prosperous tradition of cloths of silk and wool is in decline, for France and England, once their best customers, are making their own cloth. They look to the court for custom, but the Duke's taste favours brocades from Venice, cut velvet from France. Moving through the crowds, ignored by the majority, are men with full beards and long black overgarments. They are the Hebrews, given refuge by Duke Guglielmo after they were expelled by His Most Catholic Majesty of Spain. A humanist gesture, though inspired more by Duke Guglielmo's view that where the Jews arrive money follows. Over the years they have been good for Mantua's trade, and for financially embarrassed nobility. Even here, they wear the yellow badge required by the law of the Inquisition. Duke Guglielmo, when he finally gave way to pressure from the Vatican to allow the Holy Office within the walls of Mantua, gave the Inquisition a building adjacent to the synagogue, as if setting a cat next to a cage of canaries. His sense of humour was as warped as his body. And now the cat's tail twitches for, during the long year of dying, His Most Catholic Majesty of Spain issued further edicts against the Hebrews, and more have arrived in Mantua and in Venice. The Holy Inquisitor looks out of the window of his office at the tribe of Israel and shivers at the ungodliness around him, in the synagogue, and in the palace.

Earlier there was a chill in the air, and the autumn mist that lay over the lake and marshes gave the illusion that the city was rising out of the clouds. The sun has dispersed the mist and the buildings have a sharp brilliance in the clear light. Coaches roll towards the palace with retinues of guards and servants. The guests from Milan, Ferrara and Florence are arriving, each name on the list multiplied by several hundred of their necessary entourage. Along the Mincio glide the barges from Venice, bearing the great of the Serenissima. In the courtyard the Quartermaster and his staff wait with lists of who is to be billeted where. And this is all before the entrance of Margherita of Austria, on her way to her bridegroom, the new King Philip III of Spain. The quartermaster's list for her Habsburg court runs to a whole book, beginning with the words 'Her Most Serene Majesty and seven thousand mouths'.

All this to cement Habsburg friendships, to celebrate the birth of Leonora, the fifth and youngest child of the Duke and Duchess, and to demonstrate Mantua's artistic pre-eminence. In the newly-built court theatre, the Duke's set designer strikes his forehead against a pillar several times at the stupidity of the scene shifters who cannot get the drifts of silk representing Alfeo, the river of Arcadia, flowing in a lapidary way.

To avoid the sound of hammers and the cries of the designer, the musicians have retreated to the Hall of Rivers to rehearse. This is next to the Duke's apartments, and he is overseeing the rehearsal. His chief actor, Arlecchino Martinelli, retails the Duke's wishes, as dictated earlier in the day, to the actors rehearsing in the Great Hall, under the Pisanello frescoes of death in battle.

> Come se' grande, Amore,
> di natura miracolo e del mondo . . .

Claudia, leading the chorus of nymphs in the Hall of Rivers, is aware of the Duke's eyes glancing at her with a more than passing interest. He leans over to the crook-backed courtier who is frequently in his company, and mutters something to him. It is obviously a *louche* remark, for they both seem amused as their eyes are directed at her again. She is aware of Claudio's interception of the glance and sees his face darken. She watches the wall above the Duke's head as she sings, and holds the score in front of her to obscure his view. She will be safe as long as she acknowledges nothing, she thinks. He has enough to amuse him without chasing after reluctant singers. About 10,000 guests are descending on Mantua. There is the huge production of the pastoral, several concerts, a fireworks display and a tournament for him to oversee. And countless dark-eyed beauties to divert him. She cannot understand why he appears to know her so well.

Afterward Claudio is angry with her. Why was she making eyes at the Duke? he demands. The sheer injustice of men leads her to answer him angrily. And then later, at supper in the evening, her father forbids her to see Claudio on her own. But if he wants us to marry? she says, to which he replies, You are deluded, he is no more suited to marriage than a priest is. She wonders why pastorals about perfect love seem to put everyone into such a fury.

Il Pastor Fido is a triumph. The court theatre is packed out. To say that people have killed to get invited is hardly an exaggeration. Eight hours of pastoral and intermezzi, longer even than *La Pellegrina*, and then a sumptuous banquet. The Duke is everywhere, like the magnificent host he is, so that everyone feels they have bathed in his charm, have each had his complete attention. Later, in the Duchess's apartments the Duke recounts some of the more hilarious remarks of the guests, and leans over the cradle of their youngest daughter, Leonora. She is the prettiest child of them all, he declares. She is to marry no one but the Emperor himself. That will be one in the eye for her great uncle, the Grand Duke.

The guests eventually depart, satiated with music, theatre, tournaments, dances, banquets. They lean back in their carriages, their minds in confusion. The iron wheels roll along the narrow bridges out of the city, the horses' hoofs strike iron against the paving stones. The barges of Venice glide back to the Serenissima, their occupants gazing out at the gathering mists that shroud the glittering festival city.

In the house of the Pellizaris the singers try on the necklaces that the Duke has sent in appreciation of the triumphant performance. Claudia fastens the pendant of pearls and rubies and looks at herself in the glass.

'Why is it,' asks Lucia Pellizari, 'that the little Cattaneo has the best necklace? At a glance, and I know something about jewels, I would say it is at least twice as expensive as those we have been given. Did Claudia sing twice as much as we did? Rather less, I would say. No, don't worry, Claudina, I'm not angry. More amused, aren't we, Isabetta?'

'It is part of the natural order of things,' says Isabetta. 'Now it only remains for Claudia to find a complaisant husband who can turn a blind eye.'

'You are getting old and cynical – I hope that never happens to me,' says Claudia. She turns to look at the pendant in the glass again. The rubies shine like drops of dark blood on her skin. The back of the pendant feels rough and turning it over she sees engraved on it some lines she recognizes:

> Come se' grande, Amore,
> di natura miracolo e del mondo!
> Qual cor si rozzo o qual si fiera gente
> il tuo valor non sente?

She smiles to herself. It is, after all, appealing that a man with such power, such unlimited prerogative, should take so much thought over his gifts. At heart, she thinks, he was a grand romantic.

❈

The Duke was playing cards with the Marquis del Vasto, Count Carlo Rossi, and Don Ottavio Gonzaga in the Room of the Zodiac. A quartet of musicians played *divertissements* at the far end of the room. The Duke's new secretary, Messer Chieppio, was keeping a note of the score as the Marquis was notoriously quarrelsome.

Ottavio laid down a Jack of Clubs, the Marquis a King of the same suit, and the Duke a King of Swords.

'Mine, I think,' said the Duke.

'This is a magical pack which shuffles itself in the Duke's favour,' said the Marquis del Vasto.

'The luck of the Gonzaga,' said the Duke good-humouredly.

'Never joke about that,' said Ottavio. 'Dame Fortune might be listening.'

'And talking of fickle women,' said the Duke, 'have the gifts been sent to my singers?'

'This morning – with the appropriate verse on Signora Claudia's.'

'Cups are trumps, this time,' said Count Rossi. 'Make a note, please, Messer Chieppio, for those of us with poor memories.'

'The Cattaneo is not worth the trouble, really, her heart is engaged elsewhere,' said Ottavio.

'So?' The Duke was examining his hand of cards.

'Has fortune favoured you again?' asked del Vasto, discontent at what had been dealt him.

The Duke's face remained expressionless as he looked at the array of cups in his hand.

※

Claudio writes his love into his music, and because he has so many commissions for the Duke, music for tournaments, music for meal times, for the next Carnival, he has no time to speak his love. He knows there is an understanding with Claudia, but he has to talk to her father, and old Cattaneo has been uncommunicative. Meanwhile, there is another poem the Duke has sent to be set to music, with his requirements scribbled in the margins, 'three ladies and an alto, set in cantata style'. He works on till late in the evening. There are more fanfares to devise for the arrival of Madama the Duke's sister, Her Serene Widowed Highness of Ferrara. Now that the Duke of Ferrara is dead without heirs and his state annexed by the Pope, Monteverdi's hopes of a post at their court have dissolved, and he is irrevocably tied to Mantua. At times like this he thinks of the pure certainty, the measured pace of the cathedral at Cremona. And then a picture comes to his mind of the willow trees by the lake. Claudia's face, Claudia's eyes, Claudia's mouth, the hollow of her neck. He is caught in a web of longing. And where is the money to support a family? What dowry would Cattaneo provide with Claudia? He looks at the lines he has set: *O come e gran martire | A celar suo desire* . . . How painful it is: setting those lines he understands so well for a prince who has never known the torment of concealing his desire. The irony of it, and there is his brother Giulio Cesare transcribing the notes for him, peering short-sightedly at his script. They always make copies because of the carelessness with which the palace treats the originals.

Voices in the street outside and then knocking at the

outer door. Giulio opened the shutters and said, 'It's the crooked one.'

'At this time of evening?' But the housekeeper had already opened the door, and Ottavio was shown in. He had some more poems from His Highness, he said, and was bringing them round now to allow more time for composition. They were needed for Friday's concert.

'But it is Wednesday evening, and we have still to rehearse the composition I am working on at present,' protested Claudio.

His brother sighed, shook his wrist to indicate an attack of writer's cramp and left the room.

'I brought the poem around myself for I know that His Highness's wishes are difficult to meet, his view of time being different from other men's. It is a lovely poem, dear to his heart, and he would have no one but you to set it.'

'I'm grateful for your trouble. Let me see it,' and Claudio read it first to himself, then aloud. '*Si ch'io vorrei morire* . . . yes, it's pretty, full of languor . . . I would like to die . . . of your kisses, your mouth, your tongue . . . just the sort of song that would appeal to His Highness.'

'He sees it as one for a virtuoso soprano. He would like it set for Signora Claudia. He thinks it would be an excellent test for her voice.'

'It is not right for her voice.' He had spoken sharply, without a moment's hesitation. To appear more considered, he added, 'It needs a more florid, mature singer.'

'On the contrary, what appeals to His Highness is the youthful voice, and the emotional intensity of the song. What appeals to His Highness is the voice of La Cattaneo. Oh, Claudio, don't you remember what I told you, how many months ago was it? Never wait for the right moment – you will find it has passed you by.' Ottavio shook his head. 'Why does no one ever follow my advice?'

'Claudia loves me,' said Claudio. 'I have no doubt.'

'But how is she to know that you love her, unless you

marry her? How is anyone to know? Speak to her father to-morrow, get his consent, with or without dowry. If you wait any longer, the Duke will arrange his own terms for the marriage, and you will have to bear the ridicule of the court. It's not in my own interest to give you this advice. I do it purely from sentiment.'

Purely from sentiment. How the words masked the rawness of actuality. The swaying coach, Isabella's tears, her voice, But I love him, Ottavio. Too close to the sun, all of them, and some would be burned.

'I shall speak to Cattaneo as soon as I have finished the composition,' said Claudio.

Ottavio shrugged. What could you do? These people had no idea. He left the house of the musician, near the canal, and followed his torchbearer through the dark streets back to the blazing lights of the palace.

Cattaneo's house was on the straight street that led to the island of Te. He listened to his prospective son-in-law, and said, 'There is little to spare, and my other children to think of. You will be earning more in a few years. Your compositions are published in Venice, in Milan, even in Nuremberg. You will have no need of my few scudi in a year or two. In the mean time, why not ask for an advance from the Lord Duke's office?'

'I do not wish to interest His Highness in my marriage.'

'As a servant of the court, you cannot marry without his consent, so you may as well profit from his interest. That's my advice.'

The letter to the Duke asking permission to marry the court singer Claudia Cattaneo made no mention of money. Permission, pure and simple, was sought to join two of the Duke's servants in matrimony. A reply came back from the Court secretary. His Serene Highness found it inconvenient to consider personal matters until after the Carnival and the various spring festivities for which a full complement of musicians were necessary. He suggested that Messer Claudio remind him of his intentions again in May.

Wherever Claudia goes, she is watched. At rehearsals Claudio watches her as she sings *Si ch'io vorrei morire*, his mind torn between the wish for her to sing his music to its full intensity, and the awareness of the song's message to the Duke. At the concerts she is watched, by the Duke, and by those close to him. She sees the wry glance from the Duchess towards her consort, the dark observant eyes of the Duke's courtier, the impertinent stare of the dwarf seated on a stool by the Duke's feet. And the Duke's eyes, the pale light in them indulgent and amused, as if he already knows her.

Then there are her parents, watchful now that Claudio has declared his intention, and has not been able to say when the wedding will be. There are her fellow singers, intrigued at her ambivalent status, betrothed yet not betrothed. It gives them something to gossip about in idle moments. She feels the significance of a glance and a smile from the Court secretary as he passes her in the corridor. A mere courtesy, nothing more, she tells herself, she is not to delude herself that there is some mischief afoot.

So when an arm is linked through hers as she enters the Room of the Zodiac, to escape the Carnival throng, there is a certain inevitability about it. The few candles in this room light the glitter of the stars on the domed ceiling but leave the greater area in shadow. For a moment, so sure is the arm of not being rejected, she thinks that Claudio has followed her but she is aware of the velvet of the sleeve, of the rounded, muscular strength within, of the height of the shoulder above hers, and she sees through the mask the unmistakable eyes of the Duke.

From a long way off, from another country, she can hear the sound of music and laughter, but here the air is thick with silence. The Duke says, 'You were looking for me,' and she smells the wine on his breath.

She is not sure whether it would be politic to deny this so she laughs as if it was simply a jest. 'I was in need of some air,' she said. 'The heat from the people and the flames made me feel faint.'

'And I was looking for you, too, so now let us find somewhere further from the heat and the people.'

She feels anxious but his voice is lighthearted and then as she hesitates he says, breaking into comically accented German, '*Kommen sie mit, meine liebe,*' as if they are sharing a joke. It is hard to refuse but she delays, 'I have to be with the musicians, I shall be missed.'

It is as if she has not spoken. His arm linked with hers, he moves towards the door and they are in a corridor, walking past the stone eyes of his ancestors' sculptures. She hears their footsteps on the marble, and sees their shadows heightened in the candlelight to the ceiling. They have come to a double door of carved ebony inlaid with ivory, which the Duke opens. They are in a large panelled room, with pictures glowing jewel bright in the light of a blazing fire. On the wall adjacent to the fireplace she sees the rosy pink flesh of a naked Venus with Cupid, regarding each other with complicity. The Duke removes his mask, and says, 'At last we're away from the crowd.' The room is not empty though, for sprawled on the chair nearest the fire, a goblet of wine beside him, is the recumbent Archimedeo. The Duke shakes him by the shoulder and the dwarf sits up, dazed from the fire and the wine, gradually taking in the sight before him, that of the Duke with his arm around one of his singers.

'Excuse me, Your Highness,' says Archimedeo.

'Out!' says the Duke. Archimedeo scrambles down from the chair and makes his unsteady way to the door, which he closes behind him. The sound echoes down the corridor.

At this point, the door closes for all of us, for there are

only two people inside the room. Neither has ever spoken of what was said between them afterwards, and as its effect reverberated through the years, we can only look at what we witnessed outside the door and guess.

Archimedeo, not wishing to be deprived of inside information, put his eye to the keyhole and could see, from his limited view, the Duke guiding Claudia, his arm still around her waist, to the portrait of Venus, the Correggio *School of Love*. The singer cannot fail to be impressed, thought Archimedeo, shifting to the right as he tried to see round the limit of the keyhole. It was so frustrating that all he could see now was the fire, and the chair in which he had slept. He waited for the two of them to move back into his line of vision.

He heard footsteps behind him and a hand grasped the back of his collar, almost throttling him. Another hand had hold of his crotch, careless of his manhood. Archimedeo yelped as he was carried through the air, seeing the hard marble floor directly beneath him, until he was finally dumped, fortunately finding his feet, at the end of the corridor. He looked up at his assailant to see in the flickering light of the candles, the scowling face of the Duke's courtier.

'Just because you are the same height as keyholes does not mean they were placed there for you,' said Ottavio.

Archimedeo recovering his breath and his balance, retorted, 'And just because I am small doesn't mean I should be treated like a dog.'

'Get back to the carnival, and do what you are paid to do, which is to entertain, not to spy.'

But now they heard other footsteps coming from the direction of the Room of the Zodiac, striking hard and hurriedly against the floor, and turning into the corridor at such a pace that he was almost upon them before he could stop.

'Where is Claudia?' The musician's eyes had the white,

startled appearance of a deer in flight. He stared at Ottavio and demanded, 'Where is she?'

'I haven't seen her,' said Ottavio, at the same time the realization growing in his mind of the likely possibility. The dwarf looked down at the floor and sighed in resignation at everyone's lack of wits.

'Where is she?' demanded Claudio again and this time Archimedeo nodded his head towards the ebony door. All three stood, as immobile as the door itself, watching it.

'Mother of God,' said Claudio.

'What did you see?' said Ottavio to Archimedeo.

Archimedeo looked at him scornfully, as one who has put a price on his privileged information.

The handle of the door turned and the Duke appeared suddenly. They could see two highly coloured marks on his cheeks, as of anger, and he walked swiftly in their direction, his heels striking hard on the floor. As he drew near, he seemed to notice them for the first time, his eyes sweeping past Ottavio and then, at the sight of Claudio, turning as cold as ice. Fire and ice, contrasting humours in one glance as he walked past. The watchers listened to his footsteps in the distance, looked at each other and then at the door. A few minutes later Claudia emerged. Her face was flushed, her eyes confused, and she raised her hand to her mouth as she saw she was observed.

For a moment she stood in the doorway, surrounded by the firelight, in which the silk of her dress glinted red. Then she walked towards the witnesses, until she reached Claudio. She looked at him, and her eyes brimmed with tears as if seeing only unhappiness. They waited for her to speak, but without an explanation, without even a word, she walked on, leaving them staring after her until she was lost to view in the Room of the Zodiac.

Naturally, everyone's memories and conclusions of that night were different. At the time Claudio turned his eyes from Ottavio, murmuring only as before, 'Madre del Dio.'

Archimedeo swivelled from one to the other, waiting for someone to speak.

'Get away, you eavesdropping toad!' said Ottavio.

'My, you're a black scavenger, said the raven to the crow,' retorted Archimedeo, and moved away fast from Ottavio's approaching foot. So in the end, all was speculation, and as neither Ottavio nor Claudio talked about it afterwards, a story which altered with each telling was embroidered by Archimedeo to suit his listeners. In one version, the Duke had emerged from the room with deep red furrows scratched in his cheeks. In another, more popular version, Claudia had come out clutching at her disarranged bodice, her face flushed with passion. Yet another had him peering through the keyhole to see the pair of them *in flagrante*. No one really believed that version, which Archimedeo retailed in a hesitant way as if he realized he was going too far, but whatever the truth of it, whether she had behaved chastely or not, whether they had talked of love or of high art, something had happened between the Duke and his singer, and whatever it was, Claudia had been compromised.

CHAPTER TWELVE

*I*n *the spring* came floods like a second deluge, an omen of disaster in the last year before the new century. The River Po and its tributaries burst their banks, and the lakes surrounding the city rose higher than in living memory. Livestock was drowned, houses were swamped in mud. As the rains fell the Duke's restlessness was exacerbated by the steady drumming from the heavens, afflicting him like a nagging sore, its outward and visible sign a festering ulcer on his leg – the result, so he said, of an old battle wound. The magnificent festivities for the new Queen of Spain had led to no reward of any note, despite the Mantuan ambassador to the court of Madrid letting it be known that the post of Governor of Flanders would be welcomed.

The marriage between Claudio Monteverdi and Claudia Cattaneo was solemnized at the church of SS Simone e Guida on 20 May of 1599. Hardly a fortnight later, the Duke and his court were off for a new tour of Europe. A few days with the Habsburg relatives, then on to the pressing matter of taking a cure at Spa before further diversions in Antwerp and Brussels. The ducal entourage, by his special wish, included the court composer, leaving his bride of two weeks.

There in the stately salons, the Duke listened to the music of the new cantata and balletti of the French school while he played cards with other health-seeking princes. His composer attended the same concerts, listening with more concentration, taking notes, talking to the musicians and reporting back to the Duke. They moved on to Flanders, where Vincenzo indulged his passion for collecting in an art-buying spree. In Antwerp he visited the studio of a young artist, bought several of his pictures and invited him to Mantua as court portraitist. He will be one of the great painters, he predicted, and, moreover, is handsome with a pleasant manner. Make a note of his name, Piero Paulo, or the equivalent in Flemish, Rubens.

The travelling entourage only returned to Mantua towards the close of the year. In the whirl of parties, theatre, concerts, and intrigues, the court held passing time at bay. Outside the palace walls, the cold mist from the marshes depressed people's spirits. From his office the Inquisitor listened with righteous serenity in his heart to the mood of the citizens. At the beginning of the year, at the beginning of a new century, a new dawn of godliness must rise over Mantua. The Duke's alchemists meanwhile continued their ungodly and ineffective experiments, proving the only way to replenish the gold in the palace coffers was to increase taxes. The Duke surveyed the books in his library with satisfaction at the number now on the Index, though heaven knows if even Castiglione's *Book of the Courtier* was banned, the Index must include most books ever published. It was a constrained time, and somewhere they had lost the way to the golden age.

'They have finally done for him,' he said, reading the report from the Ambassador to Rome of the execution of the humanist Giordano Bruno after an eight-year trial. In the Campo de' Fiori they had tied him naked to the stake, with a wooden wedge driven into his mouth to stop his blasphemies. He had turned his head away from the cross held out to him as he burned, unrepentant to the last.

What did the man expect, said Ottavio, to be foolish enough to return to Italy and then to suggest there may be other worlds than ours? Such matters were no longer to be talked about. But what was this from Florence? The Grand Duke had pulled off his greatest coup. His niece, Maria de' Medici, Eleonora's younger sister, was to be married to King Henry IV of France. And the Grand Duke's musical upstaging continued, a new *drama per musica* was to be performed – *Euridice*, a work by the poet Rinuccini and the Grand Duke's favourite composer Peri. We should make sure our own composer is there.

Almost in a frenzy of restlessness, Vincenzo continued his travelling, covering most of north Italy from Venice to Genoa. His portable court was back in Mantua in time to catch their breath for Christmas. And then, once more, came the siren call of the Pope, to arms against the infidel. He departed for the crusade in Hungary with 2,000 men. Those who stayed behind shook their heads in resigned admonition. That's how the decades rule you, said Ottavio. He will be forty next year, still ambitious for glory and feeling mortality at his back.

This time the Duke spared his composer the campaign, for Claudia was approaching her time, and in the summer was delivered of a boy, whom they named Francesco after the Duke's eldest son. Ottavio stayed in the city to aid the Duchess with the administration of Mantua and Monferrato. Letters arrived from the camp outside the besieged town of Kanizsa with instructions for music to celebrate the victory of the crusaders. But as the weeks passed the letters revealed disarray in the campaign. Secretary Chieppio complained of mattresses soaked by the rain; the new young aide, Alessandro Striggio, described the weather as impossible, the Turks as unmovable. The Duke complained to Eleonora that Don Giovanni de' Medici was insufferable.

Letters to and from the camp, complaints, commands, counter-commands, to Mantua, to Florence, to Rome, to Vienna, the messengers calloused with riding. In Mantua Maestro Pallavicino sickened with fever and died. Within two days of his death, another letter was on its way in the messenger's satchel to the battlefield. Its request was couched in a humble yet feline way, suggesting that His Highness would surely consider him remiss if he did not now beg for the long awaited appointment as Director of

Music. Monteverdi's letter reached the Duke during his retreat from Hungary, relieved of his leadership by the new German commander, whose view of his competence was expressed in blunt Teutonic terms. Hardly the best moment to ask, but as the Duke's previous letter had consisted of instructions to the palace's master of ceremonies for a series of tableaux to celebrate his triumph over the Turks, no one was to know the victory was only a dream.

The letter returned with the Duke and was filed in Secretary Chieppio's extensive cabinet. His military career at an end, Vincenzo's energy now focused entirely on art. He granted the request of the new Director of Music and, by God, if political and military glory were blocked to him, Mantua would lead the world in music and art. Back and forth went the letters from wherever he was, with instructions and little time in which to realize them. Where, he wanted to know, was that artist from Flanders? Send a letter, Chieppio, to our ambassador in Brussels, to encourage the painter I engaged there to depart as soon as possible. And wasn't it about time, Claudio, that we found a new and exciting singer, rather younger than the Pellizaris, and Signora Claudia is less available now she is having children and is so frequently ill. I have been told of an astonishing girl in Rome, only thirteen, with a brilliant voice. Find out more, invite her to Mantua.

Back and forth go the letters with their demands. The father of the girl is suspicious. On the one hand, his daughter Caterina will be the pupil of a renowned maestro at a great princely court. On the other, we all know the reputation of the Duke. The girl can go to Mantua, he writes, provided a doctor and midwife in Rome first certify she is a virgin. Outrageous, says the Duke, is there no trust any more? Just to show how entirely honourable I am, she can be lodged in the household of my Director of Music. Caterina arrives, an extra mouth to feed, and already, for some reason which they hope has to do with the court treasurer and not with the Duke, their pay is five months in arrears, not only that of Signor Claudio and Signora Claudia, but also her father Cattaneo. How can they live? Where is the money to come from? Only through visits to Messer Abrameo, the usurer, who is growing sleek on the needs of unpaid court servants and spendthrift nobility.

Back and forth go the letters, about money and music, music and money. And yet all the while, his fame is increasing, he is even subjected to the flattery of an attack from the academic canon in Bologna for his new music. Discordant, says the critic, against all tradition of the *prima pratica* and of the church. But these criticisms can be brushed aside, for he knows he is on the way to even greater achievements. If only the workload wasn't so relentless, if only the climate wasn't so vile. Claudia's illness recurs in the summer. Their second child, a daughter named Leonora, contracts the marsh fever. Such a lovely baby, so little time on this earth. It seems his talent has brought them an accursed life as, dressed in mourning, they follow the small coffin to the church.

It should be most unusual, as all the actors are to sing their parts; it is said on all sides that it will be a great success. No doubt I shall be driven to attend out of sheer curiosity, unless I am prevented from getting in by the lack of space.

Letter from Carlo Magni in Mantua before the première of *La Favola d'Orfeo*, 1607

These sung things are more difficult and more beautiful than people think: they require great exquisiteness, otherwise they do not succeed.

Letter from Ottavio Rinuccini, librettist for *Arianna*, December 1607

*I*n *the garden of her summer villa* at San Martino Isabella listens to the news from court. Her youngest child is on her lap, trying to distract her attention. They are sitting in an arbour shaded by vines and lemon trees. The smell of bay laurel in the heat of the sun touches the nostrils. A cat is lying on the sunbaked earth, watching the world lazily through the slits of its eyes. Isabella stops the child from clambering over her shoulders, and says, 'Go to your Uncle Ottavio.'

'No,' says the child, hiding its head in her bosom.

'Then be quiet, and let me hear him.'

The years have been kind to Isabella. She has grown more beautiful at thirty, with an air of warmth and dignity that is fitting to her position. Her face no longer changes colour at the mention of the Duke. It is as if he belonged to another life. Which is as well, for Ottavio has proposed that she takes part in the experimental work that the musical academy of Mantua, the Accademia degli Invaghiti, is producing under the auspices of the Hereditary Prince Francesco. It is a work in which all the words of the play will be sung, and even now Claudio is labouring over it.

'But I only sing at our small court, I am out of practice with a large audience,' said Isabella. Her eyes, though, were interested, as Ottavio explained that far from being in the court theatre, it would be an unofficial production, either in the academy or in one of the halls in the palace. The audience would be small, *cognoscenti* from the academy, friends and relatives. He suspected the Duke, having been persuaded by the Duchess to give the young pup, his eldest son, some responsibility, did not want him to gain too much glory. It was ever thus, and the Duke's father before him, though the young prince was, by comparison with

Vincenzo at his age, as austere as a monk. A prig, in fact.

'As well as a pup?' said Isabella. 'Why should I want to be in a work produced by a priggish pup?'

'Because of Claudio's music; because young Alessandro Striggio, an excellent poet, is writing it; and I, as a member of the academy, will be at hand. You will regret it if you refuse. And besides, the Pellizari family have left *en masse* for Venice and won't be returning.'

'Ah, the real reason – you're short of singers and don't want to pay higher fees to get new ones,' said Isabella.

Ottavio laughed and said, 'That's the practical reason not the real reason. To tell the truth, more than anything, I would like to hear you sing at court.'

'Then I shall ask Ferrante. If he agrees, I shall come. What part do you have in mind for me?'

'Proserpina. It's the tale of Orpheus in the Underworld.'

'And like Proserpina, I shall return to the world for a while. So let us see if, like her, I can persuade my lord.'

※

Claudio works in the mornings and evenings at the score of *La Favola d'Orfeo*. He no longer expects quiet in which to concentrate since they moved to their house near the ducal palace. Their two-year-old son, Massimiliano, is a difficult and demanding child. The elder, Francescino, has taken to playing the violin. Claudio's pupil, young Caterina, exercises her voice in duets with Claudia. His brother Giulio Cesare wants to read him the latest draft of his reply to the pestilential critic from Bologna. The maid argues with the servant, messengers arrive from court with demands that the Director auditions a new singer, and meanwhile he is trying to hear the music in his head, to make it sing the words.

'Singing to a golden lyre . . . to beguile the mortal ear . . .'

Two harpsichords, ten violins, a double harp for Lucrezia Urbana, three chittarroni, sackbutts, organs, viols, cornetts, trumpets. He is not going to reduce the size of the orchestra, whatever the size of the room they are giving him. One regal organ to underline the basso continuo, and now it is time for the audition and he will have to leave La Musica's ritornello in mid-phrase, in its harmonic order against a disordered world. Six letters for La Musica, six notes in the bass theme, the musical rule of numbers, and now out into the cathedral square and fight a path through the pullulating crowds of friars, Capuchin monks and the black-robed Society of Jesus.

Venice has expelled its entire clergy in defiant response to the Pope's bull of excommunication against La Serenissima, and so Mantua has a new influx of refugees. The earlier refugees, the Hebrew, are being confined to a ghetto, apart from the family which lends money to the court. It is only another betrayal in their history after the welcome in the earlier years, but everyone knows the Inquisitor's influence on the Duke. It is not enough for him now to indulge in the sackcloth theatre of repentance on Ash Wednesday.

Claudio walks past the mendicant friars, his nose scenting the denial of soap and water on their mortified flesh. The music in his mind is ousted by thoughts of the court treasurer. Once again he has to persuade the man to unleash what is rightfully his. A while ago he had sent a letter to the Duke suggesting a way of circumventing this enemy, whose hostility towards him he cannot account for. A soothing reply had arrived from Secretary Chieppio, yet nothing had been done. So once again, he is forced to go like a beggar to the malevolent functionary for his salary in arrears. And there was the doctor's bill for Claudia, and food for the whole household. He can hardly concentrate on his work, and the year is advancing, they have to choose the singers, about which Prince Francesco, influenced no doubt by his younger brother's artistic tastes, has some strange ideas.

There will be a scene in Orfeo by a lake under some willows ... but now he is at the office of Signor 'Mal intenti', the treasurer, and this meeting will need all his concentration, all his control. The petty jealousies at court, and they even had the gall to gossip about the choice of godparents for Massimiliano. The Duke's daughter, the young Margherita, so ... our Maestro is seen as part of the family, they say. Whisper, gossip, all these mediocrities in their court dresses trying to justify their existence by bringing others down. No I will not come back tomorrow, signor. The salary was due a month ago, and I shall stay here till you find the keys to the strong-room. The audition will have to wait.

❈

Isabella is returning to court. Don Ferrante has agreed; she is, after all, a mature woman, mother of his children, and has been invited by the Duchess. He feels too old to get involved in the nonsense at the palace himself, and has entrusted Ottavio with overseeing the arrangements for her well-being. As the coach drives over the bridge to the south gate Isabella's heart leaps at the long lost but immediately familiar view of the red towers of the Castello San Giorgio. She turns to Emilia and says, 'Who would have thought it? Why did I stay away so long?' Emilia has put on weight from quiet years in the country, a husband and two children. She would have been glad not to make this winter trip to Mantua, but was loath to see Isabella there without her. Isabella's words worry her, and the way she is looking around with an agitated and eager expression. She cannot help feeling they have made a mistake.

'Oh, they have built new apartments!' Isabella exclaims. 'As if there weren't enough already. Do you think we'll get lost? We'll have to take a long string to guide us, like Theseus in the labyrinth.' She is delighted with the rooms she has been given, and the view from the windows onto the lake. 'Emilia,' she says, 'aren't you happy we've come?'

and as Emilia looks doubtful, 'We are all different people now. We have changed over the years.'

But nevertheless as the likelihood of meeting the Duke increases, so does her anxiety. She pays her respects to the Duchess and meets the young prince Francesco, whose manner is reserved, even awkward. The Duke, she hears, is away in Venice in a New Year festivity. The Duchess sighs and smiles. 'Our Vincenzo is relentless in his search for amusement.'

The next day, she hears sounds of commotion and a fanfare from the castle towers. A flotilla is approaching the palace harbour, led by the gilded barge, its standard of the black Gonzaga eagle rippling in the wind. The Duke is muffled from the cold and wearing a hat, his face obscured from view as he walks rapidly towards the palace, talking the while with one of the courtiers, and then she loses sight of him altogether in the shadow of the walls. In the afternoon, Ottavio calls on her. The Duke is to see them in an hour. Am I looking all right? asks Isabella. Is this the correct dress to wear? No, I am not nervous, only worried that after all these years I'm not in the fashion.

The Duke has moved his apartment from the graceful frescoes of the Room of the Rivers to the out-of-proportion grandeur of the new wing built by Viani. They enter the Hall of Mirrors, their reflections accompanying them along the walls, then the room of the tapestries and finally the room of the labyrinth. It is a huge square chamber, with a ceiling so high that Isabella suddenly knows what it is to be a dwarf. On the gold and blue carved labyrinth of the ceiling, she can see the same words written over and over again, *Forse che si, forse che no*. Maybe yes, maybe no.

Near the great mantelpiece which is higher than himself, the Duke is standing, with his back to them, looking into the fire. He has heard them come in, but he doesn't turn round, and she knows at once he is afraid. Ottavio coughs. 'We are here, your Highness.' He turns now and looks directly at her, and a readjustment takes place in her heart as she sees his face. Where is the golden being of her memory? She sees before her a middle-aged paunchy man, his complexion reddened, his hair dull, with patches of scalp showing through. The mask of time has descended on him, a mask that cannot be removed. She smiles at him only because she knows it is the Duke, not because she recognizes him. He laughs and comes forward, clasping her warmly, 'Carissima Isabella, and not a day older!' Ah yes, she remembers the voice, she remembers the eyes. She laughs, too, 'You are just the same!' but she feels, Oh the pity of it, in her heart. Nature is cruel.

✳

The wind blows from the east across the marshes like a knife cutting through the thickest clothes to the bone. Claudia has sent the servant to the market, and has wrapped a shawl around her head and shoulders to save her throat from the ravages of winter. She could not forgive herself if she were unable to sing Euridice because of her health. At times, she sees Claudio look at her reflectively, not so much with a human concern, more as if listening to the music in his mind and judging whether her voice will measure up to it.

Last summer, at his father's house in Cremona, he had been working on *Orfeo*, and there she had sung the part with him. In the courtyard her voice had soared through the warm summer air, and her father-in-law's eyes had filled with tears of pride at the work of his son. In Cremona she had recovered from the fever-ridden air of Mantua, and had felt her health returning. The clear air, the friendliness of the people who welcomed Claudio as the favoured son of Cremona, it was all good for the spirits. Could we not stay here, she had asked, could we not leave Mantua? But she knew the answer already. His mind was with *Orfeo*, and he moved half in the real world, half in his world of music. No one but the Duke would give him so much. Another harpsichord? No problem. Ten more viols? But of course. Even though the man who creates the music for these instruments is constantly embarrassed by lack of money. Her husband cannot understand how such profligacy and meanness can exist in one man. He blames the court treasurer, whom everyone says is dishonest. Claudia remembers, though, the fatal present of the dark blood rubies. She has wanted to sell the necklace, but there is the inscription. It would be recognized as the Duke's gift.

Little Caterina has come in with a hot bowl of punch she has made in the kitchen. The Director's pupil enjoys making herself useful around the house, though she lags behind with her lessons. She has such a beautiful voice, she thought it all came naturally, and is only just realizing the strenuous gymnastics involved in being a virtuoso. She pours a glass for Claudia, and half a glass for herself. To your health, she says, and watches Claudia as she drinks. And to yours, says Claudia, though it seems unnecessary. Caterina's skin has the bloom of a peach, and her eyes are clear pools of infinite unknowingness. Nothing has touched her, nothing disturbed her. A child existing only in the present. Claudia wonders what her future will bring.

※

Prince Francesco has the feeling of something treading at his heels. It is an uneasiness that is often with him. His younger brother Ferdinando, soon to be Cardinal, is cleverer than he. Ferdinando speaks more languages, he writes poetry, he composes, he is a student at the University of Pisa, and he spends time at the court of the Grand Duke of Tuscany. He is the Grand Duke's favourite great-nephew. His thin Medici features bring warmth to the heart of the older man, who sees a face that reflects his own when young.

Cardinal Ferdinando has written to his brother praising the new singing at the Medici court. The pure notes of the Grand Duke's castrati put the Mantuan sopranos in the shade. Such strength of voice, such pitch, such precision. It would add infinitely to the opera were they to have singers like that. As it happens, Francesco has been lying awake worrying about the voices at his disposal. The Pellizaris have de-camped, Signora Claudia is unreliable in her health, and the long-serving Madama Europa uncertain in her pitch. Ottavio's cousin, whose voice is highly praised by the Duke, has arrived but he can foresee difficulty in persuading a Gonzaga princess to attend a sufficient number of rehearsals. Only the tenor seems likely to give no trouble.

⁂

Claudia wakes in the night with an attack of fever. The sheets are soaked with sweat. She throws off the blanket because of the heat, and then starts shivering as the night air cools her damp skin. The other side of the bed is empty. She lights a candle, wraps a shawl around her, and stumbles to the close room, where she is sick. She returns to the bedroom and lies down again. She knows Claudio is working and must not be disturbed, but she sends thought messages to him, Help me. The house remains silent as she waits for his footsteps. Where are you, Claudio? In Arcadia, in Hades, in another country. When he finally returns to the room his face, seen in the light of the candle, seems curiously absent. Gradually, as if his eyes are adjusting to a different light, he notices her, and she can see his concern.

He takes her hand, and feels the heat of her fever. She can see in the midst of his anxiety for her health, another concern, that of the composer, taking into his mind another voice.

⁂

The Hereditary Prince paced up and down the room as he talked, in the way of his father, though without his panache. It was impossible, he said; he had been given a musical play that was to be entirely sung and the soprano parts outnumbered the singers available. Was Signor Claudio certain that his wife was not capable of taking the role? What suggestions did he have to replace her?

Claudio's face registered a moment's displeasure at the

prince's lack of concern for his wife's health, but he replied simply that there were no other sopranos in Mantua, in fact the only voice with the necessary range and versatility was that of the young priest who sang in the cathedral. He could not see His Serene Highness the Duke being delighted to see a castrato in the role of Euridice.

Why not? asked Francesco. And in any case he is not in charge of the production, I am. In Florence most of the soprano roles are taken by castrati. They are interested purely in the voice and the music, and that is surely what *Orfeo* is about. And in any case, I have already written to my brother the Cardinal to ask the Grand Duke for a castrato to sing La Musica, and he will be arriving any day. So I can see nothing strange about a castrato Euridice, and if my father the Duke needs a woman to ogle, there are several nymphs in the chorus, not to mention our Proserpina.

As Your Highness wishes, said Claudio. As long as the Grand Duke's castrato arrives soon. He must be here by the beginning of February, with his part learnt.

The days passed into a fortnight, to the first day of February. Francesco sent a letter to his curiously silent brother with the hope that if his much-needed castrato had not yet arrived, he would at least be on his way. Without him, he pointed out, it would be impossible to stage the play at all.

The days slipped by. The Grand Duke's castrato was not on the road. A letter from Ferdinando arrived. The castrato was complaining of the impossibility of learning the part which, he said, contained too many notes. Prince Francesco paced the rehearsal room in an agitation that affected all in the vicinity. He saw a plot in which he was enmeshed. His brother did not want his play to succeed. The Grand Duke's spies had told him of its quality and he was trying to sabotage it. And how his father would scorn him if he failed to produce the play in time for the Carnival. His entire reputation was at stake.

CHAPTER FOURTEEN

In Isabella's apartment people come and go. Her
brother has arrived with his wife and eldest children for
the Carnival and they descend on her in the afternoon.
They bring with them presents, gold ribbons, a smoked
ham from Novellara, a Madeira cake. Her brother-in-law
the Bishop pays a less welcome call. He inveighs against
the decadence of the court, and wonders that she takes part
in their frivolity. He casts a blight on the day, she tells
Ottavio. His ears are closed to any views that don't agree
with his.

Ottavio comes and goes. Sometimes it is to discuss the
rehearsals or to escort her there, at other times simply to
talk. It is noted at the palace that he is often in attendance
upon Donna Isabella. She is happy for him to call infor-
mally, after all, he is family, isn't he? There is no need for
any ceremony. He arrives without notice, hangs around
her salon if she is still being dressed, or tells her of the latest
carnival gossip while she is having breakfast. At the end of
the day he will call by after rehearsals, to sympathize with
the tired diva. Ottavio has his back to the fire, watching as
Isabella's feet are attended to by the palace masseur. The
acres of marble floors jar the ankles, she says, and she
spends so much time standing at rehearsals. She will be relieved when the Grand Duke's castrato arrives, so that
they can rehearse the earlier part and give the Queen of
Hades a rest. She is beginning to feel sorry for the
Hereditary Pup, Francesco. Every day his brow is more
furrowed, as yet another setback occurs. The orchestra has
been reduced to a handful because there is not enough
space. And Signor Claudio is obsessive about the notes. He
makes her go through her trillos again and again. He is forever criticizing the little priest who sings Euridice, as he

MASQUE OF THE GONZAGAS

has in his mind what Signora Claudia would have done instead.

'So you regret coming here?' asked Ottavio.

'Not at all, I love every minute. I return from rehearsal trilling my trillos, don't I, Emilia?'

'She is as happy as a songbird,' said Emilia, who was sitting near the window to catch the light with her sewing.

In the centre of the room, on a circular table, was a vase of hothouse lilies that scented the air. Ottavio looked at the writing on the paper beside them. Carissima Isabella, the unmistakable hand. So the old reprobate was trying to turn back time, to stir flames from dead embers.

A succession of clear bright days, unusually so for the beginning of February, have arrived. The birds are already feeling the call of spring. Isabella wakes in the mornings with a feeling of lightheartedness to the insinuating cooing of doves outside the window. The lake has a metallic sparkle in the sun and the wintry silhouette of the trees is softened by a haze of green.

The musicians have been affected by a similar levity. Every day one of them asks, with an air of concern, 'Is the castrato on the road yet?' It amuses them to heighten Prince Francesco's irritation and anxiety, though they keep quiet when the Duke looks in at the rehearsals. Their Maestro is aware of the undercurrents and takes no notice. All that matters to him when they are rehearsing is that everyone present gives of their best. He stands in front of the lectern, rarely referring to the score, his eyes on the musicians and singers, eyes that coax, encourage, admonish. His hands shape the music as if working with sculpture. At times, when the singer reaches the note he wants the right hand will be poised motionless palm outwards in front of his mouth so that you cannot see him smile. Only the expression in his eyes betrays his approval. They are alight with love of the music. He recognizes that what he has composed is finer than anything he has written before.

Isabella feels happy because he approves of her voice. She pleads with Pluto, My lord, that unhappy man . . . has so moved my heart to pity . . .

The Duke, who has been watching the rehearsal, calls out 'Brava' at the end. Claudio's face registers annoyance at the interruption. Isabella smiles at the Duke and feels, as if responding to her song, a moment of pity for him.

※

'How can you feel sorry for him?' asked Ottavio. 'How like a soft-hearted woman. He has everything in the world he could want, apart, of course, from eternal youth but even His Serene Highness must realize he is not a god.'

'You speak like someone who is annoyed that the pity is not directed towards a more deserving case,' she said.

'I never ask for anything I do not expect to be given,' said Ottavio.

'What you don't expect, you're not given. Why are you so unaccepting?'

'I have seen in my family what happens to those who expect too much.'

Isabella's curiosity was aroused. When she was a girl in Novellara she had heard whispered tales about Ottavio's father, the *condottiere* prince whose ferocity in battle was legendary, but the talk had stopped abruptly when they realized she was listening. She waited for Ottavio to say something more. He was sitting by the fire watching the flames.

'Tell me what happened to your mother, Ottavio,' she said. 'How did she die? Why did you come to Mantua?'

'It's an old story, not to be talked of.' He glanced at her angrily then looked back at the fire.

'But it's in your mind now, and you are remembering it,' Isabella said softly, and waited for him to speak.

Staring into the fire, Ottavio began to tell her. When he had finished, Isabella was silent for a while, then said, 'That is terrible, a terrible story, and very sad.'

Ottavio looked at the flames leaping, but in his mind

saw only the face of his mother. They had covered her eyes with a cloth, because no one could close them, but the lips were drawn back exposing the teeth in the swollen face. For a moment he had thought she must have been laughing as she died. She had had an apoplexy, said his father, and it had pleased God to take her from them. He had written thus to Duke Guglielmo, his cousin, and then the Duke's councillor had arrived. He left the elder son, the heir, and returned to Mantua with the younger son, Ottavio. You can have him, said his father, misshapen with his mother's sins. Yet his father's sin of murder, of poisoning, went unpunished.

'So you see, Donna Isabella,' said Ottavio, 'that is what the Gonzaga do to faithless wives.' And he laughed.

To reveal something about which you have been silent for so long makes a hostage of your listener. Isabella carried, like a small burden, the knowledge entrusted to her, aware of her responsibility in having seen the wound in him. In the evenings when they were talking or playing cards, the thought would come into her mind, *His father was a murderer.* Then she would look at the Duke, and reflect that he, too, in his youth had that whispered about him. There was the ambitious young foreigner from the north, the Scot who had ingratiated himself with Vincenzo's father, Duke Guglielmo. A knife slicing through flesh in the darkness of the night. Vincenzo banished by his father to Ferrara. She caught his eye. He was looking at her expectantly.

'Is it my turn?' she said. 'I'm sorry, my mind wasn't on the game.'

'Not on this game, evidently,' said the Duke, drawing the cards to him. 'Ottavio is also playing uncommonly badly tonight. It's no fun for me to win with such ease.'

The flowers arrive at Isabella's apartment almost every day, with little notes, commenting about the rehearsal, her beauty, the weather, anything that comes into his head. There is always a joke or a flight of fancy that makes her smile. She is disappointed if there is a day without flowers because she misses the notes. Then one day there is a bowl of peaches. The peaches are warm and scented from the hothouse. Peaches in February, it's unbelievable, it's like being in a magician's palace. She reads the note. 'To the eater of peaches,' it says. 'Remembering your liking for them.'

She imagines him in the hothouse, picking out the ripest, and she sees his hand, a young man's hand, taking a peach from the bowl and giving it to her. Bite into it whole, he had said, and the juice had run over her chin. She reaches out for one of the peaches and holds it to her face. She can smell the summer in it, she feels the down of its skin against hers. The heat of the summer invades her blood, as she remembers.

There is a sound in the antechamber that leads to the main corridor. She calls out, 'Emilia?' There is no reply, Emilia must have stepped out. She opens the door, and sees before her a sleepy-eyed boy in livery, the Duke's page. His Serene Highness wishes to know if everything in the apartment is to her liking, says the boy. His voice is a husky treble, on the point of breaking.

'It is all delightful, tell His Highness.'

'His Serene Highness will be delighted to hear that from you in person.'

'I should be delighted to tell him so.'

The page surveyed the room through his half-closed eyes, as if looking for hidden visitors, and said, 'He will be with you soon.'

The reality of life chases out the dreams. For a moment she had been tremulous as a young girl but when the man himself was before her, she felt unmoved, though you could say at least he had earned his physical decline with va-lour – it had not come upon him undeserved. And now he was looking at her as if asking for reassurance that time had stood still all these years. He was taking her hands in his and looking into her eyes. She could feel a familiarity about his touch, claiming her as his own.

'Carissima Isabella,' he said. 'I never for one moment doubted that you would return.'

'In very different circumstances,' said Isabella, gently taking her hands from his. 'Will Your Highness have a glass of wine?'

He laughed. 'You are like the Correggio Venus, with that smile.' And as he took the glass of wine from her, 'You have an air of contentment. So you are happy to be here, back in Mantua?'

'Of course I am. I have always loved being here.'

'And pleased to see me again?' He paused, mouth slightly open as if eager to say more, but holding back the words till she had spoken.

'Of that I am not so sure, now that you ask me, and we are free to talk. You wronged me, Vincenzo. You must surely remember that.'

His eyes deepened with regret at the accusation. 'I loved you too much, that I admit. I was young and impetuous. You were the sweetest, most beautiful girl I had ever seen. How could I resist loving you? You were irresistible. I couldn't bear the thought of you going to Ferrante.'

'Ah!' said Isabella, stepping back from him. 'So that was it – you thought to have me first? To spite my husband? That is disgraceful!'

He spread his hands in supplication. 'No, Isabella, don't attribute such motives to me. I loved you, and I have continued to love you, in my way. I still do, with deep affection.'

She looked at him with some scepticism, but now he stepped forward and clasped both her hands. He raised them to his lips, and then said, softly, 'Our souls are linked together, you must know that. A conjunction of our stars rules the future of our house. You must feel that as well, or you wouldn't have returned. We share a spiritual love, one that transcends all others.'

Isabella sat down in the armchair by the fireplace, facing the door. He stood the other side of the fire, watching her. She smiled and shook her head. 'Such courtier's language. I suppose you'll now begin expounding on the perfect spiritual love as defined by the poet. "All chaste lovers desire a kiss as the union of souls", isn't that what you're leading up to? Or some such stuff.'

He laughed and said, 'I'm not going to use another's words, Isabella, even though my own are inadequate. All I want at this moment is to embrace you again, with affection.'

He knelt in front of her, looking into her eyes as he extended his arms and drew her towards him. 'Nothing more,' he said, 'just a perfect closeness of friends. We are friends, aren't we?'

'Friends, only,' said Isabella, with some doubt in her voice. She could feel the ground of rationality slipping from her, as a strange otherworldliness was invading her senses. His eyes, with that pale light in them, met hers. Everything around her was changing, the atmosphere was heightening and she knew she should immediately get up and break the spell. She didn't move.

'My dearest of friends,' said the Duke. Then he sighed, 'Carissima, such warmth,' and he drew her closer, so that his chest was now brushing against her. 'Ah, your softness . . .'

'No,' said Isabella, without resisting as he raised his head to hers, and kissed her on the mouth.

'Ah, your lips,' he said. 'Like wine. They're making me drunk.' He was drawing her face to his and as he kissed her again, she could smell the scent of rosemary. Her resistance to him was melting in her remembered passion. He raised his head and murmured, 'Ah, your mouth. Like honey.' And then, 'Do you remember – the joy of two tongues in one mouth,' and his hand was caressing her calf under the skirts. She began to slide towards him from the chair. Kneeling in front of her, his body was almost engulfed in the material of her robes as his hand travelled upwards following the line of her leg through the mass of petticoats. 'The silk of your skin,' he sighed. 'The smoothness, ah, the softness of you . . . Ah, my destiny . . .'

Isabella subsided from the chair to the floor, their mouths still joined in a kiss. She heard the sound of the door to the antechamber, and then Emilia's voice called sharply, 'Madonna, Ottavio is here.'

'Get rid of him,' said the Duke in a muffled voice.

'He's right behind me,' said Emilia.

Guilty lovers move fast. By the time Ottavio had stepped into the room, Isabella was sitting in the armchair, smoothing her ruffled skirts around her, and wearing the expression of one receiving visitors. The Duke was standing with his back to the door, examining the Mantegna painting of *Wisdom triumphant over the Vices* with close attention.

'I am so sorry to disturb you,' said Ottavio.

'You have not at all. We had finished our conversation,' said Isabella. 'His Highness was taking his leave.'

'That's right,' said the Duke, staring concentratedly at the helmeted Minerva.

'In that case, with your permission, I shall stay,' said Ottavio.

The Duke looked angrily at him, but Ottavio had already taken up his position leaning against the fireplace. He gave a final appraising stare at the fleeing centaur of Lust, the crippled forms of Sloth, Avarice and Greed, then saying addio to Isabella, and ignoring Ottavio, he left. Emilia closed the door after him, placing herself outside the room.

Ottavio turned to Isabella and said furiously, 'Now, Madama, what game are you playing? It looks like whoring to me.'

'How dare you? Leave me instantly!' Isabella rose to her feet to confront him. 'No one speaks to me so.'

'Guilt makes you angry,' said Ottavio. 'How can you entertain the Duke like that? Have you no shame? Have you no memory? Do you not remember the way he used you before? Do you not remember his letter? Do you not remember calling a plague upon him? If I had thought you were still infected with this madness for him, I would never have brought you here. Have you forgotten who you are? The wife of a prince, the mother of children. How can you descend to this level? Why, he's not even beautiful any more. The man's a complete wreck.'

Isabella looked at him for a moment, and said, 'Why, I do believe you are jealous of him. You're filled with envy, Ottavio. You have no right to talk to me so, with your heart full of bile.'

'Bile would have been the least of Don Ferrante's emotions if he had seen you rolling on the floor with this man.'

Isabella's cheeks flushed red. 'That is enough, Ottavio. Please leave me now.'

'Only too glad to do so,' and he turned and walked from the room, leaving the doors open. Emilia, who had been waiting outside, slipped back in and shut the doors. Isabella raised her eyes to the heavens. 'One moment's weakness, and I'm cast as the Great Whore of Babylon.'

'He's in love with you himself,' said Emilia. 'Everyone in the palace knows that except you.'

※

Back in his apartment, Ottavio was opening and shutting drawers in the desk where he kept his papers. The rage in his heart was expressed in the slamming of drawers as his search went on among the accumulated detritus of paper for the Duke's letter. Under a file of several years' worth of tailors' bills and the architect's instructions for his villa, he found what he was looking for: a piece of folded paper with a broken seal. He placed it beside him as he took a clean sheet of paper to write his own note to Isabella. *'Madama, you entrusted me with this, in case you ever wished to read it again. Now seems the time for you to do so. I am returning it as a reminder of how your love for him ended before, because you have obviously forgotten.'*

He folded his letter around the other, and sealed it. His servant had already gone to the market, and in his impatience he went into the corridor and shouted for a messenger. Some minutes later an acned, slack-jawed man in livery arrived, muttering, 'Subito, signor, subito . . .'

Ottavio looked at him with distaste, and held out the letter. 'Will you take this to Donna Isabella immediately.'

'Which Isabella, signor? There are several.'

'Why, Donna Isabella Gonzaga, of course. Idiot.'

'There are scores of Gonzagas,' said the man obstinately.

Ottavio sighed. 'Let me spell it out,' and he wrote the full title on the letter. 'Now, if that's not too much trouble for you, will you take it to her? She's in the Romano apartment overlooking the lake.'

The messenger took the letter from him and slouched off. Ottavio said, 'How can you be so stupid and live?' As the man turned the corner and was lost to view, he wondered whether the question might not apply to himself. A strange hot sensation of foreboding rose from his stomach to his head, like a sickness. He poured himself a glass of wine and settled down to several hours of black contemplation.

CHAPTER FIFTEEN

The Queen of Hades is having a costume fitting. Her dress is of black velvet slashed with crimson, a girdle of ebony *memento mori* at the waist.

'Does it suit me?' asked Isabella. 'Do I look like Hell?'

Hereditary Prince Francesco doesn't smile. There is still no word from the Grand Duke's castrato since the ominous message from Florence that there were too many notes to sing. The composer and the poet are in disagreement over the ending. Claudio needs a happy ending for his music; Alessandro Striggio has given him bacchante tearing Orfeo from limb to limb. The designer agrees with Striggio, as there is not enough space for the machinery required for the descent of Apollo. Claudio fulminates about the lack of space. Why has he not been given the court theatre, which is instead to be taken up with a ridiculous harlequinade? One tears one's guts out writing the music, for what? They won't be able to get more than thirty people into the room by the time they have set up the stage and the orchestra. Striggio says, diplomatically, 'I am sure it will be performed again, and in a larger space. You will see, the Duke will recognize its worth.' Striggio is good at soothing ruffled feelings. He has a talent for making problems seem circumnavigable. Diplomacy has always been an art at Mantua, and he is becoming a master of it.

'Skulls at your waist, Madama. What could suit you better?' said Ottavio.

'I was not asking your opinion, knowing how twisted it is,' said Isabella. There was an awkward silence from the others in the room, at the implication to Ottavio of the word she had used. Then Prince Francesco said, 'I am beginning to wonder if we will ever get this show on for Carnival.'

One of the palace servants entered the room and called to Isabella, 'Here is a letter for you, Madonna. They say it is urgent.'

'Not more interruptions,' sighed the Prince.

Ottavio swore. For a moment he imagined that it was the letter he had sent, and that Isabella was about to read it in the middle of the rehearsal room, in front of the Duke's son, because of an idiot messenger. He felt a rush of blood to his head.

'Don't read it now,' he called out.

'They say it's urgent,' she said. She broke the seal and opened the paper. As she read, a terrible stillness emanated from her. She looked up, her face drained of colour, her eyes blank with shock.

'It's from Ferrante's brother,' she said. 'Ferrante is ill, the doctor says he is dying. I must go to him.' And then, looking at Ottavio, 'Is this God's punishment?'

'I can't bear it!' cried Prince Francesco. 'One calamity after another.'

Isabella ignored him and clasped Ottavio's hands. 'Will you come with me? I cannot make the journey alone.'

In the main courtyard of the palace, the coach waited. Emilia supervised the loading of the luggage, and Isabella waited silently, wearing her travelling dress and cloak. Ottavio arrived with his servant and luggage. 'I am sorry I sent you that letter,' he said to her, as the stable boy checked the horses' harness. 'I should not have done so.'

'You wrote to me?' asked Isabella absently. 'When?'

Ottavio whispered, 'The letter, the one I returned, did you not get it?'

'What letter?' asked Isabella. 'I received no letter from you.'

'Mother of God, where is it? You received no letter?'

'Only the one from Ferrante's brother.' Her eyes filled with tears.

'Excuse me for a moment,' and Ottavio walked swiftly to the guards' room. 'I'm looking for a messenger,' he said, 'the one with the pock-marked face.'

'Lucio? Ask for him at the post room.'

At the end of a corridor of offices, Ottavio came to a large room with a black stove in the middle and two messengers sitting either side of it. He recognized one as Lucio, wrapped in a travelling cloak.

'What have you done with the letter I gave you?' he demanded.

'Don't get so impatient. I delivered it,' said Lucio.

'What do you mean? Donna Isabella has not received it.'

'She sent no reply, that is so. I was just told to return to Mantua.'

Ottavio said slowly, 'What do you mean, return to Mantua? Where did you deliver the letter?'

'As you wrote on the letter, to the house of Donna Isabella Gonzaga at Bozzolo.'

'Not at, you fool, of. I wrote of. I wrote her title, not the address.'

The man shrugged. 'I wasn't to know. The dwarf said it was at.'

'Can you not read? Do you not listen? Did you not hear me say she was here, at the palace? Why was the dwarf involved, anyway?'

'He's often in the post room, he likes to know who is writing to whom. He said to me, "You've got a private letter from Don Ottavio to Donna Isabella, have you? Oh, she'll be at Bozzolo now. You'll have to ride hard to get there before dark."'

Ottavio swore. 'May he rot in hell, the perfidious toad. Making mischief as ever.' And then to the messenger, 'What happened when you got to Bozzolo? When you gave them the letter? Was there no reply?'

'They took the letter, but no one came back to me, so I stayed the night in the stable and returned. I was overtaken by one of their messengers as I reached here, riding like a bat out of hell. But they never told me there was to be a reply.'

'I blame myself,' said Ottavio, 'for trusting a cretin.'

'That's all the thanks I get for my hard work? Well thank you, signor, thank you so much.'

But he was talking to Ottavio's back.

'You have been gone a long time, cousin,' said Isabella as he returned.

'Affairs to attend to,' said Ottavio. 'Calls of nature.'

'You are all right for the journey? You look pale.'

'I'm in excellent health. May I see the letter from your brother?'

He read it, and there was nothing to be divined between the lines. Ferrante was ill, it said, Ferrante may be dying, according to the doctor. Imperative you return. There was no indication that things were other than stated.

'I shall never forgive myself if I don't get there in time,' said Isabella. 'Please get into the coach, Ottavio. We have already delayed.'

The coach moved off, and Isabella began to cry. Ottavio was too distracted by his own thoughts to say anything comforting. Not only was there the Duke's letter from all those years ago, but his own which accused Isabella of unfaithfulness.

'I should never have come to Mantua,' said Isabella. 'It was a foolish whim. I should have stayed with Ferrante. It was noble of him to let me come here. I should have been with him and with my children.'

'Don't blame yourself,' said Emilia. 'You weren't to know he would be ill.'

'And he has always been in good health. Who would have thought it? Perhaps he knew . . . at the very last he suddenly asked me not to go, and I refused. I said it was too late, I was expected. We didn't part on good terms.'

'He was missing you before you went. You will see,

when you get back he will be restored to health again,' said Emilia.

'That poor young Prince Francesco. You should have seen his face. "One calamity after another," he said.' And Isabella began to laugh. 'How can he follow such a father? You can see how he struggles to come out from his shadow.'

She dissolved into tears again. 'Oh Vincenzo, the poor man has ruined himself. He is a slave to his reputation. Such a monster, so lovable.'

'Will you stop talking about him. You are on your way to your husband,' snapped Ottavio.

'Ferrante didn't want me to leave, but it's so gloomy there in the winter. He said he understood, but then he asked me to stay.' She looked out of the window and began to laugh. 'Do look at that extraordinarily fat man on the donkey. How can the poor beast support him? Emilia, shall we give him a place in the coach and save the donkey from expiring?'

'As we are going in the opposite direction, I can't see we shall be of much help,' said Emilia.

'What a pity, as Ottavio is sitting here with a face like a thundercloud, incapable of saying anything.'

'I am reflecting on what awaits us,' said Ottavio. As he was. The summons, peremptory and uncompromising, the illness, unspecified. The inevitable response to a letter such as the one he had sent. The unfaithful wife had been commanded to return home, not knowing what awaited her. And her accomplice, himself, the man who must appear in the light of the letter as the Duke's pander. What awaited him?

'My mind is made up,' said Isabella. 'If Ferrante recovers I shall never leave him again. I shall stay at his side, we shall grow old together, contentedly and peacefully. I was so young when I married him, but I shall grow old and wise like him. Isn't that a nice picture?'

She laughed again, then gave a profound sigh. 'I'm so tired, Emilia. This is another long journey, do you remember that other one, and we are all older, all journeying to our graves.'

'Don't talk like that,' said Ottavio. He grimaced and looked away, then saw in the glass a reflection that resembled his mother's, the lips pulled away exposing the teeth as if laughing at death. He called to the coachman to stop, clambered out and was sick by the side of the road.

In the palace, Prince Francesco was suffering his own pangs of foreboding. 'She cannot have left Mantua,' he said incredulously.

'But what else could the lady do? Her husband is ill,' said Striggio.

'That man is never ill. He is made of iron. He is trying to wreck my play by recalling her.'

'*Your* play?' muttered the Director of Music.

But Francesco had left the room almost in tears. He went to his desk and wrote a letter to his brother, stabbing at the paper with his pen. The singer who was to play Proserpina no longer can do so. Where is the castrato? Without him our play will be entirely ruined.

Soon after, Lucio, still saddle-sore from the previous day, was despatched to the court of the Grand Duke with the new missive.

CHAPTER SIXTEEN

The fire in the bedchamber cast its light on the tapestries hanging on the walls, illuminating shadowy horses and huntsmen, a stag at bay among the *gros point* trees. In the high, curtained bed at the end of the room lay Ferrante. They could hear his breathing as they drew near, but despite the sound of their footsteps his eyes remained closed. His servant sat beside the bed with a bowl of lavender water to bathe his face. On a table in the centre lay some of the doctor's instruments and a jar of leeches.

'There has been no change in his condition since yesterday,' said his brother, Ercole. 'We have been waiting for him to speak, but he says nothing, though his eyes look at us as if there is something important he wishes us to know. His legs are powerless to hold him, and his right arm is without feeling. It's some form of apoplexy which has taken away his strength.'

'Can he hear us?' asked Isabella.

'He hears sounds, but we don't know if he understands. He tries to talk, but he cannot form the words.'

'I shall stay with him till he wakes,' said Isabella, and she sat by the bed, holding his hand in both of hers, while she prayed.

'Are you not well?' Ercole asked Ottavio, who had subsided into a chair, holding his hands to his head.

'I must get some air, this room is too hot, and it was a bad journey,' said Ottavio. As they walked outside, he asked, 'What caused him to be struck down like this?'

'He has been in a bad humour for over a week, complaining of headaches. Perhaps it was the change of weather, or that he was missing his wife. He went out hawking with his two elder sons, and they were laughing when they returned, so we thought he had recovered his spirits. An hour or so later a messenger from Mantua arrived with a letter which was taken to him. He sent word that he would dine alone in his rooms, and we saw nothing of him, until his servant went to wake him, and found him lying on the floor in the condition in which he is now.'

'How terrible,' said Ottavio, and then, his voice tense, 'Have you found this letter?'

'We searched for it, but he had hidden it or burnt it. We think there was some bad news, possibly a demand from the Duke that angered him. They have forever been in disagreement over his lands. We will only learn when he recovers. There is something he wishes us to know, of that I am sure.'

'We will learn when he recovers,' repeated Ottavio. 'Until then, I shall wait here, with your permission.'

'If you feel the Duke can spare you from his revels,' said Ercole, abruptly turning from him. 'There will be no Carnival here for us.'

In Ferrante's chamber, his daughters by his first marriage, their husbands, his sons by Isabella, his brother and three cousins had assembled by the bedside. There was subdued weeping from the women, prayers and sympathetic words from the men. The blazing fire and the mass of bodies made the room close and airless. The doctor arrived and expelled most of the relations, leaving Isabella, Ferrante's servant and her eldest son, Scipione. Ottavio sat outside the bed-chamber with Ercole, who was half asleep with fatigue. Don Ferrante's confessor arrived, and waited at the bedside for a sign of consciousness. Then Isabella emerged in tears.

'It is terrible, worse than anything I had imagined, Ottavio,' she said. 'He opened his eyes and looked at me as if he didn't recognize me, and then with such hatred, as if I was his enemy. I think he has lost his mind.'

'All people are deranged when they are coming back to life,' said Ottavio. 'It is only a matter of time before he is restored again.'

'Then Scipione called out "Father", and his eyes bulged and glared like a wild bull. Please God he recovers his wits.'

'Please God,' muttered Ottavio.

※

It is late at night. Isabella has retired to her room, on condition, she tells Ottavio, that he will wake her the moment Ferrante recovers consciousness again. Ferrante's servant sits by the bedside watching him, his head falling to his chest occasionally, then jerking awake. Ottavio takes the bowl of lavender water from him before it falls to the floor, and says, 'You have watched enough for one day. Let me have my turn for a while.' He leads the servant out to the bed set up in the ante-room to Ferrante's chamber and closes the door behind him.

He picks up a candlestick from Ferrante's bedside and takes it with him around the room, his eyes searching through the shadows for a piece of paper. He rustles through the letters in the drawers of the escritoire near the door, opens a chest and unfolds the shirts, shaking them out, closes it again, walks over to the tapestry and runs his hand behind it along the panelling. Then he approaches the bed, and sees the candlelight reflected in Ferrante's eyes, open now and watching him.

'What have you done with the Duke's letter?' he asks. 'You didn't burn it, because you wanted to show it to her. Where did you hide it?'

The eyes stare into his, the mouth opens as if trying to speak. A vein in the forehead is throbbing.

'It was so long ago,' says Ottavio. 'Even prisoners are pardoned after so long. Where is the letter?'

The eyes staring into his flicker to the right, near the bed. There is an inlaid chest standing on the table. The key is in the lock.

'Surely they would have looked here?' but he opens it in any case. It is full of coins, medallions and some unset

gems in velvet bags. 'Aha!' says Ottavio, 'this is a clever little chest,' and he lifts out its false base. Underneath lies his
letter and that of the Duke, and next to them a small packet
of folded paper. His hand in the chest slips the packet unseen into his sleeve, while with his other hand he holds the
letters towards Ferrante.

'You were right to hide these. They could be misunder-
stood, and bring shame upon us all. You never intended
anyone to see these, did you, apart from Isabella?'

Ferrante breathes laboriously. Ottavio bathes his forehead with water. Ferrante is trying to talk, his voice indis-
tinct and cracked. Ottavio goes to the table on which a
flask of wine is standing. With his back to Ferrante, he
slides the small packet from his sleeve and opens it. Inside
is a white powder.

'I shall put sweetness into your wine,' he says. 'Honey
and cinnamon to ease your throat. Come now, have some
to drink and you can talk more easily.'

Ferrante turns his head away. 'Come now,' says Ottavio
soothingly. 'Don't disappoint me, I want to hear you
speak.' Supporting Ferrante's head with his hand, he raises
it towards the goblet. 'Come, have a little, at least, and I'll
drink the rest myself. To show you that it is good.'

The head is heavy against his arm. Ottavio gets onto
the bed, easing Ferrante up, supporting his head against his
chest. He is pouring the wine into Ferrante's mouth as he
leans over him. Their eyes meet, and Ottavio murmurs,
'Just a little more, and leave some for me.' He gently lowers Ferrante back onto his pillows, and throws the dregs
of the wine into the fire which spurts and hisses.

'That's what fires are for,' he says, 'to burn anything we
don't want others to see. Shall we burn these letters? It is
better so, isn't it?' He holds his own letter out to the flames
and it catches light as he drops it. He is holding the
Duke's letter in his hand, and the temptation to read it is almost irresistible. He says, 'You may not believe me, but I

never knew what he had written,' then he flicks it into the fire and watches it flare, blacken and curl until like a fiery bird it flies upwards into the chimney.

Ferrante's eyes are on him as he approaches the bed. 'Isabella knows nothing of this,' says Ottavio. 'She would be desolate if she thought she had lost your love. It is better this way.' He leans forward and kisses him on the forehead. 'We must all sleep eventually.' Ferrante's eyes, infinitely weary with knowledge, look into his. He sighs in exhausted resignation. Ottavio waits until the eyelids close. Then he opens the door and, leaving Ferrante's servant to watch, retires to his room.

In the early hours of the morning Don Ferrante suffered a tremendous convulsion and fell into a series of fits. By the time Isabella had been called to his side he was dead.

CHAPTER SEVENTEEN

*I*n *the courtyard of the Duke's palace* the new arrival dismounts from his bay stallion. He is a tall, well-built young man with a smooth, fresh complexion, and he wears his travelling cloak with style. His boots, spattered with mud from the road, are of fine dark kid. A servant in Medici livery and a pack-horse piled with luggage follow after him into the yard.

'Giovan Gualberto Magli,' says the young man, 'In the service of His Most Serene Lord the Grand Duke of Tuscany. Sent here at the special request of Prince Francesco.'

Prince Francesco's face is alight with joy. Oh, wonderful news. Another day and they would have been ruined. Has he learnt the score? And does he know that there is one more part to learn? They need him to sing Proserpina as well.

To his credit, Giovan Gualberto does not panic or throw a tantrum. He is after all a professional singer and used to crises. He remains equable, his face benevolent, his eyes hard. That, at a guess, he says, will be double the work. A strain on his voice, the nervous energy of quick costume changes. He will need to look at the part before he can say.

'You will be well rewarded. We will pay double the fee,' says Francesco quickly.

'That's to be expected,' says the Grand Duke's castrato. 'I shall read it once I am settled into my rooms. And then I shall meet with Signor Claudio.'

So at last they can rehearse in the Hall of Mirrors, to which the select few are to be invited for the performance. The musicians, secure in the knowledge that their work will be heard now the problems have been resolved, smile at each other and at the Director. They begin the toccata, and then Giovan Gualberto, looking towards the mirrors, sings the first words of La Musica, '*Dal mio Permesso amato . . .*' His voice, high and clear as glass, fills the air to the vaulted ceiling, singing of La Musica's promise to bring peace to restless hearts and love to the coldest minds. At the end of the prologue, there is a buzz of voices and laughter from the musicians, of relief, of admiration. Prince Francesco exclaims, 'He is an angel . . . an angel of goodness.'

Giovan Gualberto looks at Claudio, and says in his light, boy's voice, 'At the second ritornello, Maestro, perhaps the strings should be heard over the organ.'

The musicians wait in anticipation. No other singer questions the judgement of their Director of Music. But Monteverdi simply smiles, and says, 'You will see that the strings are heard more strongly with the arrival of Orfeo, as the instrument special to him.'

Prince Francesco leaves rehearsals, his chest swelling with pride. Already word is going about the palace of the play's uniqueness, that it is accompanied by music throughout, every word sung, not spoken. There is a rush for invitations. Francesco knows lack of an invitation will not keep people away. They will be crowding in till the mirrors crack on the walls. Giovan Gualberto goes to be measured for his costumes, and immediately rejects the dress for Proserpina. That is an unlucky design, he says, I shall have a loose robe in velvet. And a headdress of diamonds. Prince Francesco visits the palace strong-room and returns with the diadem of his great-great-grandmother, Isabella d'Este. Giovan Gualberto looks at himself in the mirror with a critical eye, and decides, after all, on a headdress of plumes.

※

On the evening of 24 February the Hall of Mirrors is, as Prince Francesco predicted, more crowded than is comfortable. In the front of the hall are arranged the armchairs for the Duke and Duchess, and the leading members of the

Accademia. A few rows behind are wooden chairs and then two rows of benches, which is where most of the overcrowding occurs as each new arrival claims to be slim enough to need only the smallest amount of room, oblivious of the extra space taken up by their puffed and padded breeches. At the back of the hall stand those determined to see the play, with or without a seat. The musicians file in and bow to the audience. Their Director looks toward Their Serene Highnesses, waiting for the signal and then nods at the trumpets. *La Favola d'Orfeo* begins. The Grand Duke's castrato glides on to the stage in La Musica's white and gold costume. Outside the door, Francesco Rasi, the Orfeo, breathes deeply to concentrate his mind. Despite the weather, the time of year, not a cough is heard in the audience. They sit as under a spell of enchantment, reflected in the mirrors around them, silent motionless figures clothed in velvet and jewels.

Three people who should have been present are not there. In their house near the cathedral, Claudia sits by the light of the fire, wrapped in a shawl, listening to the shouts and laughter of carnival revellers in the street. She has a racking cough, and the doctor has told her not to go outside. There will be another performance, another day, he says, it is not worth risking your death from the night air. And Isabella reclines on a mattress in a bare room, dressed in black, in an abandonment of mourning. She is mourning the death of her husband, the loss of the physical presence of him, the emptiness of the unused chair, the chest full of his clothes that he will never again wear, the void at the heart of their house. Her children comfort her, and she comforts them, but there is nothing anyone can do to ease the depths of her pain. She cannot tell anyone that she is mourning for not having loved him enough. Now she realizes that grief is not to do with love, but with loss. She cannot tell anyone of the pain of her regret. She might have told Ottavio, if he had been there. But he removed

himself as soon as the funeral had been held, abruptly saying he had to return to Mantua. She had begged him to
stay; surely the Duke's business could wait. Let him go,
said Ercole, back to his festivities. Who wants to stay in a
house of death? But they have not seen him in Mantua
either. Ottavio is inhabiting a room even barer than the
one Isabella chose for her mourning. The monks don't ask
him why he is there. Penitents come and go at the monas-
tery. When he has come to terms with his conscience, he
will abandon the bread and water, the planks for a bed and
be on his way. Maybe he will sin again, maybe not. It is
not for them to know.

❈

Letters have been going to and from Turin. Vincenzo is
courting the Duke of Savoy, to arrange a marriage for his
eldest son with Savoy's daughter. Such an alliance, he
hopes, would keep Carlo Emanuele's greedy paws off
Mantua's territories in Monferrato. He calls for another
performance of *Orfeo*, for the ladies of the court. And then
they will hold a third performance in the main theatre,
with more machinery and elaborate sets, when the court of
Savoy comes to Mantua.

The candlelight flickers on the robes of Proserpina. The
designer Follino has found an ingenious material with a
shot silk effect so that Proserpina seems to shimmer with
candle flames. The masked figures of the infernal spirits
surround Orfeo, as he edges towards the daylight, leading
his Euridice. And then he falters and turns back. There is a
clap of thunder, Euridice vanishes, and Orfeo is left to his
rage and despair. Sitting in the audience with the ladies of
the court, Claudia is more than enchanted, she is in awe at
the pure genius of the images in the music. The sounds of
the birds and the running streams give way to the sombre
chords of sackbutts and cornets for the underworld, the re-
petitive rise and fall of the notes as the lost souls endlessly
repeat their actions, crying out in their anguish. At the end,

members of the Bacchic chorus slam their feet, jangling with bells, on the floor in an abandoned dance to pipe and tabor.

Once again, the performance is a wild success. The Duke is delighted, and arranges for presents for all the singers. As he passes by Claudia, with court ladies clustering around him exclaiming their admiration of the new play, his eyes catch sight of the ruby necklace she is wearing. He smiles at her with his usual charm. She is not sure whether he recognizes the necklace, but she can see his eyes, in their practised way, have assessed her and moved on.

❊

'Signora Claudia has lost her bloom,' said the Duke to Ottavio. 'And she used to be a bright, pretty girl. Do you remember?'

'Not many of us grow more beautiful as we grow older,' said Ottavio. 'Perhaps she should leave Mantua. The air is bad for her health.'

'That's for her husband to decide, and I cannot spare him. We need a new ending for *Orfeo* when the court of Savoy comes here. Something more happy for a prospective marriage than being torn apart by bacchante. The great Apollo descending to help his son. The moral would not be lost on Savoy.'

'You are a generous father. No one would deny that.'

'So Ferrante is buried, and Isabella mourns,' said the Duke. 'Let us hope his son is more amenable to my authority. Governing this state is like riding several horses galloping off in different directions. It was the misguided will of our ancestor Ludovico to be fair to each son, and now their descendants all have their petty principalities, waiting for a weakness at the centre. The will of a hundred years ago returns to haunt us. But I have done my duty. I have three sons. My succession is assured.'

'And Mantua's immortality in music and art.'

'There is something strange about you nowadays, Ottavio. You have been up to something. Can I trust you any more?'

'To the end,' said Ottavio.

※

The rewritten final act was ready; Follino had built the machinery for Apollo and designed a resplendent gold costume with princely crown. All they needed was the arrival of their guests. Carlo Emanuele delayed, and consulted his astrologers. A letter arrived for the Duchess from Florence. The Grand Duke was inquiring what had happened to his castrato, whom he understood to have lent merely for the Carnival week. Prince Francesco, chastised by his mother, wrote an effusively apologetic letter, and asked for just a little more time.

And then it became clear around June that Savoy had played their game of hard-to-get up to the hilt. A plague upon Carlo Emanuele and his daughter, said the Duke, and took his court to the beaches and casinos of Genoa. Within a fortnight he had lost more than 100,000 scudi at the tables, a quarter of the state's annual revenue. The musicians heard the news with some bitterness, none more so than their Director, torn between his musical duties and the sickness in his house.

CHAPTER EIGHTEEN

*D*ottore *Monteverdi* is not sure which of them is the more unwell: his son or his daughter-in-law. She arrived with a fever, but now in the cool air of his shaded house, she is recovering her spirits. But Claudio has a troubled mind. Even here, he is not free of the Duke's demands. There are two sonnets he is working on when he should be resting. And he has become obsessed by his prince, sometimes railing furiously at his extravagance and lack of consideration, at others talking of him as the most generous of men, the supreme arbiter of taste.

His father has read the rough draft of a letter that Claudio sent the Duke, beseeching him never again for the love of God to burden him with so much to do, in so short a time. That was at the time of the wedding of the Duke's eldest daughter. And what effect did his pleas have? Only to fuel the Duke's desire for more songs. There is no doubt in the Doctor's mind that his son has been burnt with the fire of his music. Quietness and rest is what Claudio needs, but now he is talking of going to Milan, in the middle of August, to oversee the publication of his work and that of other composers in a book of madrigals. The publisher has taken the music and transposed on to it sacred Latin texts in place of the sensual verse of Guarini, with a dedication to the Bishop of Milan, nephew of the saint of the Counter-Reformation. There is nothing he can do, in these days of correct thought, he says, except to try and ensure they don't make a pig's dinner of it.

※

'Hasn't Francescino developed a beautiful voice?'

The young boy held the note, raising his head to the heavens, and then smiled at his mother.

'Did you like it?' His eyes are large and expressive, in an appealingly serious face.

'If only your father had been here – and it's your sixth birthday.'

'I shall be a singer when I grow up,' said the boy. 'Massimiliano will be a doctor, like Grandpa.'

'You cannot always choose what you want to do. You have to follow your talent.'

'Why don't you sing any more, Mama?'

'I have been ill. You need good health to be a singer.'

'But why have you been ill . . . ?'

'No more questions. Go and play with your brother.'

She watched them in the garden, playing with a bat and ball. Little Massimiliano, not yet four, wobbled on his chubby legs and fell flat on the ground. Into her mind came the picture of Lucia Pellizari's son, falling over with the same childish lack of balance. That heat-filled day in late summer, and herself in the lake looking across the dark mirror of its surface to the red towers of the palace. Something had infected their Arcadia on that day. In the evening her fever returned and with it strange and frightening dreams.

※

For God's sake, stop the man gambling, was the gist of the Duchess's letter sent to Genoa from Lake Garda. Ottavio tried reason. Never fight against your luck, he said. Wait for a better time. The Duke sat at the tables, and stared at the cards. Sweat was running down his forehead from the heat and the tension. As he lost one game, he started another. Why must you keep playing, repeating your mistakes again and again? Leave the tables now, break the bad luck, says Ottavio. As eventually the Duke is forced to do, for he has run out of all available money. His letters to Mantua calling for more go unanswered. He turns to the bankers of Genoa for a loan, but there have been too many indiscretions with their wives in the past.

Not one of them will lend him a lire. Thank God for that, breathes Ottavio, and goes to tell the Duke he has drawn a blank. The Duke's page, lounging outside the chamber, raises an eyebrow at him and smirks. When he opens the door, Ottavio understands why. Lying sprawled in a tangle of sheets either side of the unconscious Duke are two women whom he can see at a glance are whores.

On his way back to Cremona, Claudio's heart is filled with lightness. Cherubino Ferrari, theologian to the Duke, and a good friend, has praised *La Favola d'Orfeo*, and declares he will make sure the work is heard in Milan. In Father Cherubino's garden he sang the song of Orfeo, and the Reverend Father exclaimed that he had never before heard music that so moved him. They spent the evening talking of music, and with it inevitably linked the name of the Duke. A man of exquisite and refined taste, said Cherubino, and leading the way in his passion for new music. He understands drama, it is in his bones, that is his advantage over other courts. People may laugh at his passion for actresses and singers, but at heart he is aware of the sacred nature of art. They part with warmth, and as Claudio approaches Cremona he still feels the joy of his achievement. It is not until he enters his father's house and sees the Doctor's stricken face and the eyes reddened from weeping of Claudia's maid that he knows this time the shadow of death that has brushed them before has come home to lodge.

Claudia is lying in her bed but she is not really there; she is dancing in the Hall of Mirrors, her reflection appearing and reappearing in each mirror as she passes. Giovan Gualberto has taken her arm, his white and gold robes shimmering in the candlelight, his face glowing like an angel, and she can hear a high, pure voice singing to the sound of a lute, '*Questi vaghi concenti* . . .' Oh, yes, that is her voice, 'the songs that the birds are singing as the day breaks . . .' And there is the Duke watching, with a smile of such warmth, and now he has turned to talk to someone, a figure in black whose face is hidden from view. She is looking for Claudio as she dances, and she has the impression he is near, but somehow just outside her view. There he is, she is sure, but as she turns to look, nothing is there. And fear is growing in her, the mirrors have dissolved and she is in a room with dark walls, there are stars glowing in the light of the fire that burns in the hearth. She is looking at a picture, she is in the picture, lying on a grassy bank, under the trees. Are they willow trees? Is this the lake? But no, she is in the room again, and there are pale eyes watching her through the mask, glittering in the firelight. Her heart is beating, she feels angry and afraid. She reaches out to tear the mask away. She pulls at the bedclothes furiously and beats the restraining hands.

'It is the delirium,' says the Doctor, as she lashes out at Claudio, and then she cries out, again and again, 'Where were you? Where were you?'

'I'm here, beside you,' he says, and she grows calmer. After a while she says, 'Will I get better?' Her voice is quiet and resigned.

'With God's help,' says Claudio, but he is weeping.

'You mustn't cry, you will upset the children. Where are they? Francescino, will you sing for me? Oh, the poor baby, I can't leave him, what will he do?'

'You will get better, you will recover,' says Claudio, but his father has already left the room to send for the priest. They wait for his arrival as Claudia drifts in and out of consciousness. They wait outside the room as Father Taddeo hears her confession, before he administers the last rites. Claudio sits beside her bed praying and listens to the sound of her breathing. She opens her eyes and smiles at him. Her mind has cleared, she recognizes him, and she tries to say something; there is something she wants to make clear. 'Do you remember that day by the lake?'

Claudio nods, his tears running unchecked onto the bed.

'Remember that . . .' she says. 'But you did . . . by the lake – it's in the music . . .' and then, as he bends forward to kiss her, 'If I had loved you less, Claudio, we would have had an easier life . . .'

He waits for her to say more, but as he watches he sees a cloud gathering in her eyes, and it's as if she is not looking at him but at something else through a veil. And then he can no longer hear her breathing. Quietly and stealthily she has slipped away from him.

✼

The news of Claudia's death, on 10 September, reached Mantua a week later. On 24 September, Federico Follino, the Duke's designer, sat down to write one of those difficult letters, expressing the deepest of grief, and at the same time demanding of the mourner something that he had not the right to do. 'The loss of a woman so rare and so gifted with such virtue . . .' and then comes the tricky bit, the demand for Monteverdi's instant return to the court.

He has seen in the Duke's eyes, says Follino, 'the warmth of his affection for you'. He believes that if Claudio returns now he will gain the summit of 'as much fame as a man can have on earth'. When he had written the letter he took it to the Duke for his approval.

'Excellent,' said the Duke, 'and there will be nothing better for his spirits than to get back to work, or he will fall into one of his melancholy humours.'

He knows, from hard experience, how slowly the composer works, and next year's Carnival must be the greatest ever, to celebrate the wedding of Prince Francesco and the Princess of Savoy. It must show Mantua in its full power and splendour, as a force to be reckoned with. There is not a moment to be lost.

✼

In the house by the cathedral, its atmosphere subdued by the loss of its mistress, the composer reads the text of the poetry for Arianna.

Let me die,
What do you think can comfort me
in so harsh a fate,
in such great suffering?
Let me die.

He laughs with a touch of hysteria. Had the Duke any idea of the irony, indeed the cruelty, of giving him this verse? But eventually, when he feels calmer, he looks at the words again and his mind begins to hear the musical notes.

CHAPTER NINETEEN

The painting is of a woman lying on her deathbed, her face still young, but careworn by life. One hand is resting on her stomach. A woman who has been a mother ... A younger woman kneels weeping by her side and looking down on at the dishevelled bed is a man overcome by grief, an older man by his side. Over them, like a cloud, hangs a dark red curtain which reflects the red of her dress.

Vincenzo is delighted. That clever young Fleming, his court painter Piero Paulo Rubens, heard of the painting while on a trip to Rome. The authorities had rejected it as an altarpiece, declaring Caravaggio blasphemous in show-ing the blessed Virgin dying, like any ordinary woman. The Mother of God had no commonplace death, but a mystical ascent to Heaven. Rubens bought the painting on behalf of the Duke for 350 scudi. No one else would touch it after it had been denounced by the Vatican.

It joins the wealth of paintings in the ducal palace: the *Madonna della Perla* by Raphael for which the Duke gave a Marquisate, Mantegna's *The Triumphs of Caesar*, the Titians, Tintorettos, Veroneses, and Rubens's scenes from Virgil. He congratulates the court painter, who accepts the praise in his self-contained manner. And a clever diplomat, too, adds the Duke, though he would never tell him he was first convinced of that talent by the tactful and dignified way the young man had refused to become a travelling portrai-tist of court beauties for the Duke's gallery to Venus.

So much easier dealing with painters than with musi-cians. You buy the painting and forget the painter. The musicians are around all the time, their art fluid and ever changing, according to their moods. Without their pre-sence you cannot have music, but with them there is one crisis after another. His alchemists could make a fortune if they could produce the essence of music, like a scent, and discard the musician. And now his sons were joining in, as poets and composers from Florence wrote to them, trying to impress their superior qualities over the resident Mantuan team. Well, the more talent around the better, though the Grand Duke seemed singularly unwilling to lend his castrato again.

> Alas, he does not even answer!
> Alas, he is deafer than an adder to my laments!
> Oh clouds, oh storms, oh winds,
> Plunge him beneath those waves!

Caterina is singing Arianna's lament, calling the wrath of the heavens on Theseus, her betrayer. The little Roman is fulfilling her early promise. She moves beautifully, and has developed a tragic air in advance of her seventeen years. But that's to be expected, for Claudia was both mother and sister to her in her years away from home. Arianna will be Caterina's début at court. Despite the Duke's impatience, his Maestro has held her back from performing a virtuoso role. Caterina has been shielded from the eye of the Duke in the choir of the chapel.

Claudio listens to the lament, his eyes shadowed with lack of sleep. There has been, as usual, far too short a time to work on Arianna with the Florentine poet Rinuccini, and now the Duke has thought of two other works for the wedding celebrations – a play with intermedii; and a dance entertainment, *Il Ballo delle Ingrate*. Would Rinuccini and Monteverdi turn their minds to that in their spare moments? The dance of the ungrateful souls, those thankless wretches who spurn men's love. Rinuccini laughs as he writes it. He is of a noble Florentine family, rumoured to have been in love with a Medici princess, Eleonora's sister. Your Duke treads a slippery path beside the river of ridicule, he said. Think of all the ingrates who will be watching it.

A few days later the Duchess called a meeting to be attended by the Duke's architect, the master of entertainments, the Director of Music, and the librettist. There she announced that she found Signor Rinuccini's poetry for Arianna 'very dry'. She would expect him to write with more emotion. Would he please go away and come up with something affecting? Rinuccini protested, that, with due respect to Her Serene Highness, he should know as the writer of the poetry for *Dafne* and *Euridice*, in works of this kind the music provides the emotion.

By now emotions of varying kinds were running high. The wedding was in jeopardy. The King of Spain, distrusting the united front by the states next to Spanish-governed Milan, declared the proposed exchange of territories in Monferrato, part of the wedding contract, illegal. Mantua was now in a dilemma. On the one hand, the Duke had no wish to bring the armies of Spain and Milan down on his head. On the other hand, it would be equally dangerous to renege on an agreement with the fiery Duke of Savoy. While Alessandro Striggio, as Mantuan ambassador to Milan, exercised all his art at diplomacy, the marriage celebrations were postponed. A revival of Peri's *Dafne* was hastily put on for Carnival instead.

So little Caterina, as well as learning the part of Arianna, is engaged in singing the role of Amor in *Dafne*. Her face is pale, her eyes too bright. It's the seasonal illness, says the palace doctor. The vapours from the marshes, combined with the strain on her throat. Caterina has a costume fitting for Amor's gauzy wings. There is a short tunic of the flimsiest silk to try on.

'Can I not have more covering?' she asks.

'Haven't you seen Amor in the paintings?' says Follino. 'Do you want to ruin the dramatic effect?'

Caterina, La Romanina, charms the audience as Amor with her voice and appearance. The Duke watches her with an indulgent eye, half paternal, half predatory. But now her feverish cold becomes something more serious as her temperature soars and her body is covered with a poisonous rash. She has smallpox, says the palace doctor, and she is taken to the infirmary. Reports come back of an improvement in her condition, then a deterioration, and then her death. The poor child, says the Duchess. So young, what a tragedy. The Duke calls for a magnificent burial, and Viani must design a suitable tomb. And who can the Director of Music suggest in her place? The Director is at a loss. His Arianna dead, his pupil, who lived as a daughter in their house. Caterina with her innocent, unknowing eyes, unaware that her future would be stolen from her. And what of the Roman girl's own father, cursing the day he allowed her to breathe the Mantuan air? At night Claudio returns to the empty house and seems to hear whispers around him, snatches of music, a girl's laughter. No time for mourning, there is tomorrow's music to arrange. He is working himself to death, says his brother. Claudio does not listen. He is immersed in his struggle to fuse the words and the music in an alchemy of sound. At night he falls asleep in his clothes, too exhausted to go to bed.

The Duchess, for whom the story of Arianna is close to the heart, her life having been marked by a series of betrayals, has a brilliant thought. Their own theatre company, the Fedeli, is in Mantua rehearsing a play by Guarini for the celebrations. Virginia Andreini, known as La Florinda, is a talented actress, and accomplished singer. La Florinda is delighted to accept the role – an audience of thousands, a dynastic marriage to celebrate, and music that will display her power of drama and song. What a moment of glory for her!

The preparations continued, more frenetic by the day. With a glance over his shoulder at Florence where the Grand Duke was preparing for the wedding of his own son and heir, Vincenzo ordered ever more lavish effects. Into this festival was poured the energy that years ago had gone into real battles. A tournament, to be devised by Prince Francesco, mock naval battles on the lake, firework displays, and a battalion of plays, concerts, intermedii. Battles ensued between rival composers. Rinuccini had stolen the stage device of Amor and Venus descending on clouds from Prince Francesco's own play, complained Striggio, who had been called in to aid the prince with his poetic skill. 'I am only answering the Duchess's criticism that our play was too dry,' said Rinuccini. 'And for good measure, I have Apollo for the prologue and Jupiter descending at the end, so don't even consider using them.'

Each day a new whim to meet, and meanwhile Prince Francesco, abandoning his play, had gone to Turin to meet his bride and sign the marriage contract, the disputed territories being left in abeyance until the King of Spain was otherwise engaged. After delays, caused by the Duke of Savoy's several changes of mind as to whether he would travel to Mantua, the bridal pair were approaching the triumphal arches and flower garlanded streets of the city.

> Athens prepares for you
> magnificent festivities, and I remain
> as food for beasts on lonely sands . . .

La Florinda wonders, as she rehearses Arianna's lament, whether the Director of Music himself is much longer for this earth. When she sees his face, gaunt with overwork and grief, her heart bleeds for him, though heaven knows the acclaim he will surely meet when Arianna is performed will be some recompense for his pain.

It is a fine evening at the end of May, and there are thousands in the courtyard, crowding to get into Viani's theatre constructed for the occasion. The Duke has pronounced that only the foreign guests are to be admitted. There is no room for citizens of Mantua, though nonetheless many

have arrived, aware of a great event on their doorstep.
The invited princes, cardinals and ambassadors from cities
elsewhere are counted in on copper tokens, to prevent a
stray Mantuan native slipping by. Three thousand, four
thousand, and still they are crowding in, those behind
pressing on those in front in their concern not to be left
outside. The guards taking the tokens are overwhelmed.
The captain of the guard tries to restore order, and then the
Duke's General of the Army, Carlo Rossi. The hubbub is
increasing to hysteria, when the Duke, hearing events spin-
ning out of control, goes out to quell the mob of distinguished guests.

Seated in their thousands, the distinguished guests stare
at the curtain. Behind the stage, out of sight, the musicians
tune their instruments, and then at a signal from the
Director, begin the first chord. The curtain flies up – Viani
has devised a system of weights which makes it vanish in a
blink of an eye, thus providing the audience with their
first surprise of the evening. On his cloud Apollo descends
to the shore of the rocky island as one musical instrument
after another begins to play, until there is a celestial symph-
ony. The audience sit entranced as they realize the reports
they heard of the *Orfeo* were true – the Duke's composer is
a magician, conjuring up the most turbulent of emotions
in the notes. And when La Florinda, looking directly at the
audience, sings Arianna's Lament, there is not a dry eye in
the house. Her eyes, vulnerable and accusing, touch each
person in the audience. Her voice, sweet and plaintive,
overflows with the depths of her emotion.

See to what pain my love, my constancy –
and another's treachery – have made me heir.
Such is the fate of those who love and trust too much.

The words and the music strike home in several thousand
hearts. The Duke studiously avoids the eyes of the
Duchess. Prince Francesco glances sideways at his bride,

half in guilt at the thought of possible future betrayals. His brother, Ferdinando, a Cardinal at the age of twenty, listens with the serene expression of one immune from common temptations. Next to him, fidgeting and turning his head from side to side is the youngest, fourteen-year-old Vincenzino. The prettiest of the sons, with his fair hair and blue eyes, say the court ladies. And he looks as if he will be the wildest, like his father when young. Young Vincenzo is not listening to the words or the music, but staring at La Florinda's breasts with interest. Recently he has begun to realize how many shapes and sizes of the female form there are.

The Duke has devised a festival to outshine all festivals – Arianna is the beginning, and every succeeding moment provides a diversion for his guests. The Duke's chefs have been as ingenious as the theatre designers, creating a panorama of dishes at the banquets. Look at the temple of the antipasto. It has pavements of multi-coloured jelly, columns of salami, a capitol of Parmigiano cheese, an apse made from marzipan, and a congregation of boiled thrushes. The guests can hardly bring themselves to demolish it. There are platters of oysters garnished with fried frogs' legs. There are pike in piquant sauce; as many game birds as the Duke's huntsmen have been able to slaughter; milk-fed lamb; boar cooked with oranges; and as the dishes are demolished ever more are brought in from the kitchens.

And such fireworks. Lanterns and flares illuminate the battlements, bonfires are lit on the banks of the lake, and an explosion of rockets and revolving wheels scatter their sparks in the air. On the lake, circles of fire burn as the archers re-enact the Duke's battles against the Turk. The lake glows red, the air as bright as day with golden sparks from the set-piece of the Savoy and Mantuan coats of arms.

So the days and nights pass, each one bringing more

diversions. Viani has excelled himself in the intermezzi to Guarini's *L'Idropica*, indeed they far outweigh the play. He creates the towers and palaces of Mantua on stage, flies in gods and goddesses, sometimes on clouds, sometimes floating in the air, supported, it seemed, only by their wings. A garden appears full of trees and flowering plants, pergolas of roses and the sound of birds. Fountains gush perfumed water, the scent of which wafts into the auditorium. Proserpina and her nymphs dance, then in an explosion of flame, a fiery chariot drawn by black horses appears. Pluto seizes Proserpina and carries her off. And that's only the first intermezzo. There are three others to follow, with a finale of thunder and lightning that appears to take actors as well as audience by surprise. Everyone's eyes are in a state of confusion at the relentless spectacles, the unending celebration, their minds by the eighth and final day beginning to long for rest.

On the eighth day there is no rest, either, for it is the evening of the Duke's favourite ballet, *Il Ballo delle Ingrate*. It is both spectacle and commentary, containing hidden messages of court gossip. Sixteen of the dancers are to be ladies and gentlemen of the court, led by the Duke and the prince-groom.

Archimedeo has arrived with his own court in miniature, six dwarfs dressed in gaudy doublets and ruffs, brocade dresses and jewels. He walks with a stick for he has begun to suffer from gout. Even in his illness he mirrors his master, who, it is said, is troubled again by the old battle wound. You would hardly notice, though, as the Duke leads the men of the court in the dance. The gates of hell open, and from the cavern issue rotating balls of flame, and monsters of the inferno throwing flames from their mouths. The audience, crammed into the theatre, gasp at the audacity of courting such danger but by now trust the competence of the stage crew. Two nights before when Viani's blazing comet erupted into the auditorium during the intermezzo of the wedding of Jupiter, there had been cries of 'Fire!' and shouts to put out the flames.

The ingrates emerge from the gates of hell, in dresses of grey embroidered with gold and scattered with garnets and rubies to resemble coals burning among the ashes. Their hair is festooned with ashes and jewels, their faces grey and white. As they dance, sometimes embracing each other, at other times striking out in rage, Pluto pronounces their fate. They are condemned to the fires of hell for their coldness. La Florinda, as the chief ingrate, sings the song of farewell to the light, lamenting their harsh fate, and exhorting all ladies to compassion for men.

> Where are the parties, where are the lovers?
> Where are we going, we who were so sought after in
>   life?
> Learn pity, all women and maidens . . .

As they are swallowed up by hell, the cavern closes its mouth on them, revealing a pastoral landscape. The audience applaud with laughter over the *ballet-à-clef* while backstage the guards standing by with emergency buckets filled with water breathe a sigh of relief.

The guests leave Mantua, in a state of shock at the sensations to their eyes and ears. At the same time, the Duke, seeing the vacuum before him, takes off for a visit to Spa. A quietness descends on the palace. The costumes are heaped in the theatre wardrobes, the jewels crammed into chests in the palace strong-room, Viani's contraptions of windlasses, cables and weights rest idle. In his house, Monteverdi lies in a state of exhaustion at the sudden release after six months of creation, surrounded by quarrels, clashing wills, changes of mind. He has mourned for his wife in his music, in Arianna's lament, in the Ingrate's farewell to the light, and now he has time to mourn anew, in the silence of the room, the shutters closing out all but a thin shaft of the harsh mid-day light. The promise made last autumn – 'as much fame as a man can have on earth' – has proved empty. The Duke has sent the Florentine composers away loaded with presents and gold. His own Maestro has received nothing, and has even been short-changed by the Treasurer. He reflects on the gulf between the promise and the reality. Vincenzo moves in a whirl-wind, surrounded by his court, down the great stairs, out into the courtyard and away in a clatter of wheels, iron-shod hoofs, shouts and fanfares. No word of praise, no ac-knowledgement of how much his composer has given of himself in his music. Such is the fate of those who love and trust too much.

CHAPTER TWENTY

*D*ante's *lost souls* repeat their actions again and again, sighing over each mistake, knowing that they are condemned to do wrong once more, to sigh once more, through eternity. A more frightening vision than all the fires of hell. Did this vision occur to the Duke as he exercised his charm yet again, went through the same courting dance, to the same end? In the heat of the night, as he sweats over the territory that is so familiar, does he feel condemned to pleasure? Bored with the ladies at court, bored with his gallery of beauty, he is seen prowling through the back streets of Mantua to a house near the city walls. Not long after, a letter from the Grand Duke of Tuscany arrives for his niece Eleonora. He writes: We hear a common criminal in Mantua boasts the Duke's life is his to dispose of, for a large enough sum. The Duke of Mantua is enjoying the said criminal's daughter. Will you please exercise some influence over your husband, my dear niece?

But the Duke needs the sense of danger to strengthen his appetite. He has a reputation to keep up, literally. He cannot, surely, be losing his potency? 'I believe there is a beetle in South America, Ottavio,' he says, 'which is efficacious for such problems.' His botanist goes to Madrid to organize an expedition to Peru to collect rare plants and the efficacious beetle. The Duke's alchemists meanwhile brew up potions to strengthen the prince's person.

The only thing that will revive the ducal flesh is a great new love to appeal to his imagination: a woman in the form of a comet to blaze a trail of fire through his entrails. He has heard of a new singer. They say she is better than even the most celebrated in Florence or Rome. A Neapolitan, she has a voice like nothing ever heard before, they say. Adriana Basile, the fiery basilisk of the south. We'll fetch her here.

This proved easier to say than to do. Signora Adriana exclaimed in a bravura display of mortification, shock and horror, that she had a reputation to think of. Letters go from Mantua to Naples, from Naples to Mantua. It seemed the lady, despite the inducement of singing at the leading musical court, was resisting like one of the virgin martyrs, even though she had a rich protector in Naples and a complaisant husband. Eventually, word came back that La Bell'Adriana would consider the invitation if it came from the Duchess, as one lady to another. Her unspoken implication was that such an invitation would not be forthcoming.

No one makes a mockery of my husband, said the Duchess, and dictated a letter to suggest that nothing would please her more than the singer's presence at court. Protesting her virtue, and driving the Mantuan ambassador to distraction with histrionics worthy of operas yet to be written, Adriana made her slow progress north, in company with her husband, her son, her brother and sister, her sister's husband and a few of their children. She spent several days in Florence to sing for the Tuscan court, and finally the Neapolitan band arrived in Mantua. Strategically, the Duke was absent at his villa on Lake Garda. The Duchess received her instead, as one lady to another. The Duke returned to a concert arranged by the Duchess, where Adriana displayed the full range of her virtuoso talent, her eyes expressive with emotion, captivating her audience, of whom none more than the Duke.

※

If the Duke feels revived, there is another at court who feels his spirits soar. Claudio listens to La Basile sing and knows that here is an artist who will bring joy to his music. Here is a singer to inspire him, who will sing the music as celestially as the voices in his head. Even when she is silent and tunes up, she has qualities to be admired, he tells the music-loving young Cardinal Ferdinando who writes a poem in Adriana's honour.

'Monteverdi smiled today. Thank God he is content at last,' said the Duke. 'I was getting more than a little tired of his letters petitioning to be dismissed. I couldn't let him leave, to have another court claim him for their own, to hear the boasts from Milan or Florence or Rome. Claudio will stay here until one of us dies. Let him complain as much as he likes.'

Indeed, the letters the composer had sent from Cremona after the wedding festivities of 1608 pleading to be released from his service had precipitated a marital rift. How can you treat your Director of Music so, said the Duchess, when you throw jewels at your actresses, and provide a haven for any crooked alchemist with a plausible scheme? Why, the poor man nearly died from grief and exhaustion.

'Would he have written such a fine lament if he had not suffered so much?' asked the Duke. 'Don't frown, Ottavio, I'm only asking. My great regret is that the Grand Duke is no longer in this world to hear la Bell'Adriana sing. After his excessive interest in our affairs I shall miss his presence in Florence watching our festivities jealously.'

Adriana's voice soars and trills in incredible displays of virtuosity. Monteverdi is well pleased, the Duke a touch discontent. Wherever she goes, she is surrounded by her family, several of whom are also on the Mantuan payroll. Ask her to dinner and the whole tribe of them arrive: husband, son, brother, sister, assorted nephews and nieces. And she takes the jewels as her due, showered on her for her beautiful voice, rather than for her delightful person. The more you give her the more she takes, always mentioning in her thanks her sacred calling as an artist. 'The woman's a hypocrite, an opportunist, Ottavio. I think I'm losing patience.'

But with her impeccable sense of timing, Adriana knows when the moment of decision has come. It may be a veiled comment from Ottavio that in all things a time comes to deliver, or it may be her natural sense of drama; having played the high priestess of music long enough, she understands there must be a progression in Act II if she is to hold her audience. So when the invitation comes from the Duke to stay at the villa on Lake Garda, she leaves behind her entourage, arriving only with a quartet of musicians to accompany her songs of love.

The night is moonlit, a scent of orange flowers in the air, the sound of water cascading over the stone cupids in the fountains. Adriana gazes over the lake as she plays the lute. With one hand she loosens the fastening of the blouse at her neck. Such a hot evening, she says, I can hardly play in this heat, and she gives him her fan. Bring me a cool breeze, and he obediently fans her until, choosing her moment, she puts down the lute and waits.

<hr>

The Hall of Mirrors is crowded each Friday evening with a hundred from the court, half as many from the city, listening to La Bell'Adriana. The composer in black looks up from his score and smiles as she soars to the final note of the cantata. The audience applaud, and Isabella catches Ottavio's eye in the mirror as he knew she would. Look at the Duke: he is besotted. It is January in this year of 1611 and the winds blow from the Mantuan marshes even to the cloistered corners of the palace. Appearance is all. Who could attack such glory? Splendour is power. No one would confront a prince of such substance, not the King of Spain himself. The dynasty is strong. Prince Francesco and the Princess of Savoy rule the distant territories of Monferrato together, which solves domestic problems along with those of the state, as she has proved a tiresome daughter-in-law.

Adriana tunes her lute. She places it on her lap, and something about the way she protectively touches her stomacher causes Isabella to turn again towards the mirror. She catches Ottavio's eye, and mouths, 'She is pregnant.' Her hands

mime a swelling stomach. Ottavio laughs and has to turn
away to control himself.

> Come se' grande, Amore,
> di natura miracolo e del mondo!

Adriana sings and her audience listen enraptured. The
Duke has tears in his eyes. Outside the Hall of Mirrors the
wind grows stronger, rattling at the windows. A door
slams. From the tower of the Castello a guard shouts the
hour. Inside the hall, no one can see further than their own
reflection. They see their jewels and brocades, they exchange glances, they fill their ears with music, as later they
will fill them with gossip. See the mirror at the end of the
room, dark and shining. It is the future. Step through it
into the coldness outside.

PART FOUR
1611 − 1630

A thing once done is finished . . .

Alessandro Striggio, December 26, 1627

God does not pay a weekly wage; He pays at the end,
the very end, and all at one time.

Marie de' Medici, 1630

CHAPTER TWENTY-ONE

In the spring of that year 1611, floods raised the water level by nearly two metres. The city's cesspits overflowed into cellars. In the dungeons prisoners stayed on their feet until felled by sleep into the foulness. As the waters receded the air was filled with the smell of mud and stagnant water. On the marshes clouds of mosquitoes roamed like brigands looking for prey. There were an unusual number of illnesses. People complained of the bad air, and of overcrowding. There had been too many foreigners taking refuge under Mantua's liberal rule, and now they were breeding and multiplying like the mosquitoes. The city had never been designed to take so many people, nor had the surrounding lakes where a residue of silt increased the stagnation. The Duke's architect laid aside his drawings for a new loggia and temple to concentrate on engineering works to clean the lake.

The Duke looked at the network of channels on the blueprint, and asked why it was necessary to drain the marshes, when it was only a question of clearing the ordure from the lake so that it would flow as it used to. Viani said that may be true, but both he and the palace's doctors believed the marsh air caused the low fever during the summer. And in winter the mists brought catarrh and phlegm from which so many citizens, and indeed a large number at court, suffered.

'We have always lived in this terrain,' said the Duke. 'I would not wish the natural order to be altered. If we drain the marshes, and put it to farmland, we will lose the birds. If we drain the marshes, people will find other illnesses to trouble them.'

Viani put away his plans to await the departure of the court for the summer months. In the mean time, they would all have to live with the air. The palace doctor recommended that the Duchess leave earlier, for the sake of her health. But Eleonora was reluctant to leave Mantua for Lake Garda. There were too many state decisions to be made, and the Duke was absorbed in more intriguing matters, such as the construction he was planning with his architect of a Gonzaga mausoleum in the crypt of the church of Sant'Andrea, where he and his descendants would be interred before the sanctuary of the Precious Blood of Christ.

By day Eleonora was immersed in papers with Secretary Chieppio, in interviews with ambassadors, in weighing one treaty against another, in listening to the petitions of the citizens over land and businesses. Vincenzo was searching as if against time for the knowledge of the universe that eluded him. His world took him more and more into the night. The alchemists' motto, *Meliora latent* – the better things are hidden – was well demonstrated in the obscurity of their equations.

The certainty of nature cast its light through the alchemical fog. Prince Francesco's wife had, after a preliminary daughter called Maria, produced a son and heir. Little Ludovico was christened and the bonfires lit by the side of the lake, the sky ablaze with fireworks. As the new generation assured the line, the older generation faltered. Autumn approached, the waning of the year, and the Duchess's strength waned with it. Then one day, as the mists from the marsh brought a damp chill to the air, she was stricken with a fever. It was over in a matter of days. Her heart has failed, said the doctor. It is worn out from years of ill health, from the cares and worries of state. So the new mausoleum, which Viani is working on, had its first occupant.

※

The Duke leads the procession behind the coffin to the church of Sant'Andrea. His face is composed, though his eyes reddened from weeping. Twenty-seven years of marriage, the magic number of the Gonzaga, the mystic XXVII. There he is, coming away after the interment, his eyes staring blankly as if at a vacuum. What he has been afraid of all his life, the unknown abyss, lies in front of him. The loneliness is terrible, part of himself lies in the grave with her, the woman who knew him more than he would admit to, on whom he relied more than he could say. He can think of no solution but to leave Mantua again, to travel anywhere rather than be still and listen to his thoughts.

The Duchess is dead. Monteverdi and Follino work on a commemoration, which Adriana will sing, once she has recovered from the birth of her daughter. She has asked to name the child Eleonora in memory of the dear Duchess. The Duke is at the christening – he has, after all, agreed to be the child's godfather – but his mind seems elsewhere. He returns to the palace after the service and walks restlessly from room to room, gallery to gallery, occasionally stopping before a painting. He looks at the Caravaggio for a long time. The Virgin is lying on the makeshift bed, oblivious of the mourners. Eleonora lay in the high, velvet-curtained bed, above her the carved black Gonzaga eagle, oblivious of the man who had occupied her entire life. He walks on, through the Room of the Zodiac to the Room of Venus. The Correggios hang opposite each other. The first picture is of the Education of Cupid. Venus, alert and smiling, has given her son to the care of the quicksilver wit of Mercury. The second is of Venus observed by a Satyr. She lies unknowing under the trees, her eyes closed in sleep, with Cupid asleep by her side. Into his mind comes a picture of a lake in late summer, a girl naked in the water, her head thrown back, her eyes closed as she turns her face to the sun, unaware. He remembered his unforgiving anger. We are both of us widowers now, he thinks. And Isabella is a widow. There is something inexorable about the progress of life, though that does not make it less painful. But his thoughts have already moved on in search of distraction. The Mantegna *Triumphs of Caesar* calls to him from the Sala dei Trionfi. There is certainty in glory. There will be more splendour, there will be a great Carnival of commemoration next year.

The ageing man walks down the corridor lined with the busts of his ancestors. Federico, Francesco, Ludovico, GianFrancesco, eyes paler than his stare blankly through him as he passes. Behind him, punctuating his limping step, a stick taps on the marble floor as the dwarf follows the Duke.

❀

Ahi, che morire mi sento … The words sung by Adriana Basile sound in the hearts and minds of the listeners in the Hall of the Mirrors. The concert opens the carnival festivities, the first to be attended by the Duke without his Duchess. Taking her place is the Duke's sister, the widowed Most Serene Madama of Ferrara. She sits stiffly in her black brocade sewn with black pearls, black pearls in her auburn hair – some say unnaturally auburn. She watches Adriana with a critical eye, counting the cost of each note. The Duke her brother is ludicrously generous; if she were in charge the first cuts would be to La Basile's salary. Next to her, back from Rome for the Carnival, is the young Cardinal Ferdinando, watching the concert with particular interest, not only because Adriana sends him flirtatious glances, but because the poem is his own, written especially for her. The Cardinal feels there is nothing inappropriate in wearing the biretta and writing about love.

'Look at the young man, he can't take his eyes off his father's mistress,' said Isabella. By a slight turn of the head, Madama of Ferrara indicates she has heard.

Ottavio mutters, 'Silence.'

Isabella whispers, 'I'm only saying what everybody knows.'

Ottavio whispers back, 'How fortunate that everybody doesn't know everything.'

Now it is Isabella's turn to say, 'Silence.'

Adriana reaches her last trillo, her black eyes enormous and glowing with love for the music. She ends, and bows to the applause with gratified humility.

As the court is still in mourning for the Duchess, the theme of the Carnival takes a redemptive note. There will be a ceremony of the Knights of the Order of the Precious Blood of the Redeemer in the Basilica of Sant'Andrea, the singing of Monteverdi's Mass and Vespers of the Blessed Virgin in the ducal chapel, and plays and intermedii dealing with tragedy rather than comedy. Though there is no need to forego the banquets and dancing, why, you could hardly have Carnival without them. The evening after Mass and Vespers, no one found it strange that a troupe of Neapolitan dancers, in honour of Adriana and her capacious family, led the festivities in a musical procession through the palace.

Everyone is wearing their carnival masks, the theme of the Carnival is red, black and white: red for the blood of the Redeemer, black as a reminder of mortality, and white for purity. Most, in deference to the Duchess and to the Spanish fashion, wear black. The procession of masked courtiers in black velvet and brocades, led by the dancers in crimson and white and a band of musicians, wind along the picture gallery of Titians; people and pictures glow in the light of the torches. Through the room of Jupiter, the torches catch glimmers of the god in pursuit, disguised as golden rain, as a bull, as a swan, as an eagle, through the room of the Grotesques, the room of the Masks, the room of Bacchus, past the frieze of Orpheus being torn to pieces by the Maenads, past the Rape of Proserpina. Those who would be like gods and goddesses dance as they process, shuffle, hop, step, turn. They are approaching the great ballroom named after the soothsayer Manto, founder of Mantua. They are repeating the pattern of the years, thinks Isabella, the only change is in ourselves, weighed down by memories. She has a reluctance to face her younger self in the ballroom, the child of sixteen on the brink of a great adventure.

As the procession moves on Isabella drops out, slips through a side door leading from the gallery and climbs the steps to the loggia. It is a clear evening, and the full moon casts a cold light over the water. Isabella removes her mask to allow the air on to her face. She becomes aware of another presence, a man dressed in a black open-necked jerkin who is looking on to the lake as well. He turns as he hears her, and she sees that he is young and slim, with fair hair that is ruffled by the breeze. He is wearing a black mask and his eyes shine with a pale light. She thinks, It's the Duke, the ghost of the past, as I first saw him, in the days when everything seemed possible. And then another thought: Go now, don't speak to him. She sees him smile as he moves towards her. Yes, it is the smile she remembers, and she retreats down the steps. Then, twenty years ago, she had been with friends, and they had laughed at her confusion. Now she is on her own, the grand lady, the widowed princess, but suddenly as confused as a young girl. She hears him laugh as she turns and walks quickly down the steps. She hears the sounds of revelry in the distance, but she wants no part of it, simply to leave this accursed palace and its revellers.

※

In the great ballroom, another is of the same mind. The Duke's leg is giving him pain, his head aches, and the newly created Baroness Adriana is tireless. There is something oppressive about a carnival all in black, it is like an undertaker's dance. His mask is clinging to his face, and he feels as if he is suffocating. It is too hot, there are too many bodies around, he must find somewhere quiet, away from these tedious courtiers. While everyone is clapping to the beat of the Neapolitans as they stamp their feet in a Spanish mooresque, the Duke slides unobtrusively away. He notices Ottavio looking at him strangely. There are times, he says to himself, when even a living legend needs a rest.

But the uncrowded corridors do not cool him, and he feels waves of heat rising through his body to his head, which seems to be floating away from him. He walks more slowly. His hand reaches for the wall to steady himself. He is in the gallery of the Titians, its shadows lit by branches of candles. Through the gloom he sees approaching a woman in black, whom he recognizes as she comes nearer as Isabella, unmasked. She looks at him, as if they have not met for a very long time, and says, 'I have just seen you when you were young.'

The woman is talking in riddles, and unkind ones at that. He sits down heavily on a chair. Now, as if regretting what she has said, she exclaims with concern. 'You're not well.'

'The mask,' says the Duke, 'the mask is killing me.'

She leans over him and eases it from his face. 'It was too tight for you. Why your face is almost the colour of the mask. You look as if you have a fever. Shall I send for the doctor?'

'Cool hands on my forehead,' and he clasped them. 'Ah, Isabella, will this be my last carnival?'

'There will be many more. I must fetch some help, you cannot stay there, and I cannot carry you.'

'Why are you fussing like this? I'm perfectly able to walk.' But she had hurried away in the direction of the party. He struggled to his feet and walked on. There was one final room he wanted to reach. He took a triangular candelabrum from the stand to give him light in his journey to the unlit regions. Along the gallery, then the narrow corridor and the archway, into the Apartment of the Metamorphosis.

It is an apartment he rarely visits. A museum of curios, collected by the family over the centuries, are contained in four rooms, named after the elements; earth, water, air and

fire. On the walls are pictures of Ovid's Metamorphoses;
Coronis changed into a crow, Callisto turned into a bear.
In the first room is a display of petrified objects dug from
the earth, ancient Egyptian and Greek ornaments. Moving
into the next room, la Sala dell'Acqua, he passes tables
crowded with corals, shells and marine curiosities. On the
walls Actaeon is changing into a stag, the Lycian peasants
into frogs. He moves on to the third room, where there are
cases of diamonds and rare plants, and holds the candles
up to the walls to see in the agonies of their metamorphosis, Cadmus and Harmony changing into snakes, Aglauros
into stone.

And now, he comes to the last, the room of fire, and
the candles flicker in the draught, the hot wax dripping
onto his hand. He holds the candles towards the walls.
There are the myths that have been imprinted on his mind
since he first entered this room as a boy of seven: the Rape
of Proserpina, Ceres changing the boy into a salamander,
and Theseus with Ariadne in the labyrinth. The labyrinth
of the mind, and from its depths comes the memory of
Duke Guglielmo, avaricious, cruel, intent on dominating
this bright, only son of his. Look over there, said his father,
lifting up the lamp, at the first enemy of the Gonzaga.
That is what we did to him, Passerino Bonacolsi. He has
lived with us for more than two centuries. Look at him
well, that's what we all come to in the end, whether we win
or lose. The boy had stared at the embalmed corpse of the
Bonacolsi, determined to show no fear before his father.
Now the man directs the candelabrum over the work of the
taxidermists in the room, the varnished jaws of a leopard,
the gleam of a giant boar's tusks to the shadows at the end
of the room. It is as he remembered, the corpse's walnut-
coloured skin like thin leather stretched over the bones, the
parchment eyelids closed over the empty sockets, the teeth
exposed through the dry lips as if the man is snarling at
him. But the face is higher up than he remembers, and,

uneasily, he lowers the candles towards the cadaver's body, which is clad, as he remembers, in a torn tunic and blackened breastplate.

A monstrous face is looking at him in the candlelight, with tusks and gaping jaws, a creature from the inferno. As his eyes, after the first shock, adjust to the scene, he realizes that Il Passerino is sitting bolt upright astride the monster as if riding into battle. A chill strikes his heart. Somebody in the palace, for a joke, has placed Il Passerino on one of the exhibits, a stuffed hippopotamus. Somebody must have thought it was fun. If he were still a careless boy, perhaps he would have laughed along with the joker. But now, as he feels mortality in every limb, he can only wonder at what may happen to his own body once he is powerless to defend it. And he feels, too, a chill of foreboding. To be entrusted with the safekeeping of their defeated enemy, once the ruler of Mantua, and thus to mock him. No good can come of it.

Ottavio, hurrying along the corridors with the Duke's servants, finds him lying near the entrance to the Apartment of Metamorphosis, the candles guttering at his side. They carry him to his own rooms and lay him on his bed. They wait by his bedside for him to sleep, but there is something troubling his mind. He says, Where is Chieppio? I must see the will, and insists that his doctor fetches his secretary. Chieppio is aroused from his bed, unlocks the drawer of the Duke's private papers and hurries along the corridors, the Duke's page following after him with his inkwell and lectern. He is in private conference with the Duke for over an hour. When he re-emerges, his face has that carefully blank expression, which so many people will assume as they leave the ducal chamber over the following days.

CHAPTER TWENTY-TWO

T^{*he Carnival*} was cancelled. The entire staff of doctors tried to subdue the fire that was consuming the Duke. Before he was struck down he had complained of a cold and catarrh, and now there was a fever and a burning pain in his lungs. If he had been persuaded to take to his bed in the first place, they told each other, he might not be in this dangerous state. It concerned them that, instead of fighting his illness as he had done in the past, he was contemplating a life that would continue without him. It was as if he had decided he was dying, and as the days went by, this became inevitable.

Across the long bridge to the Castello four evenings later, Prince Francesco's retinue arrived from Monferrato. In the ante-room to the Duke's bedchamber, his other children waited, in a daze of sorrow and disbelief. And so it was throughout the palace. It was not that they believed in his immortality, simply that they could not imagine life without him. The violins and theorbos lay untuned in the musicians' rooms. Adriana was prostrated on her bed in her villa weeping, refusing any comfort from her husband, brothers, sister, nephews and son. Oh, let me die too, she cried, her grief mingled with anger at the strange message that had arrived from the Duke's confessor, to the effect that her presence was not required at his bedside while they were saving his soul.

In his house near the cathedral, Monteverdi waited in a fever of anxiety. He had grown so accustomed to the Duke over the years that even his unpredictability had become a familiar trait. The future was uncertain without him. It was known at the palace of their past disagreements, of his angling two years earlier, at the time of his Vespers, for an appointment in Rome. The Duke had taken little notice of the composer's rebellion, confident of his hold on him. He remembered what Ottavio had told him about the Duke's old Maestro, de Wert: 'the Duke and he went back a long way together'. And so it had been with him in his turn. He and the Duke went back a long way – to the concerts at the Palazzo del Te, the camp fires of Hungary, the travels with the court to Austria and France. He thought of evenings at Spa, of the Duke's conversations with him into the night on the new music. It was only after his marriage that the Duke's demands for constant entertainment had nearly driven him into the ground. As his mind had taken him further into the search for the new form of music, so the demands from the palace had multiplied. Compositions to be played in the church, in the streets, atop the city walls, madrigals, masses, airs and dances. Set this poem to music, Claudio, and I want it now. And yet through all this there had been a common sympathy that linked them, as if they were both searching for immortality in music.

At the palace, the line of courtiers wishing to have one last word with the Duke stretched the length of the Hall of Mirrors. Ottavio sat by the Duke's bedside in the chamber of Amor and Psyche, red-eyed like the rest of them.

'The little salamander in tears?' said the Duke. He was half upright in the bed on a heap of pillows, but it was difficult for him to talk with the congestion in his lungs. He tried to say more, then gave up as if the effort wasn't worth it. His hand reached out for Isabella. His skin was dry and burning hot.

'Cara Isabella ... where is your son?' The breath now was coming with a great effort. He paused between the words to gather strength.

'He is at home, we weren't to know...' and then she stopped.

'I should like to have seen him. You should have brought him here...'

'Another time,' she said.

He smiled. 'There is only the present. Why don't you marry Ottavio?' and then, as she looked shocked, he gave a shadow of a laugh. 'He's been hanging around along enough. Or has the time gone ... Don't be a widow, Isabella, it's not . . .' They waited while he seemed for a moment to be choking on his congestion, and then he said '. . . not your style.'

The doors opened and Prince Francesco stood on the threshold. 'If you will excuse me, my father needs to rest. The doctors say only his children should see him now, and the Holy Confessor.'

Isabella kissed the Duke's hand, feeling the heat of his skin on her lips. 'As it's written on the labyrinth,' she said. 'Maybe yes, maybe no.' Then she hurried from the room before she burst into tears. Prince Francesco stood to one side as she passed and waited silently for Ottavio to follow.

※

After that the only people going through the room of the labyrinth to the chamber of Amor and Psyche are the doctors, the Duke's personal servants, Madama his sister, his children, and a succession of priests and confessors. The priests and confessors leave the chamber with the same blank expression that Chieppio had assumed, suppressing all emotion at what they have just heard. For two days they are with him, and the Bishop of Mantua brings the relic of the Precious Blood of the Redeemer from the crypt of Sant'Andrea, where he will soon be interred.

Finally, on 18 February that year of 1612, Prince Francesco leaves the chamber with the Duke's doctor and announces to those waiting in the room of the labyrinth: 'The Duke my father has passed away.' The Bishop raises his hand in blessing towards Francesco, as the new Duke. Chieppio fetches the will, and reads it out to the family. In his dying days, the Duke has tried to right any wrongs in the state. There are bequests to the poor, though it is left to the executors to decide who is poor, and whether deserving or not. Other sums are put to various religious establishments, with an especially large sum to the convent that Madama of Ferrara has founded. And then presents and bequests to mistresses present and past, Adriana, Agnese of the Palazzo del Te, way back to the earliest, his first, the one who had set him on his life of pleasure, Barbara, the Countess of Salo. Well, so be it, say his family. We won't quarrel with his wishes. But now there comes the instructions for burial, added after he had fallen ill.

Chieppio reads out the instructions and pauses for their reaction. The Duke wishes to be buried not in a recumbent position, but upright on a marble throne. He wants to be displayed on the throne with his sword for forty hours and thereafter to be buried in this position in the same chamber of the crypt where his wife had been placed.

'Like a Neapolitan catacomb,' said Prince Francesco in disgust. 'It must be the effect of consorting with the gang from Naples.'

'What can he be thinking of?' asked the new Duchess. 'He will make a laughing stock of himself.'

Her interjection is met with stony silence by the other children of the Duke. Madama of Ferrara, the Duke's sister, says, 'He was already ill when he made this addition, according to Messer Chieppio.'

'It was the same night as he was found outside the Apartment of the Metamorphosis,' said Chieppio. 'He had the fever then.'

'In that case, we must decide what is best for him, and that must surely be to bury him in the normal manner. Certainly, that's what his wife would have wished, had she lived.'

Madama of Ferrara does not expect an argument, and none is given. Chieppio is despatched to give the instructions, and then an announcement is posted outside the gates, the ducal ensign lowered to half mast. In the piazza people who have been going about their business hurry home to tell their families. A sadness descends on the city as they wait for what will come next.

What comes next, after the sumptuous funeral of black-plumed horses and gilded hearse through the city of mourning, is a thorough examination of the books by Francesco with the help of Chieppio and Alessandro Striggio, now recalled from Milan to act as counsellor. First to go is the colony of alchemists, who are given twenty-four hours to pack up and get out. Next, Duke Francesco prunes the list of courtiers, all those without specific functions other than looking after the late Duke's pleasures. Ottavio returns to his apartment to find it being measured up for offices for the new Duchess's private secretaries from Savoy. At least give me time to arrange my affairs, Ottavio says furiously to Striggio, who soothes him with promises of delaying action.

After that, Duke Francesco turns to the theatrical and musical establishments. The Fideli are to hire their actors as and when they are called upon to perform, rather than keep a permanent troupe at the Duke's disposal. And as for the musicians, he cannot believe they need so many. He calls for a meeting with the Director of Music and his brother, Giulio Cesare Monteverdi.

The two brothers sit at the table with the lists of the musicians and singers and their salaries, arguing against any dismissals. Eventually Duke Francesco says, 'I am cutting ten from the payroll, whether you like it or not. Unless you give me some names I shall choose them myself. Why is Lucrezia paid so much as a harpist? And look at these Basiles from Naples. Why are there so many? And the amount given to Signora Adriana is scandalous.'

Claudio defended his overpaid star singer, as one who must at all costs be kept on, for the prestige of the court would suffer if she went elsewhere. Only a few weeks earlier the Spanish Governor of Milan had been writing to demand her presence. There was truly no singer in Italy to surpass her. The brothers left the meeting with the task of telling ten of the orchestra they were no longer required, a commission to produce a ballet by the following month and to compose the music for Duke Francesco's coronation in June.

Duke Francesco has more than the debts of his father to deal with. Across the border in the state of Parma, Ranuccio Farnese has seized on the death of Duke Vincenzo as a time to reopen the wounds of the Duke's first marriage with the Farnese princess of many years ago. Reports come in of slander about the late Duke, of friends of Mantua disappearing in Parma, to be tortured and killed. After his coronation, Duke Francesco declares war on the Farnese. He reinforces his strength with a festival in honour of the newly elected Habsburg emperor Matthias, who had fought on the battlefield of Hungary beside Vincenzo in the days of crusades.

※

It is a thundery morning in late July. Ottavio, staying at a palazzo in the town when in Mantua, walks over to the cathedral square to watch the celebrations. He calls out to the stocky, bustling figure of Striggio who is crossing the piazza towards the palace. Striggio, now ennobled as Count of Corticelli, apologizes for his hurry, but he has some letters to send to Florence and Rome. The post of Director of Music is vacant. Monteverdi and his brother have been dismissed.

'Has Duke Francesco gone quite mad? He has got rid of the greatest composer we have. And what about Adriana?'

'Out of favour, but still here. She has written complaining to the Cardinal Ferdinando about being confined to her house.'

Ottavio shakes his head in disbelief. 'So even being coveted by every court in Italy doesn't save Duke Vincenzo's favourites.'

'At least they are living in Mantua, and not in Parma. The old Countess of Salo was put to the rack, then be-headed, on the orders of Ranuccio. These are not good times, Ottavio,' says Striggio, looking at him with mean-ing. 'If I were you, I'd keep my head below the parapet for a while.'

Ottavio walked to the Director of Music's house, and found the door open and an elderly sweeper clearing up scattered papers. Yes, the Maestro and his brother had gone, said the man. This morning, early, on the coach to Cremona. They wouldn't be back.

Ottavio followed Striggio's advice and returned to his villa in the western region of Mantua, Vincenzo's present to him and now his refuge. From courtier to farmer, all in the space of a week. He wrote to Isabella about the events in Mantua, the last piece of court gossip he would pass on for the foreseeable future.

In the summer Isabella stays at the villa at San Martino, in company with her two youngest children, while the elder boys come and go, in their peripatetic way, a week or two with their cousins, a week or two with their mother, then on hunting trips, boat trips. Isabella is proud of her tribe of seven sons. They were Ferrante's pride and joy, she says, and none more so than the eldest, Scipione. 'Look at him now, only nineteen, and already taking charge of the estates for me. He has plans to drain the land and build a dam, he will make this the richest principality in Mantua. And as for the court, no I don't miss it, Ottavio. There is so much work and planning to be done, and if that is not enough, I have taken up gardening. Don't laugh, it brings me the greatest pleasure. Look at the pergola, I've trained lemons and some orange trees, and have you seen my rose garden? I call it the garden of ten thousand roses. No, I'm not exag-gerating. Count them and see. And here is my most prized garden. Smell the air, the scent of the herbs as you go by.

There's sage, and oregano, basil and tarragon, mint of three different sorts, and rosemary. There are medicinal herbs, eyebright, lavender to soothe inflammation . . .'

'How many gardeners do you have?' asks Ottavio.

'Always cynical. There are five, and I am the sixth. And all the planning is mine. Do you see, here I have had steps made to the lower garden, and the path leads to a lily pond, and then to a stone seat in an arbour.'

Ottavio looks round at the garden, and sees reminders of the gardens of the ducal palace. 'So are you free of Mantua at last?' he asks.

'I haven't wished to return since the day of the funeral,' says Isabella. There is a constraint about her voice, and Ottavio waits, but her attention is caught by the two sons who are pushing each other towards the edge of the pond, and the moment has gone.

In the evening, after Ottavio has left, Isabella's mind dwells again on the day of the funeral. She is sitting in the arbour, watching in the gathering dusk the flutter of white in the air as the doves go to roost in the dovecote. She remembers the procession from the palace, the cavalcades of hooded monks and Capuchins, the black-veiled ladies of the court, and the silent crowds lining the route to the basilica Sant'Andrea, watching the gold and black hearse, the coffin bearing away the creator of splendour, the tyrant of pleasure. As the coffin rested on the plinth in front of the altar, she followed the line to pay her final respects before the laying to rest. She looked down at the open coffin, but it was not the man of her memory, hardly even the appearance of him, after the embalmers had been at work. Was this the body that lived for pleasure, lying there like a wax effigy? How ironic the motto he had made his own, *Semper viva* – alive for ever. Without our spirit we are nothing, she thought, then, aware of being observed, raised her eyes from the relic of the Duke. Looking at her across the coffin was the ghost of the night of the Carnival, without the mask. She recognized the fair hair, the eyes with the pale light. Of course, it was you, the one I have never seen, his youngest son, his namesake. The boy stared at her, smiling, until she thought, What rudeness, over his father's dead body, too, and turned away. But now as she listens to the nightsong of frogs in the marshes, his image by the coffin recurs in her mind.

CHAPTER TWENTY-THREE

A ll his life the Duke had stretched the luck of the Gonzaga to its limit, and suddenly it is as if the line has snapped. Remember Francesco's harried expression of a few years earlier, the uneasiness, as of someone treading on his heels? Perhaps the future was already a shadow in his mind. In the winter of his first year as Duke there was an epidemic of smallpox in the city. His precious son and heir Ludovico caught the infection and died before his second birthday. Three days before Christmas, Duke Francesco, who had clasped his son to him in his anguish, died of the same illness. The widowed Duchess veiled herself and her small daughter Maria in black and waited for the arrival from Rome of her brother-in-law the Cardinal.

The young Cardinal and the Duchess circled each other suspiciously. Her daughter Maria was now heiress of Monferrato, which made her, the mother, the Regent. So she claimed. Cardinal Ferdinando's answer was to confine the widow to her rooms until such time as it became clear she was not pregnant with a posthumous son, and then to despatch her back to her father without an escort, taking from her the four-year-old heiress to be brought up in Madama of Ferrara's convent. Not surprisingly, the furious Duke of Savoy unleashed his troops and invaded Monferrato.

Ferdinando, now Cardinal–Duke, though yet to be crowned, is not going to let the continuing war in Monferrato affect the running expenses of his court. It is to combine the splendour of his father's days with the intellectual acclaim of the court of Isabella d'Este. He airs his knowledge of Greek, Latin, Hebrew, law and philosophy, literature and music, and keeps pen and paper by his bed to write down poetic lines and musical phrases that occur to him in the night. As the Mantuan troops under the command of his younger brother, Prince Vincenzo, drive back the army of Savoy, Ferdinando's Director of Music Sante Orlandi recruits musicians from Rome and Florence, and another Basile, Adriana's younger sister. Orlandi raises his eyebrows when Monteverdi's name is mentioned. Yesterday's man, he says. He has never forgotten or forgiven being shown up in the rehearsals for Arianna, when he had been called in as a singer. Let him go back to Cremona and rot.

But the Serenissima has other plans for Monteverdi. The old Director of Music at San Marco has died, leaving choir and musicians in disarray. The procurators summon him for an audition. He rehearses his Mass, *In Illo Tempore*, in the morning, with instrumentalists doubling the choral parts, and it is performed at the Basilica in the afternoon. There is no argument. The procurators are delighted to offer him the post.

So, in another island city, set in the Adriatic, Claudio begins a new life at forty-six, his energy renewed. As his fame increases, as the lament of Arianna becomes a popular song in every household that possesses a musical instrument, as San Marco is thronged with all of Venice to hear his music, the Cardinal–Duke reflects on the stupidity of his late brother, and plays a curious game of enticement, torn between regard and envy for the composer. He is to be torn in many other directions before long. Half-priest, half-sybarite, his blood running with Medici calculation mingled with Gonzaga impetuosity, he is condemned to inhabit a divided self. Unknown to him as yet, there is another face behind the Cardinal's mask of erudite melancholy.

It is a day in late spring and Ferdinando has been at prayers. He spends an hour of devotions in the private sanctuary Viani has built for him. On his knees he climbs the Holy Staircase to the labyrinth of tiny rooms leading to the chapel modelled on the Roman Sancta Sanctorum. On his knees he progresses through the rooms to the sanctuary, followed by his priest. It's a painful business, and his mind in the middle of his devotions is half occupied with the bruises he has acquired. The devotions over and Ferdinando on his feet again, he goes to a meeting with his Director of Music and with Adriana, for whom he has written another poem. They have been having a desultory affair, or is it her sister he loves? He is no longer sure. He is really rather tired of these artificial protestations that lead to so little satisfaction. He walks through the ducal garden to the studiolo and grotta where the collection of his great-great-grandmother Isabella d'Este is housed. Through the gold-ceilinged studiolo with the relief of the rape of Proserpina – how many times is that myth portrayed in the palace? – to the panelled grotta where the most treasured part of her collection remains. He examines the bronzes and sculptures from ancient Greece. Of late, he has realized that part of the collection will have to be sold to pay his debts. On the cornices, like messages, Isabella d'Este has had inscribed her cryptic signs. The mystic XXVII, the candelabrum, the lottery tickets, and her favourite motto, *Nec spe, nec metu* – Neither hope nor fear. As he looks at the panelled wooden pictures of musical instruments, he hears the sound of a lute, like an echo from the past, and he feels a shiver on the back of his neck, as if she is sending a message to the descendant who intends to disperse her collection. Neither hope nor fear – the music is from the secret garden at the end of the corridor to the grotta. Now he can hear voices, the subdued laughter of girls, and then a voice singing. He walks out into the enclosed garden, among the flowering lemon trees, the scented azalea and lilies. Seated on the stone bench, a young girl is playing the lute, while her companion sings.

A strange and unusual emotion seizes the Cardinal. One moment his mind is arguing the need to sell the collection, the next all thought is obliterated by the throat of the young lutenist. It is the first part of her he notices as she raises her head to join her friend in the song. So smooth, so slender, it's as if nothing else in the garden exists as he watches the way it swells and subsides to the notes, the way her breath beats against her dress, and then as she turns her head towards him, he sees her mouth, and the fullness of her lips. He is gripped by a fiery desire; it is as if his body is already on hers, his lips already against hers. He wants to sink into her softness, to hear her cry out for him. As his senses reel, she becomes aware of his presence, and raising her eyes to his, stops singing.

There is silence in the garden as the two girls look at him. They see the Cardinal, in his ecclesiastical robes, staring at them as if he is angry. The girl with the lute rises to her feet and says, 'I am sorry, Your Excellency, we thought there was no one here.' She and her companion make as if to leave the garden, but the only way out is by the door at which he is standing. As she comes near he says, 'No, stay, and go on playing.' She is quite close to him, and he can smell an indescribably tantalizing scent of jasmine, soap, fresh linen and warm flesh.

'What is your name?' he asks, his eyes unable to look at anything but that mouth.

'Camilla Faa, daughter of Count Ardizzino.'

'Go on playing your music.'

But she and her friend make their excuses. Whatever he may say, the Cardinal still looks angry, and they know the garden is private to him. As he steps aside to allow Camilla to pass, he has an almost irresistible desire to seize hold of her arm and turn her face to his. He hears their footsteps fade down the corridor as he stands in the garden overwhelmed by emotions outside his control.

CHAPTER TWENTY-FOUR

T he road outside the villa at San Martino was filled
with horsemen, wave upon wave of Mantuan cavalry
returning from Monferrato after a summer of fighting.
Isabella leaned over the balustrade, trying to see where the
line ended. The vanguard had halted outside the gates and
now there was total confusion as the others rode into
them, and spilled out over the fields. The shouted commands only increased the chaos.

'They're not all coming in here, are they?' said Isabella.
'Oh, my poor garden!'

Six of the horsemen had ridden through the gates towards the house. She recognized three of her sons through
the dust kicked up by the horses. They dismounted and,
one after the other, embraced their mother, bringing with
them the dust of the road, the smell of horses and men's
sweat. Taller than her, their voices resonating, their bodies
lean with army rations and the tension of battle, yet in her
eyes still three boys who had come back from playing a
dangerous game. Had they been hurt? Were they all in one
piece? Oh, the relief of it.

And now the fourth horseman had dismounted, handing
his horse's reins to another of the soldiers. His face, like
theirs, was streaked with sweat and dust, but she recognized the eyes, and the smile. Prince Vincenzo, leaving his
troops in disarray outside while he joined his young kins-
men. 'To pay my respects, Madama,' he said.

'You're more than welcome,' said Isabella. 'You will
join us for food and drink, though I am not sure I can feed
the whole regiment.'

Later, they sat under the vines of the terrace, with jugs
of cool wine and *limonata*, while her boys talked of their ex-
ploits in battle. She looked at their faces fondly, listening

to them with indulgence. Scipione, the eldest, his fair hair long, pinned up at the back, and falling over his face, like a bravo; the second son, Annibale, his hair cut short, a neck like a bull, the image of Don Ferrante; and the third, young Guido just turned seventeen and attempting to grow a beard.

'So they fought bravely?' she asked Prince Vincenzo.

'You are the mother of tigers,' he said, pouring himself another glass of wine, which he drank like water to quench his thirst.

'They're still cubs to me. I hope that after this victory there will be no more fighting.'

'Some hope,' said Prince Vincenzo. 'This poxy state of Monferrato which brought us so much revenue is going to be a running sore in Mantua's side. The Duke of Savoy will never rest while it's ours, and he's playing a dangerous game, trying to set the French against the Spanish. He has given the great powers a reason to concern themselves in our lands. My father always warned us of his treachery, even during the days of Francesco's marriage.'

'Perhaps it was unwise of your other brother not to deal more carefully with his sister-in-law.'

'The Cardinal thinks he is clever, but it's all learning, no sense. He should have married the sister-in-law to keep the Savoy lunatic at bay.'

'But he is a Cardinal . . .'

'He can always renounce it, but he is reluctant to lose his holy privileges. Sanctimonious shit . . . please excuse me, Madama. It's the effect of being with your rough sons. I'm so sorry.'

Isabella laughed. 'Now you're impugning their mother, for not having brought them up well. Come, leave the wine, I think it has a rougher effect than my sons, and let me show you the garden.'

Vincenzo got unsteadily to his feet, and they walked along the shaded pergola, through the garden of roses and the scented herb garden. Isabella gathered a bunch of the herbs, and gave them to him, to guess the names from the scent.

'That's rosemary,' he said. 'My father's hair always smelt of rosemary. I remember that.'

Isabella turned her head from him, as she felt her colour rise. They walked on in silence to the orchard. The apple trees were ready to be picked, the apples weighing down the boughs. The peaches were almost over and wasps buzzed among the rotting windfalls on the ground.

'What a pity,' said Isabella. 'No one picked them, and they're going to waste.'

She reached out to the tree, and touched one which fell as if waiting into her hand.

'There you are, a fresh peach,' she said, and gave it to him. She watched as he bit into it whole. He laughed as the juice ran down his chin and held the half-eaten peach towards her.

'Now you,' he said, but she shook her head, laughing, and said, 'No, don't tempt me.'

'Oh,' he said, looking at her with very bright eyes, 'I'm not sure who is tempting who.'

※

In the ducal palace the Cardinal wrestles with his conscience. Or, rather, with Camilla's unbending virtue. She has pointed out to him there is a gulf of difference in rank, that marriage is out of the question, and she would rather die than allow such things out of marriage. And no, the promise of subsequent marriage does not make any difference. She is virtuous, her father is old and loves her dearly, and would be shamed. And no, when Ferdinando's control gave way and he tried to seduce her forcibly, believing she would accept what was inevitable, no, she cried, beating him with her fists, she would kill herself. They have reached an impasse. Marriage is the only answer, but it must be a secret marriage, so that none of the powers outside

Mantua know what a weak position he has put himself in,
to marry a woman of no influence.

A secret marriage that is no secret. As soon as his orders
for music to be written for the occasion are made known,
the entire court buzzes with gossip. He sends to Venice
with a proposal for Monteverdi to compose the music for a
libretto written by himself. Musicians are hired from
Ferrara and Rome. At the same time, carefully not mentioning the marriage, he lets it be known at the Vatican
that he intends to renounce the cardinalate, in order to be
properly crowned as Duke. As the negotiations with Rome
become protracted, he suggests that if it would ease the
matter, the cardinalate should be passed on to his younger
brother.

'Is this wise?' asks Striggio, now Grand Chancellor and
Lord President of the Magistracy. 'He has no interest in the
church. He's a soldier and, with respect, inclined to be
wild.'

'This will steady him,' says Ferdinando, whose mind
was entirely concentrated on any measure to expedite the
marriage.

✻

As the months went on, his temper was worsening, and
the opposition growing. From her convent, his aunt
Madama of Ferrara had heard of his plans. She arrived at
the palace to call her nephew to order, but too late. The cardinalate had been renounced, his priest had performed the
ceremony at the ducal chapel of Sta Barbara in the evening,
and Ferdinando had sworn before witnesses that Camilla
was his wife. Madama of Ferrara recited to him the glorious
dynastic marriages of the past with the Habsburg, the
Medici, the Este. And now this ... this ... person. She
hoped the so-called marriage would at least be dissoluble,
and committed herself to do whatever she could to end it.

Ferdinando surprised himself by falling even more in
love with his wife after their marriage. They had told him

212

that once his first passion was satisfied, he would tire of her. But the reverse was true. She was wholly good, wholly loving. It was impossible not to love her, and now she was going to have his child, the next heir to the dukedom.

Carnival followed swiftly on the coronation in the New Year, and Ferdinando's only regret was the lack of response from Signor Claudio in Venice. In his reply to the Cardinal's letter commissioning a balletto, the composer complained of the lack of detail. Duke Vincenzo, of glorious memory, he wrote, used to know exactly how many movements there should be, and would give a detailed account of the plot. Ferdinando read between the lines a certain reluctance and, on the advice of Sante Orlandi, looked elsewhere. Meanwhile, his brother had been causing more annoyance. Young Vincenzo had taken sulkily to being a cardinal. He delayed fittings for his robes; he refused to take on the duties; he came back drunk after evenings in bad company. Ferdinando was fast losing patience with him, and feared the Vatican would hear of his behaviour.

And on a Carnival night, Ferdinando's patience gave way. Prince Vincenzo had arrived for the concert in his cardinal's robes, though not straight from the final fitting, for he had been drinking with some friends. He took up an obtrusive position near the front with two of his drinking companions and a young actress from the Fideli. As Adriana finished her song Vincenzo said loudly, 'Pretty music . . . shame about the words.' It was, of course, one of Ferdinando's poems. Vincenzo, getting bored, left the room after the next song, followed by his companions.

What followed next varied according to the teller. Those on Ferdinando's side professed to be scandalized. Vincenzo's friends said it was just a joke that went wrong. 'I'm a cardinal, I must behave as a cardinal,' Vincenzo said. 'What would my brother do in my place?'

'He would climb the holy staircase on his knees!' cried the actress, known as La Bambolina.

So a procession, led by the unsteady young Cardinal, wound its way to Ferdinando's Scala Santa, and stood before the three steep parallel staircases that led up to the sanctuary.

'Who will ascend the holy staircase with the Cardinal?' asked Vincenzo. 'Archimedeo, did I hear you volunteer?'

Archimedeo had been unable to resist limping after the procession to see what would happen to the blasphemous Cardinal, but had no desire to climb the staircase himself.

'I have a bad leg,' he said.

'You will climb the Scala Santa – you're the only one who can stand upright in the sanctuary. And La Bambolina, the Cardinal says you must repent. On your knees.'

The three set off up the stairs, Archimedeo complaining, La Bambolina giving high-pitched shrieks at each step. As she reached the top, she attempted to stand. One foot caught the hem of her skirt, and she tumbled backwards down the stairs, hitting her head with a crack on the marble. Sudden sobriety doused the revellers with icy cold force.

After the unconscious Bambolina had been carried away to the palace doctor, Vincenzo went to his bedchamber and passed out. He was woken next morning by his furious brother who told him to get dressed and be ready to leave the palace for their villa at Gazzuolo until such time as Ferdinando wished to see his face. Vincenzo left the palace disconsolately with his personal servants and an escort of guards. The villa was cold and unaired, the countryside around soaked in rain, his friends slow in coming forward to share his banishment. It was not for a day or two that he recalled Gazzuolo was just a few miles from San Martino and the beautiful widow.

CHAPTER TWENTY-FIVE

It began as a joke for both of them. The maids servicing the villa at Gazzuolo were extraordinarily old and ugly, as if Ferdinando had personally chosen them out of spite for his brother. Meanwhile, a few miles away there was the widow of iron Ferrante, whose eyes had already told him she found him attractive. It would be amusing, thought the young prince, to test her resolution. It began in a similar spirit for Isabella. The boy with his ardent stare that reminded her of his father when young, who arrived always as if in a tearing hurry, galloping up the drive on his horse, who could play the theorbo, who could recite romantic poems, how could she not be flattered, or feel her heart lift as she heard the sound of hoofs on gravel and heard him call, 'Where is Donna Isabella?' through the house and then the impatient steps in the hall, pacing, like a high-spirited colt. Her sons were dispersed, Scipione and Annibale at Bozzolo overseeing the estates, the younger ones in the army, or studying at university in Padua. Ottavio had been confined to his house during the winter and early spring, his letters a list of physical ailments from gout to a streaming cold. She had sent him some remedies from her herb garden, and then, as he still complained, became irritated. That one of the late Duke's most quick-witted courtiers could think of nothing to write about but his phlegm. She sent a curt letter back telling him to find something more interesting to say.

And now there was young Vincenzo. Isabella looked at herself in the mirror, and remembered the words of the Duke – don't be a widow, it's not your style. She could not help but be flattered by this impetuous youth. It was impossible of course. He was eighteen years her junior, his future was mortgaged to the needs of the state, and what

Mantua needed, particularly in view of Duke Ferdinando's disadvantageous marriage, was an alliance with a strong state. This she told him, when he first suddenly, outrageously, proposed to her, having had his kisses rebuffed.

'This is dangerous nonsense,' she said. 'You know that you have a different future – you cannot follow your impulses.'

'I am only happy when I am with you,' he said, kneeling in front of her. 'How can you be so cruel when I love you so much? I love everything about you, I breathe and sleep thinking only of you.' And he listed all the things he loved about her, beginning with her eyes and ending with her feet, which he made as if to kiss.

'Stop this stupidity at once,' ordered Isabella. 'This is only a game for you.'

'No, it isn't, not now,' he whispered and drew her towards him and kissed her. 'I love you more than all the kisses in the world. Oh, Isabella, make me happy.'

'No,' said Isabella softly. 'I cannot.'

'Isabella, marry me.'

'No.'

'Why all this no, no, no? You will kill me with your cruelty.'

'No, I'm being kind,' she said. 'Be content with only a kiss.'

'One more,' he said immediately, drawing her to him, and then he gasped, 'Dio, Dio, how I love you,' and rested his head on her lap like a child. Then Isabella knew the *commedia* they had been playing of Harlequin and Columbine had changed into a more perilous drama.

And it was around that point in their unresolved tension, that Ottavio found them on an evening in May. Isabella was walking in the garden and the young prince's arm rested on her waist. She saw Ottavio's eyes darken with anger, and when Vincenzo had departed, he confronted her, 'What game are you playing now? Surely you must know that boy is half-mad, and not only that, but half your age as well.'

'Thank you for so gallantly reminding me of my age,' said Isabella. 'Apart from your having no rights over me, has it not occurred to you that there are other friendships between men and women besides carnal matters? Perhaps he sees me in his lost and confused way as giving him maternal love.'

'Maternal!' exclaimed Ottavio, and then, with a smile, 'Well, I suppose you could have been his mother, considering your love for his father.'

'How sad,' said Isabella. 'Whenever I see you, Ottavio, I'm subjected to malice. You do not seem a friend any more.'

'If you only knew how good a friend I've been,' Ottavio said with bitterness. 'I've brought damnation on myself, because of you.'

Isabella was intending to disengage herself from the quarrel by leaving the room, but the words he had spoken were so wild that she paused by the door and looked uncertainly at him. 'What do you mean, damned because of me?'

'An expression of speech,' said Ottavio quickly. 'It meant nothing.'

'It must have meant something, or you wouldn't look as if you were biting your tongue. I have never asked you to do anything that was against God. I don't understand what you mean.'

Instead of answering, he said, 'You must not marry Don Vincenzo. It would bring unhappiness to everyone, including him. You delude yourself if you imagine he is in love with you, any more than you are in love with him. It is his father in him that you love.'

'You are talking stupidly now.' But as she looked at him, it seemed as if there was another presence in the room, and she could hear in her mind the laughter of the Duke.

You see, his voice was saying inside her head, it's as the astrologers said, a conjunction of our stars rules our house. As much a prey to his astrologers, as to his alchemists, and yet even after his death their destinies were linked.

'How he would have laughed to see the woman he seduced in turn seduce his son,' said Ottavio. At the coarseness of this remark, her mind turned from the question of linked destinies to the immediate need of disarming the man who had once kept her secrets, and who now could use them against her. She realized the destructive power of his jealousy directed at her love.

'Ottavio, do you remember, many years ago when I trusted you I gave you a letter for safekeeping? There is no need now for you to have it, yet you have never returned it. I should like it back in my possession.'

'What letter?' asked Ottavio, and his eyes slid away to avoid meeting hers.

'You know very well the letter I am talking about. From the Duke. I said I should like to read it again one day. Now is the time to do so – not least because it's no longer safe in your hands.'

Ottavio turned away, looking towards the fireplace. 'The letter is burnt. Don't ask me any more.'

'Oh, how splendid!' exclaimed Isabella. 'But I will ask. It was my letter. You had no right to destroy it. When was it burnt?'

'Don't ask me, I can't bear to think about it. For God's sake, let it rest.'

But Isabella, seized by curiosity, was the more persistent. She stood in front of him so that he could not leave the room without pushing past her, and refused to be turned from the subject. Gradually, under her relentless questioning, he relived the progress of the letter from the palace to Ferrante's house, his search for it, his burning of it, in order, he said, to try and make amends for his mistake, in order to save her.

Isabella was silent for a moment as she took in the enormity of what had happened, and then she said quietly, 'So now I know that my husband's last thoughts were of anger and deception. That you destroyed his love and trust in me by your carelessness. That my love for him went for nothing in his last moments. Searching his room while the poor man lay dying. How could you do it?'

'I was trying to save your life,' said Ottavio vehemently. 'He would have killed you had he recovered, do you not realize? Do you not remember what I told you about my mother, what happened to her?'

Isabella suddenly cried out, 'You killed him. You killed my husband!'

Ottavio had turned pale at the words, and he protested, looking directly at her, 'No Isabella, no, I only destroyed the letter. He died from his illness.'

'Oh, did he?' said Isabella, her mind alert to an implicit knowledge underlying his denial. 'Ottavio, you look as sick as you did on that night, when Ferrante died. Now I can see that it's true what they suspected then, and I always told them it couldn't be, that you wouldn't have done so. His servant left you alone with him and a few hours later he was dead. So it's true, Ottavio. You are a murderer, as your father was. You poisoned my husband.'

'No,' said Ottavio. 'I did not . . . the poison was his . . .'

The words remained in the air, the implication clear to both of them. They looked at each other silently and then Isabella began to scream, as she had done when Ferrante had died. Her screams sounded through the corners of the house, across the gardens, and there were shouts and the sound of feet running as several of her servants arrived to find out what had happened. They saw their mistress lying on the floor sobbing, and Don Ottavio standing there looking as if he had been turned to stone. They paused uncertainly, not knowing what to make of this scene, then Emilia, who had run in from the garden, snapped at them,

'Stop staring and get back to your work. Madonna doesn't need a crowd of gawpers. Away with you.' She shooed them out of the room, and shut the door. Isabella rose from the floor, and pointing at Ottavio, cried, 'He is the one who should go. He is a murderer.'

'I saved your life. I saved your life,' said Ottavio as if repeating a charm.

'How dare you judge my husband by what your father did! Your father was evil and mad. Ferrante was good and he loved me.'

'Madonna, come away, let us leave him,' said Emilia, taking her arm.

Isabella continued to stare at Ottavio, and cried, 'I can see what you are now. You are as cursed and evil as your father. And my sons will avenge their father. Where are they, where is Scipio, where is Annibale, Guido, Ferrante?'

There was a murmuring outside the door from the listening servants. Ottavio said to her, 'One day you will realize that whatever I did was for you.'

He left through the doors to the garden and then walked as swiftly as he dared to the stableyard where his horse was tethered. He gave the stableboy a scudo, and the lad, unaware of the commotion within the house, thanked him with a beaming smile and held the horse for him to mount. Ottavio spurred his horse to a gallop as he left the yard, hearing behind him someone shouting at him to stop. An hour later, the stableboy held one of the horses for Emilia's son, bound for Bozzolo with a letter in his satchel for Prince Scipione.

※

It is as if she has lost Ferrante over again. Isabella lights the candles in her chapel and prays for him, that his soul will be at peace, that he will be blessed in paradise, not suffering in purgatory. Early next morning, Scipione and Annibale arrive at the head of fifty armed men. Scipione goes in to see his mother, and leaves shortly afterwards, taking the road towards Ottavio's house. His men surround the villa, as the brothers dismount and, with swords unsheathed, crash through the door into the hall. They can find only an elderly servant, for the younger men have made themselves scarce, leaving the place unguarded.

'Where is Il Gobbo, the poisoner?' demanded Scipione.

The old man, his eyes dazed by the sight of steel and studded leather, pleaded to be spared to live in peace. His master left before dawn, and did not say when he would be back.

'He will have gone to Mantua. We will find him there,' said Scipione. 'If you send him a message, tell him that he may die in Mantua as well as here. Tell him distance is of no object to us. He doesn't escape our vendetta by his mere absence.'

As a declaration of intent, should its owner return, he drew his sword across the portrait of Ottavio as a young man, ripping the canvas apart at the throat.

CHAPTER TWENTY-SIX

*T*he faces of the Titans are contorted with pain as, crushed by the falling pillars of their palaces, they are overwhelmed by Jupiter's wrath. Eyes bulging, mouths open in agony, they stare out from the walls. Above the clouds, Jupiter watches their destruction. The giants in their pride set themselves up against the gods, and now he is bringing them down.

The Hall of the Giants is the *pièce de résistance* at the Palazzo del Te, and has a curious echo that distorts and magnifies sounds into the rumble of falling masonry, the rushing of a storm. Every now and then a concert is held there as a test for musicianship.

'I came here with Monteverdi when I was a boy,' said Ferdinando. 'He first gave me my knowledge of music. He taught me the theorbo and the harpsichord, and I played in a concert here. I remember how he tested the acoustics, marking the floor with chalk where each instrument was to be placed. He was a genius of precision.'

Ferdinando does not say so, but the remark reflects on his present Maestro of Music, Sante Orlandi, the man from Florence, the man who happened to be in Mantua at the time Monteverdi was dismissed, and who stepped neatly into the vacant post. Far from enhancing the music this evening, the room's echoes create discordancy.

'Do you think our Claudio would come back to Mantua? You know him better than I, Ottavio.'

Ottavio, sitting next to Ferdinando, saw an opportunity to distance himself from Scipione's men, several of whom, he had heard, had arrived in the city. Monteverdi would take time; he would be slow in making a decision; it would need much argument to persuade him, which could only be done by going there. If Ottavio were, say, resident in

Venice he would be in an ideal position. He waited for Ferdinando's reaction.

Ferdinando considered. Perhaps, he said, you can go there in the autumn. And then he began to talk about his son and heir, delivered of Camilla. A beautiful boy, Giacinto, but aunt Madama of Ferrara had refused to attend the christening.

'Life does not become easier, does it?' said Ferdinando. 'I am only thankful for music to lighten the spirits. I think I would die without music.'

Ottavio visited Alessandro Striggio in his office the next day to find out the latest news on the Camilla problem. Duke Ferdinando is under a great deal of pressure, said Striggio. I have a file full of letters on the marriage. The disagreement with Savoy rumbles on; France is involved; the Emperor may even think of annexing a strategic state such as ours if we have no strong alliance. There are factions at court, encouraged by Madama of Ferrara, who say poor little Camilla is a liability. If he is to hold to this so-called love match, he will have to compensate with great alliances for his brother and sister. He is twisting this way and that. One day he is hot for Camilla, one day cold. He doesn't know his own mind any more.

※

Ottavio shadows Ferdinando throughout the summer. Being close to the court is protection against the bravos of Bozzolo who may be lurking around town. So he is there, in Ferdinando's palazzo a few miles from the city, when the courier arrives from Gazzuolo. The palazzo is a hugely expensive and unnecessary addition to the houses scattered throughout the state, a monument to Ferdinando's pride. Each successive Duke makes his mark by building anew, and so it is with Ferdinando, despite the fact there is no longer the money to spare. The courier, refusing to entrust his letter to anyone else, climbs the stairs to the *piano nobile* and seeks out Ferdinando. He gives him the letter and retires to the next room to await a reply. Ferdinando hands the unopened letter to Striggio, saying, 'Something to do with my wretched brother.'

Indeed, it is, says Striggio, as he reads the letter. He is sorry to say that Prince Vincenzo has contracted a secret marriage, to the widow of Don Ferrante. It took place at the parish church of her village, witnessed by one of her brothers, two of her sons and members of her household.

Ferdinando sinks into a chair with shock. His eyes are staring into the future as he murmurs, 'Povera mia casa!' They have built their House to the envy of the gods, and now it is crashing down around them.

It is early morning, but the heat of summer is already invading the house from the sunbaked land. The shutters that were opened at daybreak are being closed again. Isabella has told Emilia to leave the bedroom shutters open. She looks at her lover, now her husband, beside her. He is sprawled on his back, one arm stretched behind his head on the pillow, the other still reaching towards her. He had held her hand as he fell to sleep and for a long time she had been unable to loosen his grip. Now as the sunlight slants through the window across the bed she observes him asleep. As he lies with his face to the ceiling, his eyes shut, she watches the movement of breathing, the firm chest muscles, the smoothness of his stomach and the arrow of hair running from his navel, reflecting gold from the sun.

'Oh, my sweet angel,' whispers Isabella.

He opens his eyes, sees her looking at him, and smiles. 'Are you content?' he asks. 'Do you like what you see?' His hand reaches out to her, and he lazily moves towards her. 'I was dreaming of you while I slept, and now I'm awake and still dreaming. Look what you've done to me.' She watches the expression of tender absorption on his face as he moves over her, until she closes her eyes from the pleasure and the pain that course through her. He cries out in triumph as he comes and then collapses on to her and falls asleep. 'My poor, tired little husband,' says Isabella solicitously, lying under his weight, looking upwards at the fresco of Cupid and Venus among garlands of roses. A grey salamander runs along the cornice, flicking its tongue at insects. Isabella watches its path across the ceiling. The earth is a lover, the air is a lover, even the salamander is a lover. *Amante e il cielo, amante la terra, amante il mare*, and when I first heard those words, Vincenzo, you were in another woman's womb, and I was in love with Vincenzo. But young Vincenzo, still sleeping, is oblivious to this riddle.

The days passed through the heat of the summer to the early autumn mists. She had forgotten, Isabella told Emilia, the joy of sharing a bed, of reaching your hand out in the dark of the night to find your beloved lying beside you. And he was happy, wasn't he? He no longer drank as if looking for salvation at the bottom of his glass. Emilia said, indeed, he was far less wild about the eyes, though she hoped he wouldn't become tame, she didn't care for lapdogs. He was a soldier at heart, and needed the excitement of the chase. Which is why I have sent for Scipione's huntsman, said Isabella. To give him the joy of chasing after wild boar and other harmless creatures.

On a day in early autumn, Vincenzo and Guido, Isabella's third son, were pursuing a stag that was fleeing towards Gazzuolo. Across the flat lands they saw a band of horsemen on the road from Mantua, their breastplates glinting in the sun. Vincenzo reined in his horse, and waited. They were from the Mantuan cavalry, and he was missing his friends among them. But as they came closer, he could not see any man he knew. The captain hailed Vincenzo with the usual courtesies then handed him a letter. It was from his brother, and its message was brief. To allow himself to be escorted to Mantua by the men he had sent.

'And if I don't allow such a preposterous thing?' he said furiously.

The captain assumed a regretful air. 'We have orders to take you back in whatever condition you make necessary. Freely among us, or tied head and foot on the back of a horse. I am sorry, my Lord Prince, those are our orders.'

Vincenzo swore vengeance on the lot of them when he became Duke, and then bowed to the inevitable. He rode with them on the Mantuan road, leaving Guido to convey to Isabella his love, his regrets and his expected speedy return after confronting his brother. But he was not, after all, bound for the city. His brother had prepared for him to be held at a fort to the north. There he was to be imprisoned until such time as he renounced his scandalous marriage, remembered his position as Cardinal, and declared himself a true penitent. The Father Inquisitor, concluded Duke Ferdinando at the end of a ten-page letter, was taking a close interest in the case.

⚎

But then the Inquisition was taking an interest in everything that moves. Its powers extend into every part of life, the books you read, the pictures you look at, the friends you know, even your thoughts if it could only see into your mind. In Venice the printing presses have been reduced from a hundred to a dozen. The more outspoken *avvisi* are issued clandestinely, with neither the names of the writers or the printers on them. But Venice for Ottavio is a place where he feels he can breathe freely again, without looking over his shoulder for an assassin.

He is staying at the Mantuan Residency, a short walk from the Grand Canal and from the Piazza San Marco. He takes one of the gondolas that glide like black swans along the canal. 'From where?' asks the gondolier, looking at his clothes as if they are foreign to the Venetian style.

'From Mantua.'

'Where the divine Claudio comes from. The maestro of San Marco. You know him?'

'I knew him well, years ago.'

'You have heard nothing, until you have heard him at our basilica. The angels fall from heaven listening.' The gondolier looks soulfully ahead of him as he sings a verse of Arianna's lament while he poles the boat along. They reach the open water and turn towards the Piazza San Marco. Ottavio stares in alarm at the sheet of water covering the square. It is as if the sea is reclaiming the city.

The gondolier laughs at his expression. 'Don't be afraid, we're not sinking under the sea. It's the *acqua alta*. Would you care for some pattens, Signor Mantovano?'

Ottavio buys, at *prizzo alto*, a pair of wooden pattens which keep his shoes above the salt water and walks with unsteady footsteps to the basilica. As he enters the building, he steps out of the acquaceous light into a cavern of gold. The candle flames illuminate the wealth of Venice to the vaulted domes. The joyous voice of the choir soars towards the gilded mosaic saints, in praise of God, *Lauda, Laudamus Dominum* . . . He edges his way through the congregation. There, before the choir, is the familiar figure in black, like a magician, holding a thousand souls in thrall. Ottavio's mind, till then absorbed with several worries, such as officials to approach over the forthcoming visit of Duke Ferdinando, and the possible link with Bozzolo of an evil-featured man seen near the Residency, is cleared of all but the sound filling the basilica. In accord with the congregation he feels his soul soar with the music.

He knows that Ferdinando's desire to have Monteverdi return will be disappointed. As Claudio said later, 'With all Venice eager to hear my music, with the choir and musicians I have at my disposal, and the patrons who commission work from me, why should I subject myself again to the whims of a prince and the crookedness of his treasurer? Why, here in the serene republic if I don't collect my pay, they bring it to me! In Mantua I had to go to the treasurer as a supplicant to beg for what was mine. I don't believe anything has changed. Last time Ferdinando commissioned an opera from me, for which I neglected my work here, he changed his mind half-way through. How do I know he will not change his mind once I am in his employ? Why should I compete for my living with alchemists, favoured singers, and a band of dwarfs? Mantua is in my blood, as you must know, or you wouldn't suggest my return, but to be bitten again? I would be mad.'

Even as he speaks, his eyes betray a longing, though not, Ottavio knows, to return to the state as it is now. It is the country of his youth, his love and his loss that was in his mind. A fair-haired man, laughing. A dark-haired woman, smiling. His music written for them both.

'I would be mad,' says Claudio. 'And by the way, could you please ask my good friend Alessandro Striggio to find out what has happened to the pension due to me? It was promised me by our late Duke.'

Back in Mantua, Striggio sighs as if he has heard it all before. 'That cursed *fondo* ... he's always writing about it, and I send notes to the Treasury. But what can you do? A former maestro's pension comes lower down the scale than the costumes for the dwarfs' harlequinade.'

CHAPTER TWENTY-SEVEN

Speaking of dwarfs, there are many more at court than in the days of Duke Vincenzo of glorious memory. From a dozen to over a score. They process the corridors as if they are the masters of the palace. Archimedeo has been building up his mirror court for years, three of whom are his own children. Legitimate, too, for the marriage was celebrated in the Duke's private chapel. Archimedeo, grey-bearded and crippled with gout, is borne by four of his fellows on a litter. The front-runner calls in a peremptory voice, 'Make way for the Lord Duke's dwarf.' Courtiers who do not move out of their path have their shins barked by the poles of the litter. No one objects to the behaviour of the dwarfs, any more than to a band of unruly children. It is for Ferdinando to have them called to order, in any case.

Ferdinando has more pressing problems on his mind. Matters of politics are painfully entangled with matters of the heart. The Medici conditions for allowing his marriage to Grand Duke Cosimo's sister have closed all the loopholes to love. Camilla must be sent to a convent, and Ferdinando's son disinherited, so there can be no doubt that the first marriage was invalid. And His Most Serene Highness of Tuscany has heard the so-called Duchess Camilla possesses a letter in which Ferdinando swears he is her true husband. That letter must be delivered to the Grand Duke before the marriage with his sister can take place. Camilla refuses to relinquish the letter but it is difficult to be resolute when there are two evil-looking bravos eyeing your child. She has no one to turn to. Her father died quite suddenly, and she has no defence against the threats to hurt her son. They take the letter and Giacinto back to court. Ferdinando is ashamed to see the boy crying for his mother, but what can he do? Those are the conditions of the Medici for the princess of the huge dowry, which arrives just in time to save the jewels he will give her being pawned.

The succession depends on this marriage, for his request to the Vatican to annul the secret wedding of his brother has been refused. The Pope upholds the union, and orders that Prince Vincenzo, instead of trying to be a Cardinal, for which he is unsuited, honours his marriage vows instead, and returns to his wife. Moreover, adds the Vatican's representative, the Pope is tired of the chaos in which the present ruler of Mantua has immersed a house that once produced great cardinals. They are banned from the cardinalate, at least for the lifetime of the present Pope.

It is essential then that Ferdinando's marriage is fruitful, and at least the celebrations in Florence impressed his enemies. But now, in the privacy of their bedchamber – though one can hardly call it privacy due to the Medici spies reporting back to her brother – the outward success has been paid for with bitterness. Caterina de' Medici is not a woman he would have chosen for his bed, had he the choice. She has a Habsburg jaw, a lack of warmth and a jealous mind fed on suspicions. As he kisses her he thinks of Camilla's mouth, but Caterina knows his protestations of love are hollow when she caresses him as he sleeps and hears him murmur Camilla's name.

※

The road to San Martino has become busy. The Savoy ambassador has called in, on his way to Mantua, he says. A courier has arrived from the French branch of the Gonzaga, with a message of support and an offer of money. 'I am not interested in money or in the succession,' says Isabella. 'All I want is my husband back. A contract is a contract. The contract, which I have held to on my side, was that he should love and honour me till death. Tell him that, wherever he has got to now.'

She knows where he has got to. He is fighting for the Spanish troops under the Governor of Milan, as a less hazardous alternative to being torn between his brother's demands and hers. She had seen him after he had been released from imprisonment, when he had fallen to his knees in front of her and sworn that it had not been his idea to ask for an annulment but his brother's. 'My poor husband,' said Isabella, lightly touching his face, 'what is to become of you? I can see the spirit of your father fade from your eyes.' He stayed in her bed that night, and left the next day with his troops, and that was her last sight of him, wearing an air of false cheerfulness as he rode away.

'My little husband, you and your brother will have to learn what it is to dishonour your word,' she says to the miniature he has left with her. 'Your father had more spirit, he sinned with bravado, not with subterfuge.'

'Let them both go to hell,' says Scipione. He has ridden over from Bozzolo and is enraged that Vincenzo has left. But in any case he is going to give them something to think about. He will go ahead with his plan to dam the course of the River Oglio for his mills, which will be profitable for him. Mantua will lose an important tributary and its lakes will drop by a third with odorous results.

Isabella smiles at her son, who wears his riding boots in the salon and his hair long, in contrast to the pomaded courtiers. 'So let them wallow in their mud,' she says. 'We will grow rich at their expense.'

※

A man with a clever and subtle mind does not acknowledge an impasse. If Isabella will not give up her rights quietly, then she may be removed. Ferdinando's informers tell him that Prince Vincenzo stayed the night with the wife from whom he should be estranged, and she is now rarely seen out of doors. It is rumoured she is pregnant. Ferdinando sends a warmly phrased letter expressing concern for her health as her loving brother-in-law and suggesting she would be better looked after by his own doctors and servants in a very comfortable villa he has near Mantua.

Thanks, but no thanks, says Isabella. Which of your servants would serve me the poison?

※

Poison? The seed of another idea lodged in Ferdinando's mind. It germinated as he held conference with the Father Inquisitor in the hall of the labyrinth. Under the ceiling's motto of life's uncertainty, the two men sat either side of the high fireplace and discussed a solution to the Isabella question. The Inquisitor's quiet voice calmed Ferdinando's troubled spirit. They both have Mantua's best interests at heart, said the Inquisitor, enfolding him in a sympathetic but curiously opaque gaze. Nothing is more tangled than the conflict between the material and the spiritual. I sense a conflict in your heart, my son. He waited, allowing the pause to rest between them, for Ferdinando to break down as so many of these princes do when forced to look within.

But Ferdinando, trained at the Vatican, has control of his temperament. There are more important things than to give way to the melancholy he carries within him. In a voice as quiet as the Inquisitor's, he answered the problem was not his but his brother's, and though there was no one else in the room to overhear, he began to speak in Latin. His brother was bewitched, there could be no other explanation for his obsession with a woman nearly twice his age, and not only that but from a family whose loyalty to the state was questionable. And she had had the devil's own luck in holding to her claim. Can you imagine such a marriage to be valid, with the prince a Cardinal at the time? Yet the Pope upheld this unholy union.

The Inquisitor held up his hand to silence him, and said reprovingly that it was not for either of them to question the Pope's will. But, of course, if she was a witch, it became a matter for the Holy Office of the Inquisition. What proof was there of her witchcraft?

Ferdinando said he remembered his brother mentioning her herb garden. She grew herbs that were used in witch-craft. She may have poisoned his food with spells.

The Inquisitor shook his head, That was proof of nothing but the Lord Duke's suspicion. He would need witnesses. And then, almost as an afterthought, he asked if Donna Isabella were beautiful?

'A beauty against nature,' said Ferdinando angrily. 'She is forty, the mother of seven sons. They say her beauty is witchcraft as well.'

The Inquisitor smiled for the first time. 'Is it the beauty that causes harm or the beholder's thoughts?' he asked, re-verting to Italian. 'When you have proof, come to me again.' He raised his hand in blessing. 'May your spirit find solace in God's will.'

Ferdinando remained alone in the room of the labyrinth, looking at the portrait of Duke Vincenzo and the inscrip-tion in gold round the edge of the ceiling – VINC. GONZ. MANT. IV., with its blatant lie, Conqueror of the Turks. The portrait was painted soon after Vincenzo had become Duke, and he is young and slim, aware of the fine figure he cuts in high ruff and the breeches of the time, absurdly puffed, showing off long well-shaped legs. Ferdinando looks at him in envy and wonders at the dazzling sleight of hand that came to his father so easily, and has quite de-serted his son.

※

'What are your men doing outside my gates?' asked Isabella of the Captain from Mantua, the same officer who had arrested her husband.

The Captain said, in the same reasonable tone of voice that he had used to Vincenzo, 'We have orders to prevent visitors, apart from those necessary to the running of the household, Madama. And I am afraid we cannot allow you to leave the house, except escorted by guards.'

Isabella's face reddened in anger. This cipher of

Ferdinando's telling her what to do in her own house. 'I will not hear of it,' she said. 'Where is my son? He comes under the heading of those necessary to the running of the household, Captain.'

'I am so sorry, Prince Scipione is no longer at Bozzolo. He has fled with his brother, we think to Milan, to escape arrest for the theft of Mantua's waters. We are commanded to question your servants on certain matters, those in your employ at the time the Lord Duke's brother began his attendance on you. Please excuse me, Madama.'

The captain bowed and left the room. Isabella heard him giving orders to his men, and then there were sounds of shouting and wailing from other parts of the house. She ran to the door, but a guard outside was facing her, barring the way with a pike. An hour later, released from the room, she retreated to her bedroom. She sat in front of the mirror, aware of the way her face had changed. Eyes with the expression of a hunted animal looked back at her from the glass. She saw strands of silver in her hair she had not noticed before; the life seemed to have drained from her skin. That this change in her fortune could happen so quickly, and she knew there is worse to come. She could not call on Emilia's good sense, for Emilia, along with her husband and three other servants had been arrested and transported to God knows where. For the first time in her life, Isabella felt truly alone and in need of a friend. She wondered, What would Ottavio do if he were here? She felt mildly surprised that she, who had wept so much and so readily in the past, could find no tears now that life had hit her with all its force.

CHAPTER TWENTY-EIGHT

*W*hen *Duke Vincenzo leaned over the cradle* of his infant daughter and said she would marry no one but the Emperor himself, he did not foresee that he wouldn't live to arrange the match. But Ferdinando has pulled it off. His father would have been proud of him. The midnight sky turns to gold with the explosions of Catherine wheels, rockets and flares; beacons are lit every few paces around the lake, to celebrate the arrival of the Emperor to claim his bride.

With such a great marriage for his sister, and his own illustrious union with the Medici, Duke Ferdinando can put a brave face on to the world again. But while the distinguished guests and the citizens enjoy the fireworks and the flowing wine, he knows it is a façade. Caterina, his Duchess, is barren. The fault of the Medici, say his doctors. No, says Caterina, it is because my husband doesn't love me. Whatever the reason, it is necessary that his brother is freed from his marriage to make a more suitable match. He seems ready at last to fall in with whatever Ferdinando wants, accusations of witchcraft included. A bewitchment that was cured after he was sent to Spa for his health. A letter from Ferdinando had preceded him addressed to Mme Gilbert, procurer for the nobility, with instructions to look after the heartbroken prince.

❈

In San Martino Isabella heard with anger of the treatment of her servants by Ferdinando's men. Emilia's husband suffered a broken nose, a dislocated arm and several cracked ribs. Emilia's face was discoloured with bruises, but we wouldn't tell them what they wanted, she said. They were trying to make us say you had practised witchcraft to bind the prince to you.

A few days later a letter arrived in which Prince Vincenzo, with much affection, asked his estranged wife to come to Mantua for a reconciliation. She was considering the journey when the priest of San Martino arrived to tell her in confidence that the process of examination had already started at the office of the Inquisition in Mantua. There were two witnesses to the accusations of witchcraft, and it was only a matter of time before they would interrogate her. If you go to Mantua, my daughter, said the priest, you know how it will end.

A bonfire on the piazza, said Isabella. She looked out of the window towards the guards at the gate. She could hear their voices, and one of them must have been telling a joke, for there was a sudden burst of laughter. The fields that stretched towards Gazzuolo were verdant in the spring rains.

'Do you remember the day you married us?' said Isabella. 'An evening in August, the air still hot from the sun. It was a true marriage, and the Pope upheld it. Against the arguments of Duke Ferdinando, and all he persuaded to support him, and what an array he called, the King of Spain, the Medici Regent Mother of France, his friends among the Cardinals. Ferdinando pulled every string he could pull, and yet the Pope would not annul the marriage. And because of this, they would kill me. It is for the Holy Father to decide the case. I want him to hear the evidence. I demand to be tried by the Pope.'

※

It is the sensation of all Italy. The Mantuan princess, whose case has been debated for months, has arrived of her own free will, to be imprisoned in the Castel Sant'Angelo in Rome, her only condition being that the accusers and their witnesses are also called to appear. The sales of the *avvisi* soar, as everyone is eager to hear the princely dirt. While they're about it, they recall another beautiful victim of the Gonzaga duke. What has happened to la bella Camilla, languishing in a convent? asks *Il Intrepido*. And now here's la bell' Isabella, locked away in the Vatican's jail.

In the ducal offices Ottavio finds Striggio plunged in gloom. Ferdinando is desperate to forestall the trial by means, Striggio says, he would rather not discuss. But Ottavio has already heard from a careless remark of the Count's secretary that a letter from Striggio has gone to his friend the Marquis Tassoni in Rome about the possibility of hiring a Neapolitan assassin specializing in poisons. How do you feel about the wheel of fortune now, Count Striggio? says Ottavio. The writer of the songs of Orfeo ends up consorting with the underworld.

Striggio gives him a guilty, sideways glance. It is with great reluctance, he says, that he even considered such a means. But look at the alternative. Without an heir from either of the brothers, the succession is plunged into confusion. Mantua will be torn apart by the conflicting claims. The life of one woman for the security of the state . . .

❋

The day of the process begins. In the courtroom Isabella, dressed like a nun in a plain black dress with a headdress to cover her hair, sits in the chair for the accused, her lawyers in the adjacent seats. On the benches opposite are the black-robed Mantuan lawyers crouched over their papers like crows over carrion. When Isabella looks at them they avert their eyes.

The clerk reads the charge: that Donna Isabella Gonzaga of Novellara, widow of the late Don Ferrante, mother of Don Scipione of Bozzolo, at San Martino dell'Argine, near Gazzuolo, in the state of Mantua, did during the year of 1616 practise witchcraft against Don Vincenzo Gonzaga, brother of Duke Ferdinando, sixth Duke of Mantua and fourth Duke of Monferrato, thus entrapping the said Don Vincenzo into a marriage against his vows as a Cardinal and the will of the Lord Duke. How does the accused plead?

Isabella says in a quiet voice, looking at the judge, Not guilty.

Now the Mantuan advocate, a man of wide girth, gets to his feet, and after a pause while he rearranges his robes around him, shuffles his sleeves, adopts an orator's posture, and begins his speech. The larger part of it is in Latin, a dissertation on the quality of witchcraft, its demonic effects, its subversive influence on state and church, and the necessity to eradicate its practitioners. But, he says, and this is evidence of the benevolence of the Lord Duke, even when pushed to extremes by the harm done to his brother, they would not have Donna Isabella made to suffer the ultimate penalty. Donna Isabella had sinned through love, and surely the sins of love should be less severely punished? After all, *si eos, qui nos amant, interficiamus, quid his faciemus, quibus odio sumus?* If those whom we love, we kill, what do we do with those we hate? The benevolent prince would not wish the death of the noble princess, but simply her agreement to dissolve the marriage and leave him free to marry another.

Perhaps the benevolent prince does not fully understand the consequences of the charges he has brought, says the judge. They do not relate to an annulment, which is a separate issue, but to witchcraft. The desecration of the Holy Sacrament is an offence against the Church, to be dealt with as the Church decides, and it is not possible for such a charge to be withdrawn whatever the wishes of the accusers. Speaking of whom, why are they not in court?

If it please Your Excellency, says the Mantuan advocate, the Lord Duke is occupied with defending his territories which are under threat. And Prince Vincenzo is unwell.

Counsel for the defence rises, and suggests in a silky voice that they might consider an adjournment until the accusers were in better health or less occupied with affairs of state. The judge, with some irritation, repeats that the charge involved the Church, and the brothers' presence or wishes were irrelevant. They would hear the evidence of their witnesses after the defending lawyer's plea.

The defence says that after the elaborate edifice of the prosecutor's speech and the slender foundations on which it was built, he wishes only to state plain facts as to why the charge of witchcraft was without any substance. First, the charges had only been brought years afterwards when other attempts to annul the marriage had failed. Secondly, the moral character and good reputation of Donna Isabella could give no credence to such charges. Third, she had no need of witchcraft anyway, because it was her beauty that brought suitors for her hand. Fourth, that the Prince's ill treatment of his wife was the behaviour of one who had changed his mind about his hasty marriage, rather than of one who had been bewitched. Fifth, that a woman as prudent as Donna Isabella would not have confided to such witnesses such secrets, the witnesses being a servant of Don Vincenzo, and a former servant of Donna Isabella who had been dismissed. Sixth, Duke Ferdinando was already in dispute with the accused's family over other matters and had sent an armed force against her son, Prince Scipione. Seventh, how could anyone possibly believe such charges of Donna Isabella, who has conducted herself as someone who is completely innocent, willingly agreeing to her trial in Rome? Look at the accused. Has she not grace? Is she not surrounded by the light of innocence? I rest my case.

The defence subsides gracefully on to his bench, inclining his head towards his clerk, and looking at his papers, while the court sits in silence for a moment considering his words.

❈

And then the trial took a turn that would delight the Roman *avvisi* who, though banned from the proceedings, picked up the gossip afterwards. First into the witness box was one Federico Puelli, carver to Don Vincenzo, who averred that he had seen Donna Isabella muttering over a sauce she was preparing and had said, when he asked what was in it, Something that will do him good. Puelli, stumbling over his words and looking down at the floor, eventually was released from the cross examination.

The clerk called for the second witness, one Bianca Montagnana, former serving woman to Donna Isabella. It seemed that Montagnana was not in the best of health, as she was helped by two court servants to the witness's chair. She sat there, her head turned from Isabella, and answered the questions from the Mantuan prosecutor in a faltering voice. Yes, she had seen Donna Isabella brewing the potion. She had seen the skull of a dead man in the kitchen cupboard, and then late one night, Donna Isabella had asked her to hold the pestle while she crushed pieces of bone into it, and then she had scattered over it fragments of the Holy Sacrament, and had rendered it into a powder.

'Which of those lunatics thought that one up, Bianca?' called out Isabella.

The judge called for silence, and the defence shook his head at her, mouthing, Be careful.

Isabella said to the judge, 'With your permission, I should like to ask the witness some questions,' and then, to Montagnana, 'Tell me when you last saw me, Bianca, and in what circumstances.'

Montagnana looked at her in embarrassment as she recalled the day of dismissal. Yes, it was for lying. And yes, she had been stealing. And yes, she had been relieved that no other action was taken but her dismissal.

'So what made you then accept this farrago of nonsense against me? Who thought of it, and why did you agree to speak out against me? Tell me, Bianca, do you really wish to see me dead?'

Now Bianca began to cry, and then, wiping the tears from her eyes, she said, 'I am sorry, Madama, but they said they would kill me . . .'

There was a scraping of the chair as the Duke's lawyer

rose quickly to his feet, and protested, 'Your Excellency, this is untrue.'

The judge called for silence again, and said that he would question the witness now, as to the circumstances of her confession. The court was above any threats or influence from interested parties, and the witness, he would remind her, was sworn to tell the truth. Bianca composed herself sufficiently to recall her incarceration, in some sort of lodge outside the city, where she had been kept in the greatest discomfort and subjected to abuse and threats. She had been questioned hour after hour, and they had punched her and threatened her with their daggers. She had been locked up for twenty days, the last seven without any food, and she had finally, in desperation, agreed to their demands. Even now, she had nightmares about it, the way that she was held, her arms twisted behind her back, while he had brought his dagger an inch from her eyes, and drew it along her cheek to her throat, so that she was certain she would be killed. And he had called her a whore.

There was a murmuring around the courtroom, as she broke down into sobs, and the judge said, 'Of whom are we speaking? Who held you, and who threatened you?'

'The Count Striggio held my arms, and Duke Ferdinando hit me and cut me with the dagger. Forgive me, Your Excellency.'

'No forgiveness is necessary for you, if you speak the truth,' said the judge. The murmurs increased to uproar, and the judge's clerk yelled, 'Silence in court!'

Above the noise the Duke's lawyer shouted, 'She is lying. She is making it up. There was no such meeting.'

'Oh, so you wish to say that your witness is unreliable? Have you any others to call?' asked the judge.

There was a written deposition from Prince Vincenzo, said the lawyer quickly.

'And he's not here to be questioned,' said the judge. 'You have claimed that witness for the prosecution is a liar.

The case against the accused is unproven and is dismissed.'

The defence rose to say they would be pressing for damages from the Lord Duke for defamation and for the anguish the case had caused Donna Isabella.

'That's a matter for you, Advocate,' said the judge, rising to his feet. 'The hearing is ended.' The court had risen with him, and as he left the room the entire gathering exploded in uproar.

⁂

The *avvisi* are soon passing from hand to hand with the shock revelations ... Donna Isabella carried out of the Castel Sant'Angelo in triumph ... vindicated ... Duke Ferdinando disgraced ... and promises of more dirt to follow. A case for damages means the story will run and run. But in one of the more serious of the *avvisi* is a reminder that at the end of all the scandal, the dispute over the succession remains.

⁂

Ferdinando is sunk in depression. Nothing can raise his spirits. Even the music, without which he has always said he would die, is no longer capable of reviving him, for Adriana Basile has left. She knows a sinking ship when she sees one. She is taking well-paid engagements in Venice, directed by the great Monteverdi, the acknowledged magus of music. The further she is from Ferdinando the more impassioned his letters to her to draw her back.

Venice calls to Ferdinando as well, for Mantua is full of bitter reminders that feed his self-hatred. His son Giacinto is growing up at court into an intelligent, pleasant-natured boy, but disinherited by his father for the sake of the marriage that has proved sterile. Every time he looks at the boy he feels sick at heart. He sees as little of the Duchess as possible to avoid her recriminations, and her jealousy. And there is his brother, still not free of his marriage, railing about the woman he once loved, furious that she should hold him to his vows after all this time. It is a plot by their enemies, he knows it, to bring them down. Ferdinando turns to his chancellor, Count Striggio, his eyes and ears, now known, only half in jest, as the Vice-duke. Striggio applies his diplomatic mind to the problem as if it is a game of chess. The key is Maria, he says, your late brother's daughter and heiress of Monferrato. If we marry her to whomever we choose as heir to Mantua, it will appease the Duke of Savoy and reinforce our claim on Monferrato. It is only a question of finding an heir.

A letter arrives from his sister the Empress Leonora, recommending her brother to act in the Emperor's best interests and elect the Gonzaga Prince of Guastalla as heir. A man of good reputation, unbeholden to outside influences. To elect the Duke of Nevers from the French branch of the Gonzaga would bring the French, of ancient enmity, into Italy.

Ferdinando wavers. He writes to both sides at much the same time in much the same terms, the Habsburg King of Spain, and King Louis XIII of France, pledging to the opposing sides his undying devotion, and desire for his merits to be appreciated. But he is torn by a conflict of the heart – the desire for the son he had disinherited to succeed, despite opposition from the Duchess. More letters go to France and to his brother-in-law the Emperor putting forward a claim for his son. Then, in one of those postscript lines that slip by, almost as if his hand was being guided by fate, he adds to the King of France's letter – if his beloved son Don Giacinto were excluded, it might be as well for the son of the Gonzaga Duc de Nevers to come to Mantua and consider marriage with Ferdinando's niece Maria as the only means of preserving Monferrato against the claims of Savoy.

The King reads the letter as does Cardinal Richelieu. Letters from the King and the Cardinal are despatched by fast courier to the Duc de Nevers. Soon afterwards, without waiting for confirmation, the French Duke despatches to Italy, instead of a letter, his son and heir. Ferdinando's postscript, written in confusion, has played into the hands of the French and effectively barred the way for his own son.

CHAPTER TWENTY-NINE

A *rchimedeo* has taken over the Scala Sancta. The tiny, low-ceilinged rooms could have been built as a dwarfs' apartment, and Ferdinando ceased worshipping there several months before his death. Archimedeo attended the funeral on his litter. Poor Ferdinando, not yet forty and already entombed, his will to live undermined by the weight of his errors. Archimedeo has his own court bring rich tapestries from other parts of the palace which they cut to size for his new apartment. Cushions and pillows disappear, small chests, benches which are the right height for tables, the cradle in which Ferdinando slept as a baby. No one visits this part of the palace now. If they did, they would find one or two mysteriously vanished pieces of jewellery adorning the person of Archimedeo's daughter.

'You look as if you will be next,' said Prince Vincenzo, now the seventh Duke, as he passed Archimedeo at the funeral.

'I wouldn't bet on it,' said Archimedeo. His son had been sitting under the table when the palace doctor had examined Vincenzo, and you didn't even need such privileged information to see the change in the man. The eager boy, the impulsive and careless youth, was disintegrating visibly. The young Baroness, whom Mme Gilbert had chosen to cure his broken heart, who in her pale beauty resembled Isabella as she would have been at seventeen, how could he have known her perfumed body was a weapon of destruction? If you don't drink, if you don't eat sweetmeats, if you take this tincture and that, said the doctor, you can build your health against the illness. You may keep it at bay for many years yet.

How can he not drink? His blood calls out for it. And

illness or not, he doesn't intend to be deprived of love. The new Pope at the Vatican has overruled the obstinacy of the old Pope Paul and is in the slow process of granting an annulment, although upholding Donna Isabella's right to claim damages. I shall soon be free to marry and provide an heir for the dukedom. I shall marry Maria, and ensure the succession of our states.

Your niece, says Striggio in a careworn voice. That's more than consanguinity. Could we please think again?

But more urgent than the marriage is the need to raise money, simply to live. Like vultures, the art dealers of Venice are hovering, waiting for the moment to pounce. And for the first time in years, Vincenzino feels an anguish of spirit as physically painful as his illness. To lose those paintings for which his forebears fought, for which they paid a king's ransom, which they chose with an unerring eye for value and beauty, to create the greatest gallery of art in Europe – he cannot bear to see the collection dispersed. He walks the palace, dazed with grief. To lose the Correggio *Venus*, the Caravaggio *Virgin*, Titian's *Caesars*, Raphael's *Madonna*, the Rubens, the Tintoretto, Veronese, Bellini . . . he cannot believe that the moment has come.

Striggio sends word to Ottavio in Venice: total secrecy, please, the Lord Duke cannot bear to think of the paintings glorifying the court of another Italian prince. It is essential that the Medici and the Farnese know nothing. The Venetian vultures have found an art lover who will remove the paintings to a court of which he can be oblivious, an island off the coast of north France. King Charles I of England is a passionate collector, and he will buy the paintings by any means he can. A list arrives in Mantua, with the names of the greatest of the treasures the King requires. The list has not omitted any of his favourite pictures – after all, the adviser to King Charles is Sir Peter Paul Rubens, who remembers the collection from his days as Mantua's court painter.

Not the Mantegnas, says Vincenzo. Not *The Triumphs of Caesar*. Please God, I cannot part with them. On the walls of the Sala dei Trionfi the triumphal procession sweeps past in its glory, from the trumpeters and musicians, the incense-burners, the boys leading sacrificial beasts, the trophy bearers, the prisoners and the war elephants to Caesar on his chariot, a Caesar symbolic of the victories of Mantua's warrior princes. Anything but the Mantegnas, says Vincenzo, and escapes to the summer villa on the shores of Lake Garda.

Ottavio arrives from Venice, carrying letters for Striggio from Monteverdi on the new opera commissioned for Mantua. *La Finta Pazza Licori* is to be an *opera buffa*, with a theme of lunacy and delusion. Somehow, as the months have passed since he began to compose it, the work seems both apt and inappropriate at the same time. In the palace, because the Duke is absent, a group of citizens is being shown around the gallery of Titians by one of the court servants. Ottavio sees from the pleasure in their faces that they feel a share in the ownership of the paintings.

'Do they know yet?' he asks Striggio. One of the citizens was explaining the finer points of the Titian *Venus* to his family.

'No one knows apart from those involved in the deal. Please God no one learns until the paintings are despatched to Venice.'

'It's shameful,' says Ottavio. 'He is selling Mantua's heritage.'

'You tell him. If you can think of any other way of rescuing us from bankruptcy, I should be glad to hear it. The jewels are already in pawn.'

✳

On the terrace of the summer villa overlooking Lake Garda, Vincenzo reclined on a long couch, to ease the pain in his legs. He was wearing a loose embroidered robe, brought from the east. 'Please excuse my ill-health,' he said, 'an infection which has poisoned my blood. Look at the state of my legs.' And he raised his robe to show discoloured weals on his swollen calves. He laughed at the revulsion on Ottavio's face.

'I feel better when I am here, the air is reviving. What have you got for me? A letter from Striggio ... I'm not strong enough to look at it now. They call him the Arch-Duke; he thinks he rules Mantua, the old fox. Well, what else? Oh, that opera from Claudio. I'm not sure, I never thought much of the libretto, but that's Striggio again, he chose it. You will have some wine, and tell me the news from Venice.'

'I should like to talk about the paintings,' said Ottavio.

Vincenzo seemed not to have heard him. He gazed across the lake. 'Isn't this the most beautiful place on earth. Touched by the gods. Look at the water, so still, it's like silk.'

'Your Highness, you know it would be a terrible thing to sell the paintings. They are the heritage of your ancestors, they are not yours to be pawned.'

'Have you smelt this perfume? It is pure tuberose, sent to me by one of the dealers. Alfonsina shall wear it.'

'Alfonsina?'

'Archimedeo's daughter. Have you seen her? She has the most exquisite face with a high forehead, lips like rubies, a white complexion, and black, black eyes. And she just comes up to my waist. I was going to carry her away here for the summer, but Archimedeo has hidden her. Well, we shall find my love, I've got my men hunting the palace for her.'

Ottavio, refusing to be diverted, said angrily, 'It would be a humiliation for Mantua, and for your house if you sold the pictures. We could raise the money from the citizens of Mantua. They have pride in the collection.'

Vincenzo's eyes focused into a brief, shrewd glance.

'And do you think I don't have pride? That is why the Farnese must never hear of this, or the Medici. Tell the citizens and you might as well tell the world. Ottavio, I know what is happening, there's no choice. It is finished. Don't annoy me by mentioning it again.'

'I am indeed sorry. As your father would have been, and his father . . .'

'I was sent a beautiful parrot from the Africas a few days ago. Come and see him, Ottavio. He is the rarest bird in my aviary.'

Vincenzo rose painfully to his feet. Leaning on his page's arm, and taking Ottavio's arm on the other side, he led him towards the hall of the birds. As they entered, the screeching from the cages hurt the ears and the smell of bird excrement and straw offended the nose. Bright macaws and lovebirds clutched the bars that imprisoned them. They fluttered against their confines trying to escape towards the sun, oblivious of the frescoes behind them of temples, lakes and mountains. The painted beauty of their background was lost, too, on the birds which perched immobile, their feathers fluffed out, their beaks sunk on to their breasts. At the end of the hall was the rare macaw of Africa, its feathers a deep purple-blue and orange. It perched on a gilded stand, grooming itself busily with its beak, but then it raised its head and there was a bare patch of grey skin where it had plucked out its own feathers, and a red pit of raw flesh. It stared at them with bright, mad eyes and then bent its head again to peck at its breast, continuing the process of tearing itself to death.

❋

'The man is sadly changed, isn't he?' said Striggio, looking across the papers on his desk in the Reggia. 'Did he mention his views on the opera?'

'Only that he didn't care for the libretto, which he says you chose for him.'

Striggio sighed. 'That means he will be demanding

something else ... What a pity, this would have been a new departure, an opera with comedy. The waste of it, the unperformed works of Claudio's we have lying here – Arianna, Andromeda, Apollo, and others, gathering dust. In the days of the great Duke Vincenzo, they would have been staged. He knew how to do it, he could see from the page to the performance. Now I shall have to write yet another diplomatic letter to Venice, smoothing the Maestro's feathers. What did Vincenzino say about the paintings?'

'Nothing. They are lost to us. You are right, Lord Chancellor, the waste of it. It seems the comedy is ended.'

❀

Shall we end on this note, a dying prince and his corrupt, ageing courtiers? At times like this memory provides a comfortable retreat. Pause for a moment, and look through another mirror, into the reflection of time past. Travel through memory to another September, thirty years earlier as the comedy begins. There is noise, there is laughter, there is an air of excitement about the Room of the Rivers where the musicians are tuning up for rehearsal. The young composer in black gives a note on the harpsichord, and the sawing and plucking of instruments grows louder. Soh fah lah, chant the singers, exercising their voices along the scales. The doors open at the end of the hall and several of the musicians look towards the Duke, who is followed by Secretary Chieppio, still trying to catch his attention over some unfinished business. The Duke looks round the room, and claps his hands for silence. The rehearsal of *Il Pastor Fido* begins. The Duke watches from the front of the room, then walks over to the harpsichord and leaning over it, says, 'It is not fast enough. At this point, Claudio, the satyr should be advancing on the nymph.'

Claudio smiles. 'Your Highness is anticipating the music.'

'No, this is better for the drama, now the music will follow, in confirmation. Try it and see.'

Of course you don't argue with the Duke's stage directions, and he is right. The scene is better this way.

'You see,' says the Duke, 'it's lighter and quicker. That's how it is in Arcadia. Listen to the words . . .' and he sings the lines, his hand marking time on the lid of the harpsichord for emphasis: 'Let us use it while we may; / Snatch those joys that haste away . . .'

The new young singer takes up the line, in a sweet purity of tone, 'But our winter come, in vain / we solicit spring again . . .'

The Duke laughs abruptly as at an uncomfortable truth, and glances at the girl, Cattaneo's daughter, and then at Claudio. 'When you create beauty, you create love. That is our truth, that is Arcadia. Continue the rehearsal.'

CHAPTER THIRTY

Two o'clock in the morning. Footsteps in the corridor, hurried but trying to tread softly. A whispered conversation outside her room, then the door opens. Maria has been awake since she heard the carriage wheels outside the convent. She knows they are coming for her.

The lantern throws a huge cowled shadow on the wall. She sees in its light Mother Superior, and Sister Letitia who has come to help her dress. Maria gets out of bed. She is alert to everything around her, but as if in a waking dream. Mother Superior is whispering a blessing. Sister Letitia is holding out a skirt to step into. Maria keeps on the shift she has been sleeping in; it is far too cold to change it. She combs her hair and lets it hang over her shoulders. Sister Letitia helps her put on her cloak, and she draws the cowl over her head. They lead her out into the passage, and she can sense in their sympathetic murmuring an underlying excitement. She follows the lantern bearer and at the great oak and iron door to the convent, she hesitates, reluctant to leave its security. And then it is as if she is being literally handed over to the people waiting for her. She sees in the guttering light of the lantern a man in a dark cloak, crooked of stature. He is handing her into the carriage and she can see someone else in the shadows inside, a woman whose face is obscured by the cowl. The man gets into the carriage and closes the door. She hears snorts from the horses as the driver flicks his whip and the carriage starts forward. She turns to look out of the window, but the curtains are drawn. She is in a muffled, moving chamber in the dead of night with two people whom she has never met before. And then she can tell from the echo that the carriage has entered an enclosed space. The sound of its wheels has set dogs barking. The man gets out of the carriage as it halts, and turns to help her down. She is aware of cold stone through the soles of her shoes. She is in a large courtyard with dark walls looming above her like cliffs. There are lights in a few of the windows and she can glimpse figures moving around.

She stumbles as they ascend the long staircase leading up to the great hall and the lady from the carriage gives her a supporting arm. On the walls she sees a fresco of battle. Men in armour lie in an abandonment of sprawled limbs, eyes and mouths open in the throes of death. She is being hurried to another part of the palace, and after confusing turns she is in a long mirrored hall, and the mirrors are multiplying the numbers present in their reflections. More people are coming forward to meet her, among them an older man, sleek-haired and plump, whom she recognizes as Count Striggio, who had visited the convent earlier to explain what was expected of her as heiress to Monferrato, and to show her a letter from her mother in Turin exhorting her to follow the Count's advice. She had asked to keep the letter but the Count had said it must be filed with the other papers.

Standing behind Striggio is a boy a few years older than herself. He looks at her and she sees his pale face suffused with a sudden blush. So that is to be her husband, the nervous boy who glances at her and then away. Well, she is prepared to fulfil her duty. Count Striggio has told her already what it is. If she marries the son of the Duke of Nevers the states of Mantua and Monferrato will remain united and the succession secure. She is filled with the power of her responsibility. Her body is precious to all of them.

They are in a chapel, before an altar, she is on the arm of the boy, the Prince of Rethel, and the priest has asked them to join hands. She feels his hand in hers, cold and clammy to the touch. She hears her voice giving the responses to the priest's questions, as if it is coming from a long way off, outside herself. Now the ceremony is over, and her new husband is looking at her in a state of some alarm, at what is expected of him. The lady from the carriage, who she understands is the Duchess of Sabbioneta, is telling her that she must be hungry. There is supper prepared for them in the Romano apartment. They move along the corridors, Maria on the arm of her husband, to a salon where a table is set with food and drink. A fire has been lit in the fireplace, to take the chill off the air. It is four o'clock in the morning, and there is little conversation as they eat. Then the Duchess takes the bride into a chamber in the middle of which is a large canopied bed, the Gonzaga crest at its head. There is a silk shift laid out on the bed for her. Maria gets into bed and waits. After some minutes the bridegroom, wearing a dressing-robe over his nightshirt, appears. He stands awkwardly by the bed. He is sorry, he says, he has been told that they must do it now. Maria's uncle is dying.

Maria cannot understand why, once the marriage has taken place, they should have to consummate it in their exhausted state, but she supposes the necessity of doing so before her uncle expires must be a requirement of the succession. She waits for her husband to get into the bed, and then he holds her close to him, as if he himself is dying.

※

In another bedchamber, that of Amor and Psyche in the ducal apartments, the seventh Duke waits for death. Can it be only thirty years or so after the moment of his conception, when his father had made love to his mother at the time of *Il Pastor Fido*? Young Vincenzo, not much older than thirty, lies swollen with dropsy and rotting with gangrene, in a stench so nauseating that the servants wear scarves impregnated with rosemary essence over their noses and mouths to stop them gagging. He has seen no one else apart from Striggio, though he knows the ambassadors from Vienna, Madrid and France have been trying to have an audience with him. He is glad Striggio has kept them all away. Dying takes concentration. He cannot think of anything else.

He is aware of a crowd in the room, which has been empty of visitors till now. Over there in the corner is his mother; he remembers her expression from his childhood when she didn't believe his stories but was prepared to be indulgent. She will protect him from the creatures which have gathered at the foot of the bed, their goblin faces watching him greedily. And there is his brother, in cardinal's red, as sanctimonious as ever. He turns his head away from him to see Ottavio, standing next to the ducal confessor. The man is holding a handkerchief to his face, so he must be still in this world. Vincenzo says, trying to make light of it, 'I'm disgusted by my body too.'

Ottavio says, 'It comes to us all.'

'But so soon,' says Vincenzo, and there are tears in his eyes. Seeing Ottavio has reminded him of days at San Martino. Isabella, her eyes on him as he takes the peach, her look of complicity as if she already knows and loves him. The warmth of the sun, the peacefulness of the garden, the muslin glimpsed at the edge of her dress. The softness of her skin, the sweetness of her embrace. He had obliterated this afterwards in his anger at her obstinacy in holding him against his will, no, his brother's will. And then, as he remembers his spoilt love, another wave of anger comes over him, and his hands clench under the bedclothes.

'Father,' says Vincenzo, looking towards his confessor. 'Something more.'

Ottavio understands the glance of the priest. 'I will go now, God be with you,' and leaves the room empty of all but the Duke, his confessor and the ghosts of his past. He sits outside, as requested by Striggio, who is taking a few hours of sleep, to prevent anyone else approaching the Duke. Four hours later, around eight in the morning of Christmas Eve, in the year of 1627, the seventh Duke, last of the line, gives up the fight against the corruption of his flesh.

※

So it is settled then, the French duke's son and the heiress of Monferrato allied against the Emperor's claimant, the Prince of Guastalla. Striggio feels like a chessmaster at the moment of checkmate. But he has become so immersed in the diplomatic moves of chess that he has neglected the human element, the emotions that overturn the rules of the game. The union that looks like a neat tying-up of the lines of succession, instead of bringing peace, is a catalyst towards war. The Emperor is outraged. This obscene, enforced marriage, the consummation at the deathbed, the whole event taking place without his knowledge and consent. And the chicanery of the forged letter from the girl's mother, the real letter, withholding permission, arriving after the event. There is only one way of answering it. More letters go back and forth, and finally as Carlo of Nevers insists on holding on to his claim, the orders for invasion go out to the Imperial generals, and to the armies of Milan and Spain.

Ottavio watches the workmen easing *The Triumphs of Caesar* from the walls. It is a complicated operation for the material is frail, already showing signs of wear, and the canvasses are vast. After they are packed into crates for transportation he follows the procession towards the barges that will take them to Venice. A group of townspeople are waiting by the quayside, in their faces the sadness of losing the great Mantegnas and with it the remainder of Mantua's greatness. But the French Duke doesn't care a fig for Italian art, and he needs money for the coming war. King Charles of England will get the pictures he has been coveting for the last few years, and for which he is prepared to diminish his own army. 'And may our bad luck go with them,' says Ottavio, as the barges move away from the quay.

CHAPTER THIRTY-ONE

Dreams of vengeance have haunted Prince Scipione for years. There is an account to be paid by Mantua for the wrongs done to his mother. Now the opportunity has arrived, for in his hand is a letter from the new Duke, with instructions to hold the fort on the River Oglio against the Imperial troops advancing from the north, until the arrival of the French and Venetian armies. The Imperial commander is the Baron Aldringhen, seasoned in the brutalities of the German wars. It as if the instrument of vengeance has been delivered to him.

And what an instrument! He has only to look at Aldringhen's face, the hard, glittering eyes, the mouth set in lines of avarice and cruelty, to know that he has met the scourge of the Dukes of Mantua. As he agrees terms with the Imperial Commander and gives him the keys to the fort, Scipione's imagination cannot encompass the vengeance that will follow, or that it will engulf them all. The Imperial Army is not off his lands before the rabble among them begins its spree of looting. Refugees crowd the roads to Mantua as they flee villages and farms for the safety of the lake-encircled city.

⁂

Ottavio is secure in the Residency in Venice which has joined the Mantuan side against the Emperor. You would hardly know there was a war on, apart from the absence of the young men who usually hang around the Rialto. They are now being marched towards the battlefields of terra firma. The talk in Venetian society is more of the wedding of Count Mocenigo's daughter. Everyone who is anyone is crammed into the torchlit apartments of Mocenigo for the great novelty of the evening. The Maestro of San Marco, the divine Claudio, has produced the first drama with music to be seen in Venice. The opera is called *The Rape of Proserpina*, favourite legend of the Gonzagas. The guests, already delighted by the banquet and dancing, fall into raptures at the wonderful spectacle, the gorgeous scenery, and the virtuoso singing of the Basile sisters, Adriana and Margherita. Mantua's loss is Venice's gain.

It is only when the Venetian and French armies are defeated that talk turns to war, and a debate on the wisdom of siding with a state that has brought about its own downfall. The Mantuan letters to Venice are becoming desperate. We must have more troops, writes Striggio, now ennobled to Marquis as reward for his services to the new Duke. And then comes the news that the Imperial rabble have brought with them something even more terrible than war. The German soldiers are already dying from the infection of the plague, and they have spread it wherever they have travelled. It has swept through Lombardy, from Milan to Mantua. The besieged city is filled with the dead and dying.

❀

The barge from Mantua arrives in the depths of a hot night in early June. It looks like any other in the darkness, and no one would guess what it is bringing to Venice. But as Striggio is assisted from the deck onto the quay, he sways and almost falls. 'It is nothing, just exhaustion from the journey,' says the Marquis. 'Let me get to the Residency, I have work to do.'

The next morning, he sets off with Ottavio towards the ducal palace. 'They must give us more troops. They must have more troops to send,' he says, hysteria in his voice. Ottavio knows that the Venetians have already sent as many as they intend.

'The basilica,' says Striggio, as they cross the Piazza San Marco. 'I want to say a prayer. I can't get it out of my mind, the sound of the deadcarts, the cries, the smell. Some of them die in the streets, and lie there in damnation.

Bodies heaped up in the carts, sprawled naked on top of each other, all dignity gone. Layer upon layer of them in the pit, and the thin covering of earth rising with the fumes of corruption. And across the lake Aldringhen's men wait and their cannons bombard the palace. They had a direct hit to the room next to Princess Maria while she was giving birth. I can't tell you what it is like to be there, death waiting without, death rampaging within. It feels like a dust all over me. I can't get the stench of it out of my nose.'

Mass is being celebrated in the basilica. 'I must take mass,' says Striggio. He sits in one of the seats near the choir.

'Is Claudio here?' he asks. 'I must see Claudio. Is that him, over there?'

'Where?' Ottavio follows the direction in which Striggio is looking.

'There, in black, the thin figure, do you see? No, it's a shadow. My eyes, Ottavio, the pain in my eyes. I think I am ill.'

The Marquis Striggio was taken by chair to the Residency, and put to bed. For several hours, he lay in a delirious fever and then the boils began to swell under his arms. By this time, the doctor had put the Residency in quarantine, but too late, for in the afternoon three more cases were reported in the area of the Piazza San Marco. Ottavio, confined to the house as a probable carrier of infection, sat at a distance from the sickbed as the priest administered the last rites.

'Remember me to Claudio,' says Striggio, his eyes searching out Ottavio in the darkening room. 'Tell him I have gone to the place from which only Orpheus returned. Now my words come back to me. "Whosoever ascends the mountain finds that a fall must follow." I knew that then, and now I'm proving it true. I believed it was for the good of Mantua, but it was for my own ambition. To be always at the centre, holding the threads, controlling the

moves, but in the end I was the instrument of forces outside my control. . . Remember me to Claudio. Will he perform *Orfeo* again? It was good music . . . I wrote good
poetry . . . remember me . . . as a poet . . .'

Striggio died a day later. So it was not for him to witness
the fall of Mantua on 18 July 1630 when for three days and
nights Aldringhen's soldiers sacked the city, looting, vio-
lating and butchering the population, though the plague
had already depleted the larger part. The Emperor, moved
by the tears of his wife at the ruin of her city, sent orders to
end the carnage, but by then, only 8,000 people were left of
a city that had numbered 100,000 at the start of the siege.

Those who do not value their lives are condemned to
go on living. Around him in Venice, the signs of quarantine on doors signalled the spread of the plague, which
Striggio had brought with him like an angel of death.
Ottavio waited to be struck down. Instead of the plague, a
fever of restlessness came to him. As he walked the silent
streets, an overwhelming need to see Mantua nagged at his
mind. The barge in which Striggio had arrived still lay at
its moorings, and, with the siege over, the boatmen were
anxious to get back to see what was left of their homes.
They set off on a hot morning in early September through
the lagoon to the river that led towards Mantua. Standing
on the deck, Ottavio smelt the sea water give way to the
smell of the river and the mud of the estuary. As the sun
slanted to the west, its rays lit the red tower of the Castello
and the white spire of Sta Barbara. The skyline of the city
looked as it always had but as they drew nearer, he could
see the scars of cannon fire on the walls, and then the
charred remains of the merchants' storehouses of silks and
wool that lined the quayside.

In any ordinary year at that time of day the piazza
would have been busy with the evening *passeggiata*. The few
silent passers-by he saw had masks across their noses and

mouths to avoid inhaling the stench of the plague. He held a handkerchief soaked in vinegar and herbs to his face as he walked towards the palace. As he passed near the steps of the cathedral he heard the sound of high-pitched laughter, and his eye was caught by a young woman who was grinning at him. Her clothes were torn and filthy, a sight that used to be unknown in the city. She cried out, 'Are there any more of you? Eight, nine, ten, eleven, twelve,' and then that high-pitched laugh again. Sitting on the steps near her an older woman stared with unfocused eyes, her lips moving as if in prayer.

Ottavio said, 'God be with you,' and averted his eyes from their pain, there seeming nothing else he could do. He had reached the entrance to the palace where there were only four guards to be seen. The plague that had devastated the population had cut an equal swathe through their numbers. One of the guards shouted out, 'Your business?'

'The envoy from Venice,' said Ottavio. 'I have a passport of good health.'

'Then why come to Mantua?' laughed the guard, with the same hysterical edge as the woman at the cathedral. 'You must be mad.'

They made no move to detain him, their only wish being to leave this inferno of a city. Unimpeded, Ottavio continued through the main courtyard where wagons were piled high with plunder from the palace. The sale of paintings by the last Gonzaga was as nothing compared with the looting by Aldringhen, who had cordoned off the palace for himself. Curtains and tapestries had been torn down, carpets rolled up, and the last of the pictures loaded into the German wagons as spoils of war.

Ottavio wandered through the corridors, feeling sick at heart at the destruction around him. The glory of the Dukes of Mantua wasted, and who was there to blame but themselves? In the gallery where the busts of the ancestors were displayed, there were squeaks and scufflings of rats, and a hound slunk away at his approach, its ribs corrugating the scabby hide. He walked up the steps that led to the loggia, and sat on the parapet looking out over the lake towards the far shore, where the tents of the imperial army were pitched among the willows. Someone had lit a fire in the middle of the loggia, using musical instruments as kindling. The remains of a neck of a viol was among the charred ashes and notes of a score discernible on a fragment of paper. Apart from that, the loggia was as it always had been, there being nothing of value to remove. Memories of the past filled his mind. The Duke, sitting on the parapet where he was now, looking across the water, his hair ruffled in the breeze. The young girl staring with curiosity, her hand to her mouth. He understood now why he had made this journey. It was in search of Isabella, and his restlessness centred into an overwhelming need to see her. Scipione's vendetta had not ended, but then, thought Ottavio, what's one death more or less? As he returned to the town to hire a horse for the journey, he wondered, in passing, whether Archimedeo was still alive.

Outside the gates of the villa at San Martino a watchman from the health committee repelled visitors. He pointed emphatically to the sign of quarantine. The horseman from Mantua was tiresome in his insistence on gaining entry. Can't be done, said the watchman, turning his eyes from the purse of money being held towards him. Can*not* be done. More than my job's worth, signor.

Ottavio swore at obstinate little officials everywhere, and rode off, but only until he was out of sight of the watchman. Then he turned off the road across the fields behind the villa. He dismounted and, leaving his horse grazing, approached the wall by the orchard. Where the trees had grown nearby, the boundary wall was in disrepair and it was easy to climb over, grabbing a branch for support. He dropped into the grass on the other side, and crouched there looking around him. It seemed that no one had been near the garden for some time. The grass was long and bleached by the sun and as he walked through it clouds of small butterflies rose from the seed heads. Sunlight caught the artichoke thistles in an aura of light and parasols of dandelion fluff floated in the air. From the laburnum trees dried pods hung on the branches like rows of desiccated bats. There was no sound apart from the cicadas. The villa was shuttered and silent. He walked up the steps to the terrace, his footsteps striking loud against the stone and waited for someone to come to the open window but it was as if he was the only living being around. From the depths of the house he heard a dog barking. He stepped into the hall and waited and listened.

He was aware of light footsteps on the wooden floor somewhere overhead, and he began to walk up the stairs. A woman's voice called, 'Who is there?' He looked up to see a woman he recognized as Emilia, her hair now grey, standing at the top of the stair. She raised a hand to her mouth, in shock, and called out his name. As he continued towards her, she gestured him away. 'Don't come any closer, we have the sickness. Didn't the watchman tell you?'

'He told me. Where is Isabella?'

Emilia raised her hand to stop him, and said, 'She is sick. You shouldn't be here. No, don't come near. I have had the sickness, I've recovered but now Madonna is ill.'

A cold hand touched Ottavio's heart. 'How ill?' he asked.

Emilia retreated from him to the door of the antechamber, spreading her arms protectively against it. She looked at him steadily. 'I think she is dying. You must not see her. It would be too great a shock. Please leave us.'

'Not until I have seen her,' said Ottavio, standing in front of Emilia, as immovable as she. 'You must let me ask her forgiveness. How could I go on living if I couldn't at least beg that of her? Let me see her, Emilia. It may be, who knows, that she might want to see me. Ask her.'

Emilia's eyes filled with tears. 'There have been so many

deaths from this plague. My husband a month ago, and I only thank God that my son has been spared. Her son Guido who was with us died too, and it took away her will to live, seeing him dead. She nursed me when I was ill without thought for herself. I would have died too, but she sat with me day and night, and then she became ill. Oh, my poor lady, after all her troubles, not to live to a peaceful age.'

'No one is at peace when a country is at war. Please let me see her.'

Emilia stood uncertainly for a moment, then said, 'If you promise to leave as she wishes, I shall ask her. The delirium has left her but she is very weak.'

She opened the door to the antechamber and Ottavio followed her in. She said, 'Stay there, come no nearer,' and slipped through the door to the bedroom, closing it behind her.

He waited for some time before the door opened again, and Emilia emerged. She shook her head. 'She says she would not have you become sick as well.'

'I don't care if I die,' said Ottavio. 'Was that the only reason? Did she seem happy at hearing my name?'

'She smiled as if remembering a happier time. Be content with that. Now go.'

'I must have her forgiveness,' said Ottavio, and as Emilia moved towards the door of the antechamber to show him out, he slid behind her and opened the door to Isabella's room. The shutters had been drawn against the daylight, but he could see, in the glimmer of light through the cracks the bed at the end of the room and lying against the pillows, Isabella. Her hair was spread loose against the linen, her face in shadow. Her head moved slightly at the sound of his steps. She whispered, 'Ottavio, is that you?'

'Yes . . .' and he was aware of tears running unchecked down his cheeks as if there was an overflowing well inside him.

'Don't come any nearer. You will catch the infection.'

'It doesn't matter,' said Ottavio, and moved swiftly past Emilia's attempt to block him. He knelt by the bed and took Isabella's hand, pressing it to his face. The skin was burning hot and through the lavender water with which she had been bathed he could smell the sickly odour of the illness. Her eyes were sunk in dark shadows, as though the sockets were already showing her death mask, but there was still a lucidity in their fevered brightness. The darkened swellings of the disease spread discoloured patches on her neck.

Ottavio looked into her eyes, watching for their response. 'If I die, then my debt is repaid,' he said. 'But I must die with your forgiveness. Will you grant me that, Isabella?'

He saw a faint smile on the cracked lips, then she whispered to him, 'I must not go in anger, and you are so willing to die . . . I must forgive you. I leave your account to be settled by God . . . Kiss me, Ottavio.'

He heard Emilia cry out, 'No!' but he had already leant forward and kissed Isabella on the mouth, breathing in the infected air of her lungs. Then he climbed on to the bed and lay beside her, one arm across her breast. The sleeve of his shirt stirred to the movement of her breathing. She turned her head and smiled at him.

'I'm remembering, Ottavio, the summer in Novellara, when I was fourteen. Lying under the trees, the green light through the leaves, and you telling me about the life at court. Do you remember? And you talked, as we lay like this, about Vincenzo, and I listened, and I fell in love with your image of him. It was all your fault, Ottavio, for filling me with dreams.'

'So I'm to blame, as ever?' murmured Ottavio, his face next to hers. 'Was there a time when I was right?'

'It doesn't matter. I forgive you everything, even your love.'

Ottavio leaned over her and kissed her again. His hands tangled in the hair that was damp with sweat and his arms raised her towards him. Emilia shouted, 'That's enough! Get off the bed!' and she began to pull at his collar. Ottavio said to Isabella, 'My love goes with you,' and then he yielded to Emilia's grasp, and slid off the bed. He watched Isabella as he backed from the room, and Emilia closed the door firmly and stood in front of it.

'What will you do now?' she said, looking at him angrily. 'Go out and infect everyone you meet?'

'I shall stay here and wait for Isabella,' said Ottavio. 'It won't be long.'

'You can't stay. Scipione will have you killed when he knows.'

'I'm dead already,' said Ottavio. 'What difference would it make?'

'I will not have blood spilt in this house,' said Emilia. 'You must go immediately before anyone else knows. Go now, for God's sake go. What do you think Scipione would do if he knew I had let you see her? For my sake, at least, get out of here.'

'For your sake, I'll go,' said Ottavio.

He left the house by the way he had come in, over the orchard wall. His horse was grazing where he had left it. Holding the reins loosely he walked on, the horse following, his mind divided between seeing whether there was any life at the villa he had left so many years ago, or returning to Mantua. It won't be for long. I am a dead man walking, bringing death with me. Maybe on the road, maybe in Mantua; sometimes it strikes fast, sometimes it takes a week or more.

The great bowl of the sky overhead stretched to the shimmering horizon, enclosing him in its world. He walked along by the river until he saw three women, near the bridge of the Mantua road, washing clothes in the water. One of them had folded the ends of her skirt into the waist so that she looked as if she was wearing voluminous pantaloons. She slapped the clothes on the boulders at the edge of the stream. He changed his course so that he didn't come any closer to them as he followed the river downstream on its way to the Mincio.

He was aware of children laughing, and as the river curved round and he came nearer to it, he saw the children, two boys and a girl, splashing in the water. The boys were thin, brown-skinned and naked, the girl, probably no more than six, was wearing a cotton shift, which was soaked as the boys fanned water at her with their hands. Their shouts of laughter were mingled with alarmed shrieks from the little girl as, realizing the inequality of the battle, she turned and scrambled up the bank to the field. She stood up unsteadily and then, seeing Ottavio, began running towards him as if seeking a protector from her rough playmates. Whether he resembled an old father or uncle, he couldn't know, but she smiled at him with the total trust and innocence of the very young as she reached out towards him.

He tried to ward her off, shouting, 'Keep away,' and then, as she unheedingly continued towards him, he turned and plunged into the river. The water closed over his head and he heard the rushing of the stream in his ears as he reached the pebbled river-bed. Then, as his lungs were bursting, he raised his head above the water to gulp in the air. The children were on the bank, watching this strange man standing fully clothed in the water. He shouted at them to get away, and immersed his head again. The water reached his lungs, and he began to choke, raising his head above water, coughing and spluttering into the air. By now perturbed at the behaviour of the man who seemed to be trying to drown himself, the children retreated but he remained in the river, letting it flow past him. Eventually, after they had gone, he climbed out on to the bank, emptied the water from his boots and lay in the sun, his clothes steaming as they began to dry. He looked up at the trees, the silvery leaves of the willows, the green of the poplars, and the sky above where drifts of thin cloud formed and re-formed in shape. He could hear goat bells and the dry whirring of cicadas as they celebrated the sun with their music.

Isabella will die, I will die, but everything we saw and heard will go on, the cicadas, the river, the sun, the light through the trees.

He rises to his feet, approaches his horse and holds the reins firmly as he mounts. The horseman follows the course of the river as it flows towards the lake.

EPILOGUE
1643

*I govern the fortunes of men. This child surpasses in antiquity
Time itself and every other God. Eternity and I are twins.*

Amor in *L'Incoronazione di Poppea*, 1643

*C*arnival. It is always Carnival in Venice. As soon as the winter mists rise from the lagoon, veiling the façades of the palazzi, people obscure their own images with masks. Black figures with ghost-white faces, eyes glittering through impassive blankness. With the masks comes the freedom to be other than who you are. It was not I whom you met, it was not I who behaved thus, it was the unknown one. The masks assume their own character, send out their own messages. That mask is looking for love, this one is looking for trouble. And so let me remove the mask, and what do you see? An old man, stooped, with deep lines around his mouth, left there in bitterness. And yet the old man is not bitter any more, so his face is as much a mask as the one he removed to see himself in the mirror.

I look into the mirror. Yes, I am still here, Ottavio, the crooked one, accepting my life sentence of – how many years is it now? Seventy-five. The same age as Claudio. Our common link, the years and the memories. Many of his duties at San Marco are taken now by the Assistant Director, in deference to his age, but it as if the music within him will not allow him to rest. He has finished a new opera, working with the poet Gian Francesco Busenello. It is to be produced at the public theatre Grimani. He smiles when we talk of it, at his house near San Marco. I am content, he says; I have done something more with music than ever before. The music and the words are as one. You will see, Ottavio, you will understand it better than many. Make sure you are there.

I hear little from Mantua nowadays, and I exist in Venice on the rents from the estates I have not visited since that time which I don't think about. They are all dead:

Striggio, the French duke, his son. Most of the musicians have left for other courts. The widowed Regent Maria rules for her son until he comes of age. Mantova la Gloriosa is no more. The palace, bereft of its treasures, has been partly refurnished by the kindness of other princes. Furniture from the Grand Duke of Tuscany, silver from Parma, 100 pairs of oxen with as many farm workers from the Duke of Modena to till the ruined fields. There are even tapestries and pictures stolen back by friends of Mantua from the tail-end of the eighty-seven wagons carrying Aldringhen's convoy of loot.

Sometimes of an evening, Claudio and I will talk about our times in Mantua, usually of the music, or of our Duke, sometimes of Striggio, rarely of Claudia, never of Isabella. Lately he has been considering a return visit, probably, he says, the last time he will see the city before he dies. For a man whose health was ruined during his years there, he survives very well. How many of us reach that age? Perhaps another from that time, judging by the letter to me from the Regent Maria. Recently they were moving furniture into the Camera degli Sposi, and found a very old and ill-tempered dwarf in residence with his daughter. He had refused to move, saying that he had come to be with his ancestress, whose portrait was in the Mantegna fresco of the old Marquis Ludovico's court. Maria was more amused than annoyed, and so the Chamber of the Bridegrooms has become the palace of Archimedeo until such time as he dies.

And now the Carnival reaches its final days before Ash Wednesday, and the gondolas convey their masked passengers along the canals to the new public theatre near the Fondamente Nuove for the opera by Busenello and Monteverdi, *L'Incoronazione di Poppea*. Torchlight reflects in the dark water, and the chatter of anticipation heightens as they approach the torchlit theatre at SS Giovanni e Paolo. We walk up the slippery steps to the square in front of the building, and then into the auditorium itself, already warm and smoky from the light of a thousand candles. I take my place in the box of another member of the Accademia degli Incogniti, the Academy to which the poet Busenello belongs.

'They say Anna Renzi is in excellent voice, but the castrato is complaining of a sore throat,' says my friend, l'Assicurato, the Assured One. 'He wanted an apology made, but Monteverdi told him his voice would improve with use.'

''Twas ever thus. The evening would not be complete without complaints from the castrato. Have you heard anything about the music?'

'Special, very special,' says l'Assicurato. 'It does justice to Busenello's poetry.'

In the box on the other side of the auditorium, another party has arrived. And suddenly, it is as if the years have turned back. A tall, fair-haired man in a mask is standing at the front of the box surveying the audience. I see the glitter in his eyes as he meets mine, and then they move on as if searching for someone else. I know I have seen it before, the head held as if scenting the air. A younger woman, the man is probably in his middle years, is escorted to her seat in the front of the box. She is wearing a silver mask, with diamonds that catch the light. I can see two other men in the shadows of the box's interior. I turn to my friend l'Assicurato, who knows everything, to ask him who the newcomers are.

'Not Venetian,' says l'Assicurato, in a voice that implies that therefore they are not of interest. 'Probably from the Veneto, come here for Carnival.'

'The man reminds me of someone I knew, a long time ago.'

'Ottavio, you have had a long life, I would have thought by now everyone you see reminds you of someone you once knew,' says l'Assicurato with a smile.

The musicians have filed into the orchestra pit and are

tuning their instruments. And then they strike up the first chords and our eyes turn from the audience to the stage for the prologue of Fortune, Virtue and Love. Fortune in a gown shining with gold, Virtue in a plumed helmet, and then Love, a boy half their height, boasting that it is he who governs them both. Things happen at my command, sings the childish treble, as the opera begins, and Ottavio realizes why Claudio told him he would understand it better than most. There is Otho mourning the waste of his love, and there is Nero celebrating the carelessness with which love comes to him. The plumed and golden Nero, whose voice, as Claudio predicted, needed no apology, is now capricious, now loving, now cruel, and it seems that Claudio is reliving through his music his years at Mantua. In the music is expressed all the emotion of the characters, and the emotion of the composer. The audience silently watches the stage as if under a spell of enchantment.

And now as Otho reproaches Poppea for loving Nero, the orchestra begins a canzonetta duet. That insidious, sliding beat – Ottavio recognizes the lilt of the dance music, and into his memory comes the night of the Carnival ball when Isabella first met the Duke, the procession of dancers in the ballroom of Manto. Shuffle, step, hop, turn, two by two, and then the Duke is turning to meet the tail of the procession, and Isabella is unmasked. Ottavio glances across at the box opposite and his heart, along with the music, misses a beat. The young woman is leaning over the edge of the box to see the stage better and has taken off her mask. He can only think as he stares at her, It is Isabella! She glances at him, and away again, as any girl would, seeing herself stared at by an elderly man.

And now as the opera draws towards the finale, the lovers, Poppea and Nero, look towards the audience as they sing their duet. If I have lost myself in you, it is there that I shall find myself again, and lose myself anew. Love triumphant over virtue, bending fortune to its will. Love, the invisible, unforeseen decider of men's fates. L'Assicurato sighs, 'Bravo, Gian Francesco, a triumph, what a genius! And Monteverdi,' he adds. Then, turning to Ottavio in sudden concern, 'Va bene?'

'It's the heat of this theatre,' says Ottavio, 'I felt faint for a moment.' And then, seemingly unconnected, 'Claudio never wastes a good tune.'

Now the last chord sounds and the singers bow their plumed heads to the audience, who are cheering and throwing flowers at the stage. Busenello, and then Monteverdi, acknowledge the applause. Many in the audience stamp their feet, cheer, hoot, and whistle. Claudio surveys them, his austere face alight with the joy of hearing his music performed so beautifully and received so well. He looks up at the boxes. A thin, elderly man in the black habit of holy orders bows in acknowledgement of the applause. Someone in the stalls is shouting for the whole opera to be performed again, and the singers are laughing and shaking their heads. There is a communal shuffling, gathering of cloaks, the sound of chatter as of a cloth being lifted from a parrot's cage as everyone compares notes on the opera. Laughing, calling greetings to each other, they crowd down the two staircases to meet the congestion of the audience from the pit.

Ottavio has seen the people in the box opposite leave ahead of l'Assicurato's party, and among the many heads in the foyer he has lost sight of them. Then he glimpses through the crowd the fair-haired man again. He has thrown his cloak round his shoulders, which falls in folds over the sword by his side. He is talking to one of the men of his party. The young woman is nowhere to be seen. Ottavio cranes his head and wills the man to turn round so that he can see his face. The assured tilt of the head is familiar, the way his right hand rests on his hip, but just as he begins to turn he puts his mask on again, and there is only the enigmatic white blankness, the glint of the eyes in the hidden face. They are looking directly at Ottavio, and they seem to be asking a question. A simple one, perhaps. Do I know you? His left hand touches, very lightly, the hilt of his sword, and he looks at him again. He turns to speak to the man at his side, who glances back towards Ottavio, and then, by a slight gesture of the head, seems to be inviting him to follow.

Now Ottavio knows that they must meet and he tries to make his way through the crowd. It is more difficult than he had supposed. People obstinately refuse to get out of his way, as he dodges and weaves. He can see the two men ahead, near the door, and then his way is blocked again.

'Excuse me, signora,' as an elderly lady in black cloak and beaked mask steps into his path. He glances down at her and sees at her neck the blue fire of sapphires. His mind reels. What ghosts are these coming back to him? His hand reaches out to the jewels and he remembers that same hand tearing at the same necklace, the sapphires falling to the floor of the coach. He whispers, 'Isabella?' and the elderly lady smiles and takes off her mask. Now there is no mistaking her. Even after these years she is little changed.

He cries out, 'Emilia!'

She smiles, 'Don Ottavio, but who else?'

He stares at the necklace, and says, 'So you kept it all these years.'

'I was the only safe person with whom it could be kept.' She looked at him levelly. His mind was still trying to link the pieces of the past with the present. He said, 'Is Prince Scipione here?'

'You saw him just now, with his brother.'

Another missed beat of the heart, half apprehension, half excitement.

'And the girl who was with them in the box, who resembled . . . who resembled Isabella?'

'Is his daughter. His eldest son is here as well.'

'Emilia, I must see Scipione, face to face.'

'That wouldn't be wise,' said Emilia. 'You are an old man, you should live and die peacefully.'

'He wants to talk to me, I am sure of it. And I must see his face. I must see how he looks now. There is something I want to know.'

'Ottavio, who never leaves well alone. What is the point of raking up the past? It is best forgotten. Look, I think your friends are expecting you to join them.'

L'Assicurato is calling across the foyer to him. Ottavio calls back not to wait for him, and follows Emilia through the foyer. She turns to him again as they reach the open air.

'Ottavio, as she was dying Isabella forgave you. That should be enough for you. Scipione doesn't forgive, he knows you would try to meet him one day. What is the point of dying like a dog and being thrown into the canal? Is that what you want?'

'I want to see his face,' said Ottavio obstinately.

'If that is the only wish you have left, then you had better come with me,' said Emilia, in a dismissive tone. 'They have gone on ahead to the palazzo. We will follow in the second gondola.'

They have reached the quayside. Through the night mist they can see fading into the distance the torches of departing gondolas. Two of the Bozzolo servants are already in the second gondola, and one of them helps Emilia on board. She turns to Ottavio, but as he moves towards the boat, a stout woman pushes past him, crying, 'Wait for me, Signora Emilia!' She holds her hand out towards the gondolier, and then sits down heavily in the last remaining seat. Ottavio moves forward, but the gondolier shakes his head. 'No standing passengers, signor.'

'Where are you going?' calls Ottavio.

'It's off the Grand Canal, in Dorsoduro,' calls Emilia. 'Follow us.'

Ottavio gets into the next boat. The gondolier says, 'I am not going to Dorsoduro.'

'You are if I pay you double fare, twice over there and back,' says Ottavio.

'Plus double waiting time,' says the gondolier. He is wearing a white carnival mask and a hooded cloak.

Ottavio sits facing the prow, aware of the gondolier standing behind him and the even strokes of the oar, the soft splash of the water as they glide after the other boat. He sees in the light of the torch Emilia's face as she looks round for an instant. The gondolas turn into the Canale della Misericordia. Either side rise the dark cliffs of tall buildings, unlit by any sign of life. The torches from the gondolas illuminate the mist in swirls of white smoke. Outside their range the mist is a blanket of blackness, obscuring all but their immediate surroundings. Ottavio is aware, more by the chill of the air than by sight, that they are entering the Grand Canal. The chill reaches to his bones and he pulls his cloak more tightly around his frame.

He says to the gondolier, 'Wisdom does not come with age. To be out on a night like this . . .'

The gondolier does not reply, the splash of the oar punctuating the silence. Ottavio sees the torchlight of the gondola in front through the mist.

'Don't lose sight of it. Put in more strokes, or we'll fall behind.'

He looks back at the gondolier and sees the two black pits in the white mask regarding him steadily. He is shivering from the cold, and from an intense feeling of aloneness. The light of the gondola in front of them is receding, and he can no longer hear any sound beyond the lapping of the water against the side of his boat. The mist grows thicker, swirling into distinct shapes. And now, the torch dwindled, faded, and he is looking at darkness ahead. He calls out, 'Emilia!' but the mist, which has obscured sight has also muffled sound.

'Well,' he says to the gondolier, 'it seems the lady has given us the slip.'

The gondolier pauses at his oar, and the boat drifts slowly through the water.

'Where to?' asks the gondolier.

But Ottavio is listening to an inner sound. He watches the mist hide the city as the refrain of the music runs through his mind. Listen to it now, calling through the centuries. That was how we were, how we still are. It is the mirror of our souls. Can you not hear us, through the shroud of time, calling to you through the music? Listen now, look at our eyes in the mirror.

'Where to?' says the gondolier. But there is no answer to his question. Presently, in the silence of the night comes the sound that is only heard in the night, of something heavy falling into the water. The gondola glides on with even strokes, lighter now without its passenger.

L'Incoronazione di Poppea was Monteverdi's last opera. From the time of his seventy-sixth birthday in May 1643 the composer embarked on a six-month tour of Lombardy where he was received with acclaim in his favourite cities. In Mantua he fell ill and returned to Venice where he died on 29 November of that year. He was buried in Sta Maria Gloriosa dei Frari, in the Lombard Chapel.

The House of Gonzaga never recovered from the sack of Mantua, and by the end of the century the state was annexed by Austria, while Monferrato became part of the states of Savoy and Milan.

The pictures bought by Charles I were sold by the Commonwealth after his execution, though Oliver Cromwell retained *The Triumphs of Caesar*, which are displayed at Hampton Court. The Renaissance collection of the Gonzagas is now dispersed through the world's galleries, at the Louvre, the National Gallery, the Prado, the Kunsthistorisches Museum, among others. In Mantua the frescoes by Giulio Romano at the Palazzo del Te and by Mantegna at the Ducal Palace have survived.

By the end of the seventeenth century Monteverdi's music had given way to later baroque composers. Most of the Masses he wrote for the choir of San Marco were lost, as were all the earlier operas for Mantua, apart from his first, *La Favola d'Orfeo*. Of the opera which had cost him most emotionally, *Arianna*, only the Lament remains. During the twentieth century his music was rediscovered, and with it the understanding of his role in the development of opera.

The novel revolves around historical events and most of the characters are based on people of the time. I should like to acknowledge with gratitude my debt to Professor

Denis Stevens, CBE, Monteverdi scholar and translator of Monteverdi's letters and madrigals, who was generous in sharing his knowledge of Monteverdi and the Mantuan court. I also thank Professor Patrick Boyde of Cambridge University for allowing me to use his translation of Arianna's Lament. Westminster Library, and particularly the St John's Wood branch, were extremely helpful and patient in searching out rare books, from the sixteenth-century translation of *Il Pastor Fido* to a pre-war out-of-print history of Mantua. I read a number of books, which included, among others, *The Letters of Monteverdi* by Denis Stevens (OUP, 1995); *Monteverdi* by Denis Arnold (J. M. Dent, 1990); *Monteverdi* by Paolo Fabbri (Cambridge, 1994); *Claudio Monteverdi: Orfeo* by John Whenham (Cambridge, 1986); *Claudio Monteverdi: Songs & Madrigals* by Denis Stevens (Long Barn Books, 1998); *The Gonzaga – Lords of Mantua* by Selwyn Brinton (1927); *A Prince of Mantua* by Maria Bellonci (1956), *Music & Patronage in Sixteenth-Century Mantua* by Iain Fenlon (Cambridge, 1980); *Theatre Festivals of the Medici* by Alois Maria Nagler (1964).

The Fourth Duke of Mantua, Vincenzo Gonzaga, was famous for his extravagance. An enthusiastic collector of talent, he was patron of Rubens, Monteverdi and the poet Tasso. He embarked on several wars, after various domestic scandals. There were three crusades against the Turks, all of them costly and inconclusive.

Isabella is a fictional creation, but draws on the life of the real Isabella Gonzaga of Novellara, who was mentioned by Monteverdi in a 1611 letter as being among the musical audience at Mantua. Her secret marriage in 1616 caused a scandal and her refusal to allow a divorce upset the power balance in North Italy. The trial of Isabella is drawn from Guido Errante's *Il Processo,* part of the *Archivio storico lombardo,* published in 1916. Her son's antagonism to the Dukes of Mantua, the siege of Mantua and its result, are historical facts.

As for Ottavio, he is a fictional creation drawn from more than one life – a spirit of the times, a witness, and occasionally manipulator, of history.

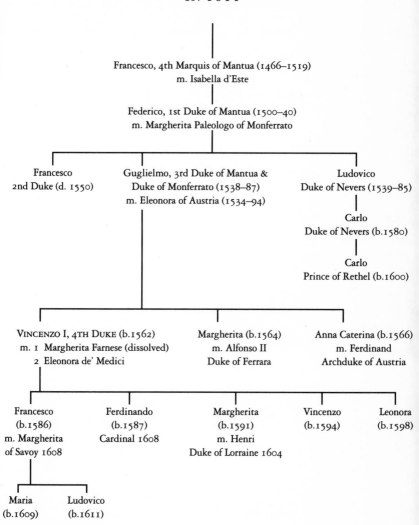

THE GONZAGA SUCCESSION
IN 1611

Francesco, 4th Marquis of Mantua (1466–1519)
m. Isabella d'Este

Federico, 1st Duke of Mantua (1500–40)
m. Margherita Paleologo of Monferrato

Francesco
2nd Duke (d. 1550)

Guglielmo, 3rd Duke of Mantua &
Duke of Monferrato (1538–87)
m. Eleonora of Austria (1534–94)

Ludovico
Duke of Nevers (1539–85)

Carlo
Duke of Nevers (b.1580)

Carlo
Prince of Rethel (b.1600)

VINCENZO I, 4TH DUKE (b.1562)
m. 1 Margherita Farnese (dissolved)
2 Eleonora de' Medici

Margherita (b.1564)
m. Alfonso II
Duke of Ferrara

Anna Caterina (b.1566)
m. Ferdinand
Archduke of Austria

Francesco
(b.1586)
m. Margherita
of Savoy 1608

Ferdinando
(b.1587)
Cardinal 1608

Margherita
(b.1591)
m. Henri
Duke of Lorraine 1604

Vincenzo
(b.1594)

Leonora
(b.1598)

Maria
(b.1609)

Ludovico
(b.1611)

The Angelic Darkness
Richard Zimler

San Francisco, 1986 – a city where Dionysian liberation is beginning to pall beneath the first shadows of a strange new darkness. Bill Ticino's fruitless and numbing marriage finally breaks up. Plagued by insomnia and spiritually lost, Bill finds a lodger as the solution to his problems: a handsome, charismatic Portuguese man named Peter, whose pet bird is a hoopoe named Maria. Bill finds himself drawn into a world of kabbalistic storytelling, charms and ritual. Peter ignites Bill's repressed obsessions by telling him emotionally charged tales of hidden meaning.

One night they venture together into the Tenderloin district, a dead-end world of prostitutes and transvestites. Bill begins to see that his new tenant has plans that will force him down a perilous sexual and spiritual path, with the power to both redeem and destroy.

'The candid first-person narrative generates suspense, as well as a deep concern for the narrator . . . Zimler is skilled at evoking an eerie San Francisco underworld' – *Publishers Weekly*

'A beautiful book. Zimler writes with great emotion and humour. This story of love and mystery invites the reader along on a rite of passage – a voyage of discovery of a man in search of his own emotional and sexual identity' – *Elle*

'A daring journey into a world of mythology and spirituality, with a shocking climax. It explores the deepest layers of the human subconscious without compromising a surprisingly simple and accessible narrative style. Filled with astonishing stories and spiced with subtle and exotic metaphors, it's a great follow-up to *The Last Kabbalist of Lisbon*' – O Diário Económico

Easter
Michael Arditti

The parish of St Mary-in-the-Vale, Hampstead, is preparing for Easter. In his Palm Sunday sermon, the Vicar explains that Christ's crucifixion and redemption are taking place every day. He little suspects that, before the week is out, he and his entire congregation will be caught up in a latter-day Passion story which will tear apart their lives.

Michael Arditti's magnificent new novel is both a devastating portrait of today's Church of England and an audacious reworking of the central myth of Western culture. Taking the form of a traditional triptych, it is at once intimate and epic, lyrical and analytic. Shocking events unfold against a backdrop of meticulously observed religious services. High Church ritual, evangelical revivalism and the ancestor-worship of the English gentry are all subjected to merciless scrutiny.

In a fictional climate dominated by materialism, *Easter* stands apart in its bold exploration of the nature of God, the problem of suffering and the existence of evil. With an unforgettable gallery of characters ranging from a Holocaust survivor and an African princess to AIDS patients and Queen Elizabeth II, it provides a dazzling and funny panorama of contemporary society. In its radical fusion of the sacred and profane, *Easter* throws down a challenge to believers and non-believers alike.

'Arditti writes about Western Christianity, as it is manifest in the present Church of England, with pungency and satirical frankness. His style has Joycean echoes. Against a background of the conventional liturgies he places awful actualities in the lives of preachers and practitioners' – Muriel Spark

'This book uncovers the truth about the Church, and does it with wit and power. It ought to be essential reading for anyone who cares about the way we live and believe today' – Richard Holloway, Bishop of Edinburgh

'In his fascination with the difficulty of goodness, and his coupling of comic plot with philosophical purpose, Arditti is a worthy successor to Iris Murdoch. *Easter* is a big book in every sense' – Patrick Gale

The Twins
Tessa de Loo

Translated from the Dutch by Ruth Levitt

Two elderly women, one Dutch and one German, meet by chance at the famous health resort of Spa. They recognize in the other their twin sister they believed to be lost. They begin to tell each other their life stories the last chance to bridge a gulf of almost seventy years.

Born in Cologne in 1916, the twins are brusquely separated from each other after the death of their parents. Anna grows up with her grandfather, in a primitive farming and Catholic milieu on the edge of the Teutoburgerwald. Lotte ends up in the Netherlands because of her TB, living with an uncle who harbours strong socialist sympathies. Bad relationships between the families and the intervening war cause the contact between the two sisters to be broken. When their paths cross again so late in life, Lotte, who sheltered Jews in hiding during the war, is initially extremely suspicious of her newly-found twin sister. But through Anna's painful stories she is confronted with the other side of her own reality: the sufferings of ordinary Germans in wartime.

In this monumental novel, Tessa de Loo compellingly weaves the story of two twin sisters separated in childhood with that of two countries opposed in war, and depicts, in a simple yet harrowing prose the effects of nature and nurture on the individual.

'All-seeing, it is brimming with scenes that are moving and sometimes disturbing' – *Der Spiegel*

'A magnificent book. It reveals a kaleidoscope in which drama, comedy, farce and poetry combine to create a novel that must be read' – *Die Woche*

Time Exposure
Brodrick Haldane
in conversation with Roddy Martine

For almost six decades Brodrick Haldane moved among the rich and the famous, photographing everybody who was anybody, including the Queen Mother, Bernard Shaw, the Aga Khan and Margaret, Duchess of Argyll. *Time Exposure* is a witty and charming portrait of an age peopled by extraordinary characters.

'The original society paparazzo, snapping the Duke of Windsor and Wallis Simpson in exile, Charlie Chaplin and a youthful JFK' – *Sunday Times*

When Memory Dies
A. Sivanandan

A three-generational saga of a Sri Lankan family's search for coherence and continuity in a country broken by colonial occupation and riven by ethnic wars. *Winner of the Sagittarius Prize 1998* and *shortlisted for the Commonwealth Writers Prize 1998*

'Haunting . . . with an immense tenderness. The extraordinary poetic tact of this book makes it unforgettable' – John Berger, *Guardian*

Isabelle
John Berger and Nella Bielski

A compelling recreation of the life of Isabelle Eberhardt.

'A tantalizing enigma, Berger and Bielski's filmic approach is appropriate to her literally dramatic life, and the symmetry of the imagery is an indication of the artistry of this work' – *Observer*

The Last Kabbalist of Lisbon
Richard Zimler

A literary mystery set among secret Jews living in Lisbon in 1506 when, during Passover celebrations, some two thousand Jewish inhabitants were murdered in a pogrom. THE INTERNATIONAL BESTSELLER.

'Remarkable erudition and compelling imagination, an American Umberto Eco' – Francis King, *Spectator*

Tomorrow
Elisabeth Russell Taylor

In August 1960, a number of ill-assorted guests gather at a small hotel on the Danish island of Møn. Among them is Elisabeth Danziger, whose happy memories of growing up in a brilliant and gifted family are overshadowed by darker ones, over which she struggles to achieve control.

'A memorable and poignant novel made all the more heartbreaking by the quiet dignity of its central character and the restraint of its telling'
– Shena Mackay

Present Fears
Elisabeth Russell Taylor

'It is hard to pinpoint what makes these stories so unsettling. Their worlds – some border territory between genteel suburbia and dreamland – are imagined with an eerie thoroughness. The inhabitants are all out of kilter, and terrifyingly fragile; spinsterish middle-agers paralysed by sexual fear; anxious children in the centre of parental power games. Russell Taylor's abrupt, elegantly engineered anticlimaxes leave the reader with the disquieting feeling of waiting for the other shoe to fall' – Sam Leith, *Observer*

The Tangier Diaries 1962-1979
John Hopkins

American novelist Hopkins arrived in Tangier at the age of twenty-four and ended up spending almost two decades in Morocco, mixing with a wide cast of characters, Paul and Jane Bowles, William Burroughs, David Herbert and Malcolm Forbes among them.

'Hopkins writes as powerfully of place as of people, capturing the steamy bustle of the Kasbah market and the awesome mystery of the Sahara'
– Michael Arditti, *Daily Mail*

Fear of Mirrors
Tariq Ali

Lovers want to know the truth, but they do not always want to tell it. For some East Germans, the fall of Communism was like the end of a long and painful love affair; free to tell the truth at last, they found they no longer wanted to hear it.

'When Ali's imagination goes wild he is superb' – *New Statesman*

Eddy: The Life of Edward Sackville-West
Michael De-la-Noy

Heir to Knole and a peerage, novelist, discerning critic and brilliant pianist, the intimate of Bloomsbury writers and painters, Edward Sackville-West was born with the proverbial silver spoon in his mouth. Through diaries and previously unpublished letters, we see a life dogged by chronic ill-health and a masochistic psychological make-up.

'Nobody can fail to respect the skill and industry which De-la-Noy has devoted to bringing Eddy Sackville-West back to life in this elegant and sympathetic biography' – *Sunday Times*

False Light
Peter Sheldon
Foreword by Francis King

Karl is a handsome adolescent in Vienna between the wars. He has every advantage, but all is not as it seems in a situation full of political tensions and erotic undercurrents.

'An absorbing read' – *Gay Times*

Double Act
Fiona Pitt-Kethley

'This poetry collection reads like it's been written by a sexually charged Philip Larkin. Both witty and scathing, it avoids the tender eroticism often employed when discussing sex and instead goes straight for the jugular' – *D>tour Magazine*

Eurydice in the Underworld
Kathy Acker

The last work of new fiction Acker published before her death from breast cancer in late 1997, *Eurydice* is Acker's response to her diagnosis. Its 'raw truth is shot through with surprising lyricism and tenderness' – *Observer*. The collection also includes Acker classics such as 'Lust', 'Algeria' and 'Immoral', on the banning in Germany of *Blood and Guts in High School*.

'Kathy Acker's writing is virtuoso, maddening, crazy, so sexy, so painful, and beaten out of a wild heart that nothing can tame. Acker is a landmark writer' – Jeanette Winterson

The Transylvanian Trilogy: They Were Counted (Book 1)
Miklós Bánffy
Translated from the Hungarian by
Patrick Thursfield and Kathy Bánffy-Jelen
Foreword by Patrick Leigh Fermor

Paints an unrivalled portrait of the vanished world of pre-1914 Hungary, as seen through the eyes of two young aristocratic Transylvanian cousins. Against a backdrop of grand shooting parties, turbulent scenes in Parliament and the luxury of life where good manners cloak indifference and brutality, is set the plight of exploited Romanian peasants.

'One of the most celebrated and ambitious classics of Hungarian literature, in a translation of great elegance' – Jan Morris

His Mistress's Voice
Gillian Freeman

Victorian London: Simon, a young Jewish widower with a small son emigrates from Warsaw to London's East End, staying with family there until he takes up the position of cantor at a smart Reform synagogue off Lower Regent Street. His liaison with Phoebe Fenelle, a leading actress of the day leads to dire consequences for her husband – or does it?

'Her writing is pure pleasure' – *Evening Standard*

ARCADIA BOOKS
are available from all good bookshops
or direct from the publishers at 15–16 Nassau Street, London WIN 7RE.
Write for a free catalogue.